THE EDEN MAN

THE EDEN MAN

Paul Lyons

ANDRE DEUTSCH

First published 1988 by
André Deutsch Limited
105–106 Great Russell Street London WC1B 3LJ

British Library Cataloguing in Publication Data

Lyons, Paul
   The Eden man.
   I. Title
   823[F]   PR9619.3.L9/

ISBN 0 233 98262 0

Printed in Great Britain by
Billing and Sons Limited, Worcester

To Steph, Jessie and Kim

one

PEACH O'Hare sat cross-legged on a piano stool facing the window of the tiny garret which served as a kitchen in his squat. His back was straight. One hand rested on either knee, the palm turned outwards. The first rays of the rising sun shone on to his face. Long years of practice had enabled him to sit thus immobile for hours. On the outside he was utterly still, except for the faintest trace of a grin which flickered like the morning sun around the edges of his mouth. But inside, he was awhirl. His heart beat. Something was happening to him at last. His fate was drawing near. For an hour he'd sat in the 'Pharaoh's Tomb', as he called that low-ceilinged void just under the skull-cap one enters with any prolonged attempt at self-awareness. He'd thought of Love. In the 'Pharaoh's Tomb' love is impossible, even the deepest and truest, even self-love. Love must come from without, from a higher source, like a camel walking backwards out of the eye of a needle – which is how small the 'Pharaoh's Tomb' felt at that moment. And it was. A circle had begun to form. A ring shining in this space of the Crown Centre, where he'd never before seen a thing. A round disk, like the rising sun outside his kitchen window, was forming in that darkness. And suddenly it was easy to think of all the people he loved. Especially Morag. And as the thought of each of them entered the 'Pharaoh's Tomb', one by one, it was answered by a steady heart-beat of true Love – from within him, but also from beyond him. And the ring grew brighter. In an hour the sun outside his kitchen window would light the whole world – and, oh, what if, like that sun, he could answer every human being in the world with a steady heart-beat of true Love. He drew a deep breath and steadied himself. He must *do* it, not just think it. And he returned his gaze to the great golden ring forming inside the pyramid of his darkened mind.

Someone was bumping around in the bedroom next door. He could hear covers being kicked back. And then what sounded like cursing. Still, these sounds didn't disturb his stillness. For they stayed, clear and understood – except for the cursing – in his ears only. For in the 'Pharaoh's Tomb' all he could hear was the blood roar of silence.

A tousled woman in a dressing-gown stumbled into the kitchen.

'Late,' she muttered. 'Christ, I'm late . . .'

It was five o'clock in the morning. What did she mean, 'late'? Where was she going?

He re-entered the 'Pharaoh's Tomb'.

'Oh Christ,' she burst out, as though not noticing that he was meditating. '*And* I feel queasy . . .'

Though more worrying, this too could wait till his inner sun had risen.

She staggered across the kitchen and gripped his knee which was thrust up in the full lotus position. Steadying herself, she reached across him and dragged a saucepan out of the cupboard.

Even with his eyes shut he knew it was the little one-egg saucepan he used for his breakfast. When his meditation was finished, he would boil an egg in it, have two slices of toast, a cup of coffee, and go to bed.

She stumbled back into the bedroom with it.

A moment later he heard the tap being switched on, hard, into the tinny bottom of the saucepan. But wait a second! There was no tap in the bedroom. The only tap in the top of the house was the cold one, here beside him in the kitchen.

The ring of light in his head was growing by the second. It was expanding past the lineaments of his skull, which it lit from within, like a strong light through bone china. It expanded beyond his head, a spiritual sun rising from within. His body gagged at its power, wondering whether such an impersonal force could be called Love. It was as far removed from his everyday love as a furnace from an unstruck match. Its spiritual fire reached down his spine till it tingled against leather and upholstery buttons. If this was Divine Love, he must let it do with him what it would. He must give himself to it. Though one part of his mind kept wondering what the hell Morag was doing in the bedroom.

Suddenly she burst back into the kitchen. In her hand was a glass cube. She placed it carefully on the windowsill in front of him.

'Look,' she cried to his closed, ecstatic eyes.

He opened them.

At first he thought it was the after-image of the ring of Divine Love, floating before him. But there, in the little cube of glass, in a terribly external test-tube, a golden circle was forming in what looked like the yellow, morning sunlight, but was in fact Morag's piss.

'I knew! . . . Oh Jesus . . . I'm pregnant! What do you think, Peach?'

'It must have been when I did that yogic birth control.'

'I suppose so. What do you think, Peach?'

He ran his fingers through his hair, massaging his scalp. The mystical moment is a pariah. It is untouchable by thought, or feeling, or the subtlest reflexes of the body. So that, passing out of it, it seems like a nothing. It *is* nothing.

'It's not how I saw things going – having a family.'

The mystical moment had shrunk to a pinpoint of stillness, a weightless fulcrum trying to balance an unknown future with a past that seemed almost as unknown, though it was his. The fire still sang faintly at the base of his spine. But now it seemed that its only purpose was to make his coccyx wonderfully sensitive to the slashed padding of the piano stool and the loose button umbilicalled to it. The ring of Love had vanished in the bright sunlight. But Peach was used to these transitions.

'What do you think, Morag?'

'It'll mean changes, Peach.'

With his legs still folded, Peach swivelled around on the piano stool to face her. Under its lid, beneath his awakened pelvis, were stored Book One and half Book Two of the complete Beethoven Sonatas, a long-unfingered volume of Czerny Five Finger Exercises, a mildewed Minute Waltz, and 'The Rustle of Spring' folded into brown leaves. He had a piano stool, and music to put in it. But though he could play, he didn't have a piano. Not in a squat. He hadn't touched one for seven years. Instead, he'd spent the last quarter of his life sitting bolt upright on this piano stool making the Music that Has No Instrument. He sat down to it each morning as solemnly as a concert pianist drawing up his stool, shaking out his coat-tails, freeing his cuffs – with no piano! Suddenly Peach felt that he was only half a man. And now he was going to have to play the part of a whole one. He leant tentatively against the wash-stand. Its rim chilled his spine. Two years of nothing but cold water seemed to have passed into the very porcelain. Even now, from deep in the plumbing, where it had been cut off, the hot water tap was gagging dryly, like a frozen vacuum cleaner. A night's worth of coffee cups was stacked beneath it, to be washed with the water he'd boil his egg in. He carefully unfolded his legs which were beginning to cramp.

'What do you mean?'

'It'll change everything. We'll need . . . things. Security.'

'There's loads of people bring up kids in squats. And they look all right to me. Look at Sid and Ruth.'

'Well, they've got more money than we have. Sid's working now.'

'Well, I'll work. I'm not afraid of work. Or change. It's what meditation's all about.'

'I didn't mean it like that, Peach. Your meditation *is* your work. But you may have to get something part-time. And Ruth and Sid are applying to be rehoused.'

Peach looked through the kitchen door at the hole in the roof. Though he would have to repair it some day, he liked this hole. It was really a manhole for access on to the roof, but it didn't have a cover when they moved in and though Peach had climbed up and jammed a piece of hardboard under the slates it had slid off in a recent storm. Since when the weather had been balmy with the coming of spring, and a pile of old curtains under the hole was smelling of new life. The hole looked up at the back windows of the hotel behind the house. And last Saturday Peach had had a long conversation with some German youths who had thrown an empty beer-can in. Beyond the sleazy hotel windows was the blue sky, swinging upwards to the Divine Source. Perhaps the new little spirit in Morag's womb had come in through the hole in the roof.

Is meditation work? Is stillness something you can put on the table in lieu of a pay packet? Of course it's the most important thing in the world. It is the only thing that can satisfy the human heart. It is the ending of greed and the annihilation of war. It is the harmless furnace. And yet. And yet . . . Sixty billion people can't be wrong. Waking all around him, at this very moment, like spark plugs, to another day's internal combustion. To work. Is meditation, then, work? Perhaps stillness dances in the engine within every man and woman. And doesn't need a lifetime sitting on your bum.

'Are you happy, Morag?'

'Yes. Are you?'

'Yes. I suppose it's . . . wonderful.'

Peach stood up. He walked to the window, bent, and looked out.

'Do you know what I fancy doing?' he asked her.

'No. What?' said Morag, thinking of a walk on such an auspicious morning.

'Gardening. I just thought of it. Outdoors work. Building something worthwhile. I'll be able to take the baby with me . . .'

'But you don't know anything about plants, do you?'

'No. No. *Building* gardens. Landscaping. You know. Putting

up trellis for climbing shrubs, laying paving, turfing. I could do that. Even bricklaying – don't you remember when I worked on that building site? – I could do that too. Little flowerbed walls, and plinths – to put pots on.'

He was walking excitedly back and forth, the two steps across the kitchen, every dozen or so turns bending to look out of the window. Spiritual energy moves spirally around the spine, like a snake round a lightning rod, coiling from positive to negative, circling from plane to plane of existence, the great glass rod of the spine charmed by its circuit, conducting the meditator into Another World. And now, compressed and candescent after three hours' concentration, this spiral was bouncing Peach back and forth across the kitchen on the spring of some possibly endless excitement. He glanced out of the window for the twentieth time. The hornbeam up the road was tapping its buds, as hard as the heads of drumsticks, against the saffron casing of the broken street lamp, skiffling sunlight from it. Three children were walking along a wall. For years, right up till today, Peach had pitied them growing up in an inner city slum. But this morning the whole world was new.

'Right then. I'm off.'

'Where to?' said Morag.

'To find some work.'

'Look, there's no rush, Peach. You haven't been to bed yet.'

'I couldn't sleep anyway.'

It was true. He felt as though he would never need to sleep again. His exhaustion was translucent.

'Why don't we go up to the park then? You could go busking if you wanted to.'

'No. Everything has changed! If I don't do it this morning, I never will. I'll get a newspaper. Look at the noticeboards. There's bound to be something.' And all at once, across North London, he had a vision of himself building the Garden of Eden in people's back gardens.

'But you haven't got any tools. You need a van. It's a long time since you were on that building site.'

'Today I feel I can do anything. I'll start small. I'll go up to Hampstead. There's plenty of gardening up there.'

'But you haven't even got enough for your bus fare, have you? Or to buy a newspaper.'

'I'll walk. It's a nice morning. I'll find a newspaper on a bench. You'll see.'

two

FINDING work didn't seem so rosy when Peach stepped out into the traffic jam in Westbourne Grove. So much energy! So much human will-power, turned mechanical. Standing on the corner of the Kentucky Fried Chicken looking for a break in the traffic was like watching someone else's stop-start nightmare, without being able to wake from it.

When after twenty minutes' steady walking he saw the vast stream poured to a standstill on the Harrow Road Flyover, Peach O'Hare stopped dead and contemplated this thought: What if all the harnessed explosions in all these internal combustion engines were a million psychic explosions, blasting away rigidity and conditioning, letting the great force he'd felt on the piano stool pass through all men and women with its freight of light? Like being harmlessly hit by a stationary juggernaut. What if all the human energy and will-power put into these machines and concrete structures were channelled into love, into spiritual acts of love. They could turn to light in the wink of an eye. No demolition required, just continual transformation. And there, standing at the foot of the Metropole Hotel, by the stalks of the Flyover, Peach had a vision of the spiritual London which would rise out of the mists these engines gave off. Westminster City Library was in it. Railway House was in it. The Flyover. Even the Metropole was in this new, invisible London. The Metropole as a spine filled with sunlit honey carried from More Than One Country of Origin by human bees. It was a tall, centrifugal drum, spinning its own honeycomb of windows, whirling the sweetest honey on earth from the tourists. The pallid stone of Westminster City Library was Death, into which men and women passed continually, and emerged with a new book. Railway House kept the whole Past dungeoned under its great footpath grilles, clutching at the pedestrians' feet with the smell of mildewed tickets, lest the Past break free and devour the Future. Over the Flyover a mighty force swept, passing through the stationary vehicles, transforming London down to its last brick, its last grain of soot.

Peach descended the subway under the roaring traffic of Edgware Road. He stopped in the cavern by the toilets. From the long, ill-lit tunnel that led to Edgware Road Station, a spine-chilling noise was tooth-edging its way along the tiles towards him. He peered into the dimness of the tunnel. A tall thin figure, dressed in black leather, was pressed into the curved wall of the tunnel playing a red electric guitar which he balanced on his knee. It was 3-Tooth McGuire. In spite of the fact that he, Peach, was the father-to-be, 3-Tooth was up and out working before him. He may have been busking all night. He played with abandon, hunched over his guitar as though it had just kicked him in the balls. Occasionally the leg on which he stood buckled at the knee as he 'bent' a note to breaking point. Between the long guitar solos he sang snatches of lyrics to the fluorescent tube above him, which guttered like some lightshow programmed to his tortured soul. He played with an absorption so intense that it seemed to have sucked him into itself like a black hole in space, leaving a black leather locum to hold the guitar alone amongst the stars.

It was the black hole left by a collapsed star: Jimi Hendrix was the only man in the Universe 3-Tooth loved. And he'd died eighteen years ago. But 3-Tooth knew he was still alive and well. He'd only heard Hendrix play once – and that was twenty years ago. But once had been enough. God had died at Dunromin, 1 Homeleigh Drive. Hendon had cracked. The Black Hole had begun to turn. And out of it came a dark, sneering, snarling voice, deep and cold as a gravel-pit, the voice of the Cosmic Gypsy, the Electric Cathar, singing of Freedom and star-spangled lays on the other side of the Universe. 3-Tooth had stayed at home only long enough to buy a guitar and amp and learn Jimi's repertoire by heart, which had taken a month. After which his parents were glad to see him go. Then he'd even sold his collection of Hendrix discs, bought a black leather jacket and trousers, and a pair of shades, and set off on a life of electric minstrelsy, unbridled sexuality, and possible stardom. The groove took him to the tunnels of London Transport. His spine curved from long years of leaning into tunnel walls. When he was sixty his back would be a perfect template of the arched tiles. His solo renditions were often four, five or six hours long, more than could be fitted on even a triple album or double-backed cassette. No band formed around him. He slept under a bush in Hyde Park alone with his guitar, which he hugged to him like a good woman, his head on his amp. Music was his mother, sister, daughter and wife – his intoxicated Kali with purple eyelids and red fingernails, wearing nothing but a plectrum and stockings of sheer electricity, her voice-box a five-watt amp, howling in orgasm. Though the songs he played had Hendrix titles, gradually his music had changed from Hendrix to pure 3-Tooth. He claimed to have lost all but three of his teeth playing 'Electric Ladyland' with his mouth. Though some buskers said Big Al had smashed them in.

For a moment Peach ached for the freedom of the busking world. Up till now, what little money he'd brought in had been from busking, but at the moment his guitar only had two strings, and he didn't have the money to buy the other four. It was strange that such a little problem could be decisive in one's destiny. If he'd had a full six strings, he may well have snuck home now, got his guitar, busked for a couple of hours, brought home his usual pound or two, and never become a landscape gardener. It would have been easier than finding work. But two strings are two strings, and they're not loud enough to earn the money to buy the other four. Peach stood listening to 3-Tooth's music with mingled admiration and repugnance. He admired his dedication and many of his plunging riffs. But he detested his electric sound. Peach disliked electric guitars. They were machines disguised as musical instruments. His own guitar was a small Spanish one. It had cheap nylon strings. When the first one had broken – top E – he'd told himself that he wouldn't replace it straightaway, as it would be good practice to play on five strings. And it was. He picked up combinations and runs he'd never thought of before. When the next string broke – the D string – and he only had four, he justified his laziness about going and buying new ones by saying that he was learning, on four strings, new zither-like chords which he would never have bothered to search out on a full fretboard. And it was true. He could make the little Spanish guitar chime like a cimbalom. Another string broke – G – and he taught himself to play on three. At the moment he was mastering playing on two strings, producing incredible ukelele effects. When another string broke, he'd give a solo-string performance at the Albert Hall. When that broke, he'd pass into the Taoist silence and become a headbanger.

Peach entered the tunnel though it was out of his way and he knew that if 3-Tooth was immersed in his music he wouldn't stop simply to pass the time of day with a friend. The guitar became the tunnel, and the tunnel became the guitar, narrowing to a brain-damaging pinpoint somewhere inside his head, tiles rippling like sequins on a concrete suit, fluorescent tubes flashing past threading his eyes on a jujube necklace, till, although he was approaching the guitarist, who was growing larger, it seemed that he'd entered a tunnel of sound that stretched before him into infinity and from which he'd never exit. He reached 3-Tooth. He was just about to hurry past without even waving, when, without any warning, the music stopped. Peach stopped dead. And the silence hit him like a sledgehammer. They stood together in the sudden stillness, as brontosauri of bass thunder galloped up the tunnel towards the silence of Edgware Road.

'All right,' shouted 3-Tooth, tilting into an imaginary microphone. He peered through his shades. 'Peach?'

'Hi, 3-Tooth.'

'How's tricks, man?'

'Great. I found out this morning we're going to have a baby.'

'Wow man, far out. Morag pregnant?'

'That's right.'

'How's the meditation goin'?'

'All right. Three hours a night, and a bit of reading in the evening.'

'Music's my meditation, man. Don't know how you do it, Peach.'

'I just sort of try to keep still, and look at myself.'

'Na. I ain't lookin' for meself, man, when I'm playin'. I'm lookin' for Jimi, man. He's me guru. Ain't no one never played a guitar like him, man, before or since. 'N ya don' need LPs or tapes or none a' that crap, man, t' hear him. His riffs are movin' out into space, man, for ever and ever, at the speed o' sound. That's where Jimi is, man, out amongst the stars. 'N I'll tell ya a secret, Peach.' 3-Tooth glanced up and down the tunnel, which was, as usual, empty. ' 'Ee's gonna come back. The greatest lead guitarist in tha history of the world, man. 'N the first person 'ee's gonna show 'imself to, is me. Then we're gonna form a group.'

'I believe you, 3-Tooth.'

3-Tooth kicked his amp, which had begun to moan, drowning his conspiratorial whisper.

'It's started t' happen already, man. I've seen 'im – outta the corner of me shades. Struttin' down tha tunnel in 'is astral body, man. Large as life. Feedin' me lyrics.'

'Sounds great.'

'Ya need a guru, Peach.'

'No. I'll do it my way. But listen, 3-Tooth. The thing that worries me is – Is meditation work? Real work. Not many people seem to think it is.'

'I dunno, man. I just do it.'

'But does it do any good in the world?'

'What? To tha people comin' down tha tunnel?'

'Yes, them — but to the invisible side of the world too. The unseen currents of love. That's God's work, as the Creator of the Universe. And when a man sits in meditation, perhaps he's doing God's work.'

'I suppose so, man.'

'But sometimes it just doesn't seem real. And that worries me, all the time I've put into it — not having a job, and all that.'

'Meditation's ya job, man. Like music's mine.'

Peach looked up and down the empty tunnel.

'Well, I'm off to find some ordinary work now. Manual work. Bread-winning work.'

'Nothin' wrong with bread, man,' said 3-Tooth looking at the empty guitar bag at his feet.

'But the funny thing is, 3-Tooth, I've never felt freer than I do this morning.'

'Ya still should find a guru, man.'

'No. I'm going to be self-employed. See you 'round, 3-Tooth.'

'Listen, man. Before ya dash. Can ya hold on to my pitch while I go and have a leak. Started at five this mornin' and I'm bustin'. Play somethin'. Anythin' ya earn is yours.'

And 3-Tooth handed Peach his guitar.

'Don't touch bottom E before ya've pumped the wah-wah coupla times. And give the pick-up a nudge if the volume gets outta control. Won't be gone long, so it shouldn't. And don't touch the amp whatever happens. Play one o' ya own numbers, Peach.'

'I think I'll just wait.'

'Okay. Just hold me pitch. Big Al's bin nosin' aroun'.'

3-Tooth disappeared in the direction of the subway toilets.

Peach looked at the red guitar, then looked up the tunnel. Big Al! The heaviest busker in the London Transport network. If Big Al came along and no one was playing, that was the end of 3-Tooth's gig. He had been known to crash pitches even when someone *was* playing. He simply set up on the opposite side of the tunnel till his bad vibes drove the original busker away. Still, the pitch was safer if someone was actually performing. Peach looked at 3-Tooth's guitar. The box was shaped like a flat fork of lightning. It had once been red, but was now covered with paintings of flowers, the illuminated names of Hendrix songs, and an icon of Jimi which 3-Tooth had spent years working at. Peach looked beseechingly towards the toilets but there was no sign of 3-Tooth. Then he thought he caught a glimpse of Big Al with his SAS guitar bag going in the other direction, towards the Praed Street exit. Peach searched for the wah-wah. But none of the knobs, switches or levers on the soundbox of 3-Tooth's guitar had labels. He touched a chrome lever, and the little black box beside him sobbed then went dead. At least it was on. He could see Big Al looking down the tunnel. What should he play? 'Greensleeves'. It was not very assertive, but it was very English. Tourists from the Metropole would like that. But would Big Al? He looked up the tunnel again. Big Al was gone. 'Greensleeves' was in D minor. So the first note was an A.

Peach touched the A string and, for a fraction of a second, some force instinct in the string itself wound his finger in a spasm around it, and gave him a short, sharp shock. Peach jumped backwards, pulling his hand away. But as he sucked his tingling finger he noticed that the string had begun to vibrate – even though he hadn't had a chance to pluck it. The touch must have been enough. Almost silently, it moaned and echoed. This A was about three octaves deeper than he had expected. It was like Paul Robeson on Largactyl trying to hum the first note of 'Greensleeves'. Then the string's subsonic wobbling reached the lower limit of the human ear, where it became the beginning of a mighty roar. Peach had heard Tibetan mountain-horns. But this A was already louder and more terrifying than them. It was the A of 'Alas . . .', the first tragic word in the song of 'Greensleeves'. Peach looked around him. The dead fluorescent tube in the roof of the tunnel was rattling and throwing off explosions of light like a mortar. And still the note grew louder. It already seemed louder than 3-Tooth played. Perhaps it was the ghost of Jimi descending into the tunnel with his own 5000-watt wall of amplifiers. And still the note grew louder. He could be arrested, on the first day of his fatherhood, for creating a note like this in public. Yet he dared not touch the A string again, to damp it, for fear of getting another, perhaps deadlier shock. He was already trembling from the first one, and from the presence of Big Al. Peach desperately searched 3-Tooth's amp, but there was no sign of a switch that would turn the whole thing off. Suddenly a blue tongue poked out of the little black box, then disappeared.

Gingerly Peach touched the other strings. Thank God! It was only the A string that was electrified. Well, if he couldn't stop the guitar, he'd bloody well play it. Let Big Al come near if he dared! The next note was D, on the open D string, the '. . . las' of 'Alas . . .' It sounded clear and true. Except that a swish of feedback, like a sigh, doubled over the top of the note. He played on. '. . . my . . . love . . .' E up to F. He plucked the two notes poignantly, and they were perfect. Except that a sound like the beating of hundreds of doves' wings escaped from the amplifier and flew away as he played '. . . my . . .', then a great, shuddering throb of static, which may have been the wah-wah 3-Tooth had spoken of, above the '. . . love . . .' But more strangely still, none of the notes, after he had finished playing them, faded away. Like the original, mighty A, they entered the amp and wouldn't die down. And these overtones awoke others – a moaning like an electric bamboo flute, the tinny crackle of Arab goat-bells. It seemed that the black box had a memory! Peach's ears popped. Though his head was swimming he gritted his teeth and played on – '. . . you . . . do . . . me . . . wrong . . .' He huddled over the fretboard as he played, to hide his face. Latvian electric zithers awoke around '. . . you . . .' Somewhere inside the amp a didgeridoo took '. . . do . . .' and wobbled it in its Adam's apple. '. . . me . . .' was scoured up and down on a ratchety washboard of feedback, each scratch a separate quarter-tone, wondrously delineated. And still the great A string thundered them all upwards. '. . . wrong . . .' played Peach, and gasped. For he thought he heard – for a split second – a human voice, dark as a gypsy's, sneering through gravel, singing '. . . wrong . . .' to the guitar's shrieking '. . . wrong . . .' It was Jimi Hendrix! He was materialising out of a wall of unbearable noise.

Though all the strings on the guitar had stopped vibrating, none of the nine notes he had played would die away, so that the opening of 'Greensleeves' formed one vast simultaneous note. In other words – outside Time! Peach swooned. The roar was terrifying. If he played on to the end of the melody the tiles would fall off the tunnel walls. His ears ached. Would 3-Tooth never come back?

Looking up the tunnel for his friend, Peach saw an elderly couple enter it from the far end. Even at that distance, and in that light, he could see that they were well-dressed and healthily tanned in the style of tourists, and already buffeted by his music. And for a second, in that kink in reality, huddled into the tunnel wall with 3-Tooth's howling instrument, he thought it was his Mum and Dad! He knew it couldn't be. They'd made no plans to come from Australia. They'd never been to England. He knew that they would probably make the long and expensive trip when they knew they were to have a grandchild, even by their alienated son. But they couldn't possibly have heard of it yet. He'd only found out himself an hour ago. Yet the elderly couple with their camera and A–Z looked for all the world like his Mum and Dad! Could it be some terrible coincidence? And here he was, kneeling on the floor of a filthy tunnel in London, with this howling instrument in his hands . . . Would they even recognise 'Greensleeves', one of his Dad's favourite tunes, in the pandemonium? The noise was loud enough to puncture their old eardrums, used only to healthy sing-songs in the living room back home. Peach huddled like a foetus over the guitar, and turned to the wall so that his Mum and Dad, whom he hadn't seen for eight years, shouldn't recognise him.

But then, as he unsuccessfully tried to cover the noise with his body, he had an inspiration. He remembered a meditational technique of Rudolf Steiner's, the purpose of which was to strengthen the will to such a pitch that it can *wind time backwards*, till the meditator has the power to make the whole past, even the time before his birth, appear before him, wound on to the spool of the present instant: the meditator must inwardly 'hear' a familiar tune *backwards*. Peach had tried it before and knew it was uncannily difficult to do. But perhaps it would work on 3-Tooth's guitar.

The old couple were halfway down the tunnel.

First Peach plucked '. . . wrong . . .' And it stopped. The note and Jimi's voice beyond it faded slowly away. He played '. . . me . . .' and the washboard of feedback began to die away with the note that had started it. '. . . do . . . you . . .' played Peach, and the didgeridoo and zithers, and the host of other instruments began to fade away. It was as though the little black amplifier was unravelling its memory. He played '. . . love . . . my . . .' and the throbbing pang and the purling of doves flew away. A great peace descended upon the tunnel. He played '. . . las . . .' and the peace deepened.

That left the great, original A. It was still menacingly loud. And it was electrified. Peace shuddered at the thought of another shock. His hands sweated. But he must do it. He couldn't subject these good people to this ominous note. He plucked the A string and the shock jolted his teeth. But blessedly the great note began to die away. And in the profoundly gathering silence, as the A of '. . . A . . .' grew less, Peach, with his face still on the wall, heard the whirring of a movie camera. And voices. They weren't his mother's and father's. And Peach felt a pang that they weren't. He would have liked to tell them about his child. And even here, on his hands and knees in a dirty tunnel, he somehow knew that he wouldn't have been ashamed.

'Wasn't that beautiful!' said the woman.

'Never heard anything like it,' said the man.

Peach heard pages being turned.

'"The street musicians, or 'Buskers', of London", read the woman authoritatively, "are a colourful aspect of the City's cultural life."'

'I think it was something by Messiaen,' said the man.

And their well-polished shoes clip-clopped away.

When he could hear them no more, Peach turned around. There, in 3-Tooth's guitar bag, lay a ten-pound note! And there was 3-Tooth.

'You did all right, man,' he said.

Peach climbed to his feet and handed back his guitar.

'You keep it. It's your pitch.'

But 3-Tooth picked up the note and thrust it into his hand.

'You fuckin' take it. You play your way. I play mine. And besides, you're gonna need it. You're gonna be a daddy.'

Fergus O'Fury stood in a deepening hole outside the Mother Black Cap, Camden Road. Whether he was digging for electricity, water, gas or sewer he knew not, nor did he care. His hole was deepening like a thirsty pint drunk in rage. But its only 'head' was his own mop of light red hair and indignant face, now on a level with the kerbstone. Over his brawny shoulder and on to the pavement he threw great gules of clay and self-pity.

Out of the saloon bar of the Mother Black Cap stepped a man who looked like an older, greyer Fergus O'Fury. He was just as big but there was more fat in it, and less muscle, and no heart. He wiped a delicate white froth from his upper lip, stepped to the edge of the hole, studied its depth, and muttered a mouthful of 'fookin'-move-ons'. Then he picked up a brush which was leaning against the bar-room window and ingratiatingly swept stray crumbs of clay from under the feet of the passers-by into a tidy heap, which he whisked, with the one flourish, back into Fergus O'Fury's hole. Then he turned and re-entered the saloon bar where his next pint already stood on the table. Fergus O'Fury threw his pick and shovel up and rose from his hole. Was he to be in this man's power for ever, or at least until pay-time? So deep was his hole, and his rage, and so mighty was his leap that he knocked over Peach O'Hare as he walked by, clutching the ten-pound note in his trouser pocket, and holding the idea of work steady in his Brow Centre.

'Fookin' ganger man,' roared Fergus O'Fury at him.

'I'm sorry,' said Peach, jumping backwards. 'I didn't mean . . .'

Fergus O'Fury hadn't heard the word 'sorry' for ten years. A crafty look entered his rage-brimmed eyes.

'Don't you tink nuttin' of it, young fella,' he said. 'I'm the one as ought to be sorry. Rearin' up at a man for no good reason. Come on 'n I'll buy ye a drink.'

A great clay hand clapped hold of Peach's free one.

'Me name's Fergus O'Fury. You call me Fergus.'

The great arm was around Peach's shoulder making him aware for almost the first time of how light a bone-structure he had.

'I'm Peach, Peach O'Hare. Pleased to meet you, Fergus. Actually I'm not much of a drinker. I practise meditation, and I'm afraid alcohol's bad for my concentration.'

But the brawny arm, with a sweep of universal brotherhood that could crumple his shoulder like a ball of paper in its hand, was already guiding him towards the saloon bar door.

'Well, don't ye give yer concentration a tort!'

And they were inside.

'What'll it be, den?' Fergus asked Peach, drawing up two stools.

'Well, perhaps a tomato—'

'A paint o' light an' tan for dis gentleman, and I'll have a stout, and a little whiskey chaser for boat of us,' cried Fergus O'Fury.

The four glasses were set before them.

Fergus snatched up a small glass and sent the fiery liquor down his inner hole.

'Why do you call it a chaser, Fergus, if you drink it first?' enquired Peach out of a genuine interest in language.

'Because 'tis chasin' me last paint, and sure he's got a good head start on 'er,' said Fergus. 'And I'll have anuder chaser if ye don't mind, barmaid, for dis here stout is hot in de blocks!'

And with one mighty tilt of his head he tipped the black pint into his hole, quartering it with his Adam's apple.

'Ah be Jesus, Peach,' he said as he placed the foaming empty on the counter, and slapped his pockets, 'I've not a fardin' on me. But sure, dat's me ganger over dere. He'll see me right.'

Peach looked at the ganger man, but could see no right in the scowl he cast upon Fergus.

'No, no,' said Peach, 'let me.'

And his ten-pound note was out and on the bar.

'Ah, yer a fine lad. Drink up. Drink up.'

Peach tilted his glass, took a mouthful of the beer, then tilted his glass back down again, allowing the liquor to run back into the glass, leaving a sickening aftertaste in his mouth. But Fergus O'Fury was not deceived. In fact he seemed to be somehow infuriated.

'Drink up, me lad. Drink up!'

And Peach knew enough about the nuances of language to know he was in danger.

'In fucked,' said Peach at the bottom of his first pint, 'I dish mothered this morning that hymen growing to be a feather!'

'God bless us,' cried Fergus O'Fury. 'A farder! What finer ting is dere t' be in dis world dan a farder! Sure, I'm six times one, soon t' be eight meself. And I can tell ye, Peach, when yer first one is born, 'tis like steppin' into a new world. Dere's solid eart under yer boots for de thirst time – cos yor de eart under dere little bootees, if ye see me meaning. Yor de rock for dat little one. Yor de hole in which dey stand, strite and dug true. Ye don't just do a shift, den piss it all up de wall, like ye used to. Ye start drinkin' more maturely, like. Ye

26

become – if I may put it dis way – a more philosophical drinker. Yer hold yer paint better. Ye keep it close to yer chest, cos ya can no longer afford to go home 'n start breakin' up de furniture an' kickin' tings no more. I mean, let's be honest, Peach – ye still might be dirt in some folks' eyes,' and he lowered at the ganger man in the corner who was lowering at him, 'ye might be less dan a clod o' clay to some, but when ye get back home, ye become a . . . a rock . . . a footin' . . . a plint for . . . for . . . two more paints please, Mrs O'Hooley – wid chasers standin' beside boat o' dem – to drink to de healt o' de holy child!'

Tears rose in Peach's eyes.

'Woo the wily wild!' he cried, and dashed back his whiskey.

After that he had a blurred vision of manly pints, each with an open bottle beside it like a round-shouldered woman and a chaser clinking like a bright-eyed child, queuing at his elbow like travellers waiting for the 31 bus. By some iron law of carousing, Fergus ordered Peach one of these little holy families of bottles and glasses for every one he drank himself. So that after an hour the queue of beverages had grown as long and impatient as a bus queue on a Monday morning. The fresh heads of the pints were lowering into a flat bitterness at the world, the economy, foreigners and the price of a pint. The womanly bottles at their sides, though Fergus O'Fury solicit-ously balanced their lids on their heads like bent hats, were losing their froth and turning sour at the incompetence of men. The chasers clinked around them like restless children – an endless queue of drinks, its bile rising – and they were all waiting for . . . for . . . for him, Peach O'Hare, nibbling at the froth of his second pint. He was the 31 that never came. He was the treacherous inspector. The up-yours driver. The nihilist conductor. All rolled into one. He took another bottle on board, but it was hopeless, there was no standing upstairs, and the queue that was left outside only grew angrier and angrier . . .

The queue was just about to riot, when up from the rear swept a large, compendious carriage with a pale-red awning drawn by two clay-brown chestnuts with delicate white froth on their bits. It was Mother Black Cap's Courtesy Coach. The coachman was a gentleman. His livery was a clay-smeared suit with the hems and cuffs touched out in cement. With a gallant 'Let me help ye dere!' he swept open the coach door, and, starting from the rear, helped the queue on board, children first, mixing the men and women together in a merry fizz. Even the last grey pint, Peach's third, which had waited so long, was jollied into a frothing good fellow as he was handed in with a 'Hold tight dere!' and the congenial coachman who now had froth on *his* nose slammed the door, leapt up on to the postillion, cracked his whip and galloped away, leaving the face of Fergus O'Fury, red and bloated, an inch from his own resting on the saloon bar counter.

'Yes,' said Fergus solemnly. 'De birt o' your first child is de birt of a new world for ye.'

'Thrash,' said Peach ecstatically, '. . . thrash's exactly how I fail, Fog Arse. Thrash why I'm out this morning, lurking for work. Not a jab, mind you. Eyes don't want a straight jab. I want . . . to be . . . shelf-employed!'

'Ah, self-employed,' said Fergus, sizing up the ganger man. ''Tis certainly de ting t' be.'

'I used to work on building seats,' said Peach, his Throat Centre wondrously supple.

'A jiner are ye?'

'Snow, snow. I wash only a harbourer, Fig Eyes. But I washed the bricklayers and chippies all the time. I washed and weren't. Now eyes going to be a lanscape gardener. I'm growing to build the Garden of Eden in people's back pardons.'

'Sure, an' ye don't have t' beg pardon for dat, me friend. 'Tis a fine trade.'

'Eyes going to lay peeving, build flower buds, and erect trollies for the climbing grubs.'

''Tis good work, I tell ye. And out o' doors. Two more paints o' light an' tan, if you will, Mrs O'Hooley, and a couple more o' de little fellas.'

'But do you know what trebles my mind most, Fugue Ears,' said Peach. 'You know what's the question that gives me the deepest weary?'

'Wot question's dat?'

'IS MASTURBATION WORK?'

'Good God, don't speak of it, young fella.'

'Eyes do three hours' masturbation a night, and a little riding in the evening.'

'God defend ye,' cried Fergus. 'And you a farder t' be!'

'Anorgy, Figures. Cosmic anorgy . . .'

'An orgy? Don't say no more. I can see what it's done t' ye already!'

'For you know, Fear Gas, I can see that you are a man of a deeply religious sporren . . .'

'Sure, an' we don't wear 'em in Ireland, me young friend. Mrs O'Hooley . . . Mrs O'Hooley . . .'

'. . . so you must also snow that God is the Contractor of the Universe!'

'I know no other ganger,' said Fergus righteously at the ganger man beginning to rumble in his corner.

'Well, when a man sits in masturbation, Few Gears, I believe he is doing God's warp!'

'And warped it has made ye, young fella. And blind soon, too, if I know anyting. Come on. On yer feet. And no more of dis terrible talk. Some real work, dat's what you need. Some real down-to-eart work t' break this vicious habit. And blowed if I won't find ye some. Fergus O'Fury knows all dere is t' know about work.'

He swept the change from Peach's ten-pound note off the bar and into his own pocket. Then he lifted Peach to his feet and dragged him towards the door. But the door was blocked by the wrathful ganger man.

'Back in dat fookin' hole, O'Fury, or yor down de fookin' road!'

'Stick yer hole up yer arse,' said Fergus poetically, and stepped into the street, bearing the raving Peach.

As soon as he entered the light and air, the vast freedom

that had expanded his Throat Centre smote the whole of his body. He collapsed on the pavement. But Fergus O'Fury dragged him to his feet.

'Now no talk about dat terrible ting out here. Dere's women and children walkin' past. You want work t' give ye a bit o' yor self-respect back. Good, self-employed, landscape-garden' work, if I understood ye right. Seein' as how an' yor t' be a daddy soon. Well, I'll help ye. 'Tis a good trade. I'll set ye up, sure I will. Dere's nuttin' I know more about 'n work, more's the misfortune. Now − you got any tools?' asked Fergus, blushing, and lengthening the 's'.

'Tools? Tools?' cried Peach. 'The only tools you need for masturbation are . . .'

'Stop dat.'

Lying where he'd flung them, beside his unfinished hole, were a pickaxe and a spade that belonged to the ganger man. Fergus remembered the nine of Peach's ten pounds that were now swilling around in his belly. And he remembered also the ganger man's ruthless reign. And stooping down with Peach under one arm, he picked both tools up in his large hand.

'Dere you are, me boy − you got tools. I've polished that pickaxe handle wit de sweat of me own palms. Now 'tis yours.'

And he propped Peach against the wall with it and leant the shovel beside him.

'Wot about trowels? And a hammer and chisel? And a spirit-level, den?'

'Spirit travel?' asked Peach, his head rolling towards the pavement.

Beside the hole stood a portable workman's hut. Fergus plunged in and came out with a bricklaying trowel, a pointing trowel, a clubhammer and bolster. He took his own sand-wiches out of their plastic Sainsbury's carrier bag, and filled it with the tools. Then he produced a long spirit-level.

'Dere you go, me boy. You're a tradesman. Now off t' de *Camden Clarinet* wit boat of us. I tink dere's just enough money left for two small advertisements.'

When he hung the plastic bag over Peach's inert hand, his young acolyte toppled forwards on to the footpath where he lay in silence, as though he'd finally reached the state of blessed samadhi. Fergus saw that he would never walk to the *Clarinet*. At the kerb by the hole stood a battered, cement-clogged dumper-truck, which also belonged to the ganger man. Tenderly Fergus O'Fury picked Peach up, and his tools, and placed them in the bucket of the dumper. The ganger man's brush still leant against the pub window. It was the only tool he ever used. Fergus flung it in with Peach. Then he leapt into the driver's seat and they roared off up the hill to the *Camden Clarinet*.

Here, in the open-plan front office, Fergus O'Fury took two advertisement forms and went outside to where Peach was sleeping in the dumper truck. On the first form he wrote

PEACH O'HARE

He pondered. Had the young fella said he'd worked on the buildings? So he wrote

PEACH O'HARE EXPERIENCED LANDSCAPE BUILDER
BRICKWORK, PAVING, FENCING ETC.

He paused and studied his friend's face. He was sleeping like a baby. But even asleep he seemed to be pondering hard. He noted his high, sensitive forehead, and wrote

CONSCIENTIOUS WORK UNDERTAKEN BY A GOOD MAN

He then hunted through Peach's pockets and found an address and telephone number which he added to the advertisement.

He saw Peach's soft white guitar-tuning hands and wrote on the bottom

NO JOB TOO SMALL

31

For a moment Fergus O'Fury considered throwing in his lot with Peach O'Hare and adding his own name and credentials to the ad. But no. They were two different men.

So on the second form he wrote

FERGUS O'FURY CONTRACTOR
EXCAVATIONS AND GROUNDWORK

He then gave the telephone number of the saloon bar of the Mother Black Cap.

He counted up the words on both ads. It was ten pence a word. He had forty pence left. Enough for a half of bitter. He looked at his own hands, large and gnarled, shrugged his mighty shoulders, and wrote

NO JOB TOO BIG.

PEACH climbed on to the piano stool nervously. In meditation it is necessary to keep a daily rhythm, to appoint an
hour for practice – which in Peach's case was four a.m. – and
stick to it, so that an ebb and flow with the Beyond is
established, as regular as the seasons or the movement of the
stars, by which beneficent spiritual forces, whose very nature
is rhythm, may draw near. It is also necessary to lead an
orderly moral life. Peach must have met a demonic force in the
saloon bar of the Mother Black Cap. For he had missed two
days' meditation with a hangover. His memory of the encounter was hazy – like looking down into the Pit through the
sickly bottom of an empty. And even on this third morning, as
he climbed on to his stool, folded his legs, set his hands, palms
upwards, on his knees, straightened his back, balanced his
head, and closed his eyes, he felt washed out. He'd lost ten
pounds, which was three or four days' keep. He'd lost his
meditational rhythm. He'd lost his momentum to find work,
after such a rosy setting forth. And now as he sat inside this
darkness-within-darkness before another dawn, he wondered
if he hadn't lost his way long before, and was now merely lost-
within-lost-within-lost. That was the problem with not being
an adept: stillness was stillness, inside the mystical state,
profound and refreshing, but outside the mystical moment
stillness was passivity, utter helplessness, the inertia that rots
bones. And all that seemed real, in his interior world, was a
nauseous dream-memory of being bumped down the Harrow
Road in some sort of hopper, and disgorged from a cement
mixer at his own front door.

Peach bent his head back, with his eyes still shut, took one
inner look upwards, and instantly became Spirit. He had learnt
this trick long ago. It was easy. All it needed was that it should

be the most important thing in your life. A moment before the Abyss came over him, he saw the Descent of Light – still as a waterfall, striking him like lightning. He saw it, not with his eyes, for they were already seeing just blackness, but through the diaphanous place between his eyes, the tender cavity of thought in his forehead, which is called the Brow Centre. Then he had to look down. The force of it was too great. But having once seen it, he knew that he now sat inside the great roaring column of goodness. And by its Light he saw the shadow of himself spasm through his body, momentarily losing its total control of it. A shuddering stick-man. A blind will letting go of him and dying. His spine sat square in the column of Light: upright, as though it were the plumb by which he had been built. He saw, heard, felt, touched, smelt, nothing, as the great Descent passed through his Heart. Where, taking pity on his darkness, it began to open out, like a bivalve shell swinging open, passing his ribs on both sides, and the knuckles of his shoulders, its edges growing fluent, turning to a great, sobbing wing-beat. And there, nestling softly in his brain like a new-born baby sucking on his cortex, was Great, Illuminate Imagination, freed from fantasy, stripped of daydreams. And he knew that whatever It created was real.

It created the inner being of Morag before his eyes. On this side of the Abyss she was often the first thing he saw – seven stars in a mist. Appearing then dying then reappearing as quick as the fizz in lemonade. Seven stars seen by moonlight. Seven stars like dancing gnats in the afterglow of lightning. It was Morag and no one else. It came towards him, her spiritual self. He had the right to see it and invite it. For the agreement had been made to be transparent to each other on this side of the Abyss – though he could never say, with his waking mind, where and when the agreement had been made. The night all around the seven stars was his knowledge of her body. He was invisible himself. It came closer and danced in ecstasy before his eyes, seven stars with the gestures of Morag. His heart beat with love. He sat still as the column of Light passed down his spine. Seven stars, the spiritual Morag, stripped now of their

34

mist, dancing in his seven Centres. He became aware of his sexual excitement, and added it to the moment. As they joined, he *had* to love all the men and women on earth, or lose her. Sitting thus, sending his love out beyond himself and Morag now, to where their child danced, half here, half in the Cosmos, he became aware of the dead weight in his arms, which had stretched themselves out without his knowing it. And an instant later, the stick-man, whispering at the insides of his eardrums, back in swift possession of his brain, alive and kicking, hissed 'What a load of rubbish! What a load of pathetic fantasising! Pull your finger out, Peach!'

To shake him off, and forget, Peach opened his eyes, blinked, yawned convulsively, shook himself, and hurried to the stove to fix him a cup of coffee.

⋯•⟶◆>●<◀━━◆•⋯

three

PEACH remembered little of what passed between him and Fergus O'Fury. He might have been able to forget the fierce Irishman altogether, if it hadn't been for the pickaxe, shovel, sledgehammer, brush and bricklaying tools in a Sainsbury's carrier bag, stacked neatly inside the front door. Being asleep at the time, he knew nothing of the ad.

Though he couldn't work out how the tools had got there, Peach decided that he must use them. They were a sign. The forces under the world wanted him to carry on with his new career. So he walked north again, and this time reached Hampstead. He looked at the noticeboards in newsagents' windows. There were only a few ads seeking landscapers, and they were dauntingly specific about whom and what they required. He took down several telephone numbers, but even as he was writing he knew he wouldn't ring them. His thoughts turned to busking again. But then, just as he'd foreseen, he found a copy of the local paper on a park bench. It was the new edition, out that day. He turned wearily to the Services Required section of the classifieds, hoping someone would be looking for him there. But all the ads for gardeners seemed to Peach, who was frightened of confronting strangers, let alone in the guise of a tradesman, to have something hectoring and cross-examining about them, something of the soft-tough interrogation technique condensed into a two-liner, the billy stick on the bars of false pretences, then the soft offer of an hourly rate, till he broke down and admitted he was a cowboy.

Then he glanced idly across at the Services Offered page, and read his own name enshrined in a seventeen-word ode, followed by the telephone number of the lady next door, who took occasional messages for him and Morag.

PEACH O'HARE, EXPERIENCED LANDSCAPE BUILDER
BRICKWORK PAVING FENCING ETC
CONSCIENTIOUS WORK UNDERTAKEN BY A GOOD MAN
NO JOB TOO SMALL

Peach read the ad over and over, fascinated and appalled. He was offering himself to the world. And he had no recollection of doing it.

Below his ad, he read

FERGUS O'FURY CONTRACTOR . . .

The name rang a bell.

Shaken, Peach did no more job hunting that day.

Later that evening, Mrs Emmet, the neighbour with the telephone, came knocking excitedly on the door. A lady had rung asking for Mr O'Hare, wanting him to come and see a job in Camden Town – brick-paving her back garden. A lump formed in Peach's throat. Mrs Emmet had the address and telephone number. Peach, Morag and Mrs Emmet sat in the kitchen for a long time discussing this lucky break. Peach's stomach was churning. At last he stood up.

'Well, I'll be off then.'

'Good luck, Peach.'

Fergus O'Fury hadn't given Peach a tape measure, so he borrowed Morag's sewing-tape.

It was six o'clock when Peach knocked on the door of a tiny Georgian house in the back streets of Camden Town. Instead of a grim-eyed householder, hard judge of an impostor, looking him up and down for signs of the cowboy, a friendly looking woman opened the door.

'Mrs Pleasance? I'm Peach O'Hare.'

She smiled at him. There was a moment's recognition of one mental person by another – even with his hands, which hadn't seen manual work for seven years, in his pockets. But he saw no sign that this recognition spoiled his chances as a tradesman. In fact he could have sworn it enhanced her confidence in him.

'Come in, Mr O'Hare. Did you get a parking space all right?'

She wasn't trying to wheedle his lack of transport out of him, but he lied.

'Oh yes – just around the corner.'

Though there was in fact an empty space right in front of the house.

'Come through to the garden.'

The lady showed him out into a small courtyard of crumbling concrete just outside her kitchen. A tunnel of bushes and fruit trees rustled further up the garden.

'We want this concrete taken up and replaced with brick paving – in those second-hand stocks, the yellow ones. Do you do that kind of thing?'

'Yes,' stammered Peach. 'All the time.'

He took out Morag's sewing-tape, and began to measure the old patio, drawing a rough square in his exercise book. Mrs Pleasance watched him as he sat down to calculate the area.

'Do you do anything else besides gardening jobs?'

Peach blushed. Was he that transparent?

'Anything else?' he mumbled. 'No. Oh no – not for my living. I've . . . I've got a family. Though I do meditate a bit . . .'

'I meant do you do any other building work – plumbing or rewiring. Our kitchen's in a mess.'

'No. No. Definitely not. I stick . . . outdoors.'

Peach wondered how he could be so deceitful with someone

38

so cordial. He thought of his own kitchen – the hole in the roof, the cold-only basin, the two-point plug with its blue tongue. No. He could do less harm outdoors.

'Would you like a cup of tea while you're working that out?' asked the lady, seeing him frowning over his calculations.

'Yes please.'

Peach sat on an upturned bucket, with his book and pen, and calculated the number of bricks needed to fill that small space. It was twelve square yards at thirty-two bricks a square yard. That was three hundred and eighty-four bricks. Say four hundred, just to be safe. And sand and cement? How deep should he make his bedding? And should it be sand or cement? He remembered old Fred laying paving slabs at Marshall Street. He had used a couple of inches of sand, and no cement. So if he, not knowing for sure, made it four inches of cement on top of hard-core, that should be all right. He hoped. He worked it out. One hundred and eight square feet at one third of a foot deep equals thirty-six cubic feet, which is one and a half yards of sand, and say . . . how many bags of cement? It was impossible to guess. He tried to picture a yard and a half of sand. It was a long time since he'd seen one. It was a big pile. He held it in his mind's eye and tried to picture five, six, then seven, bags of cement stacked against it. He knew the ratio was four to one. Seven bags looked about one fourth of the pile. Better make it eight. He'd rung the Garden Centre before he'd come and found out the price of these materials, so it was an easy matter to calculate how much they would come to: thirty-three pounds fifty for the sand, twenty-eight pounds thirty-three for the cement, and one hundred and forty for the bricks. This made a total of two hundred and one pounds eighty-three.

Then there was the skip. He'd need a skip for the concrete and earth he dug out of the old patio, and for any left-over bricks and sand. Someone had told him skips were about forty pounds each. This brought the total to two hundred and forty-one pounds seventy-three. Peach blanched. He hadn't seen money like this since he left Australia. And how would he pay for these things when he barely had his bus fare home?

Then came labour. Which raised the questions: How long would it take him? And how much was he worth? To both questions there was no answer. He didn't have a clue. But he had practised alchemical visualisation. Now he used the same technique to visualise himself, step by step, doing this job. He was an optimistic person, and one visualisation – digging out the concrete and carrying it through – flowed into another – bringing in the sand and cement and bricks – which flowed into another – floating a foundation – which flowed into another – laying the bricks – and into another – pointing them – and into another – sweeping up and getting paid – with a dreamlike ease. It was like watching Golgonooza going up in one of Blake's prophetic poems. The days it would take him seemed demarcated with a regularity and rhythmic simplicity that was almost timeless. Five and a half days. Call it six. Six days as rock-like yet rhythmical as the Six Days of Creation. And there he was, in imagination, transforming this crumbly patch of concrete into a glowing, golden-bricked patio like the pavements of Jerusalem. A strange excitement stirred him as he gazed at the moss and grass in the cracks of this diabolical piece of concreting. Here he was, confronted with concrete and earth, with brick, sand and cement – and he was still meditating!

The lady brought his tea.

'How's it going?'

Six days? No, call it five and a half. In case grass came up through the cerulean pointing of Jerusalem's streets. Then how much was he worth? He'd heard that bricklayers on big sites got fifty or sixty pounds a day. So he was worth, say, twenty-five. Or was he? Perhaps he was only worth fifteen, or even ten. But if he charged ten, she might think he didn't know what he was doing. Which he didn't. And besides, you can't live on ten pounds a day. Though he could, easily. Better call it twenty pounds a day. That came to one hundred and ten pounds for five and a half days' labour. Call it a hundred and fifteen. No, one hundred and five. He didn't want to price himself out of his first job. He made his final addition.

'It'll come to . . . three hundred and forty-six pounds eighty-three pence – all in.'

'Are you sure?' asked Mrs Pleasance.

'Well perhaps . . .' How much should he come down?

'It doesn't seem very much, that's all. Isn't it quite a big job?'

But Peach was carrying enough guilt already.

'No,' he said. 'Thank you very much. That's it.'

'Well then, that's fine by us. When can you start?'

'Let's see. It's Friday now. Would Monday be all right?'

'What time?'

'Nine o'clock.'

A Mozart piano sonata was coming from the upstairs window. Peach stopped and listened.

'That's my husband.'

'Golly. I thought it was a record.'

'So . . . nine o'clock—'

'Sharp. Monday morning.'

It was eleven o'clock that Sunday evening, and Peach and Morag sat in bed in their homely squat. Morag's shawl, hanging in the window in place of a curtain, turned the street-lamp's harsh saffron into a golden net and cast it into the room. A pane of glass had fallen out of the window, and Peach had reglazed it with a plastic bag, which now breathed gently in and out, like a polythene lung with EAT MORE FRUIT on it. Morag's bracelets and necklaces, hanging on nails around the room, glittered like treasure her swaying shawl had trawled from darkness. Their double bed, which took up most of the small room, was in fact two single mattresses lying side by side on the floor like soiled lovers and tending to drift apart when they made love. They'd always slept like that. Morag had brought her own single mattress when she came to squat with him. Peach had meant to stitch them together, but had never got round to it. Morag's loom was set up on a small table under the window. Though she turned out enough shawls, coats and rugs to keep herself, and a little of him, he always saw the loom strung with new, unfinished work. So that on this dark and balmy evening it seemed that, like Penelope, she had unpicked her lifetime's weaving back to this one panel of the coat of many colours. On the mantelpiece above the ruined cones of the gas-fire stood Peach's small collection of books on meditation, religion and myth, a monument to a future's work left undone.

Now, on the night before his first landscaping job, he sat in bed with Morag and watched the windowpane breathe.

'She was so nice,' he told Morag for the fiftieth time. 'And I was expecting some old battle-axe. I just must do a good job for her.'

'Of course you'll do a good job, Peach.'

'I've ordered everything from a garden centre up in Highgate. Except the bricks. No one seemed to have any second-hand stocks. You don't think she'll mind if I ask her to pay for the materials for me, C.O.D.?'

'It doesn't sound like it.'

'I've only got enough to get there and a bit for some lunch.'

'Perhaps she'll give you an advance, so you can get home.'

'I'm going to put in a three-inch concrete foundation, Morag. I'll do that first. Then another inch or so to lay the bricks on . . .'

'Look, Peach. Don't worry about it any more. You'll do a lovely job. Go to sleep now. You need some rest.'

'But I only got up six hours ago. I won't be ready to go to sleep till . . . till about when I'm supposed to start work.'

'Well try.'

And Morag kissed him and threw her Paisley scarf over the lamp, and the room waded into a waist-high field of dusky cornflowers. She slid down into her half of the bed and shut her eyes. Peach lay down too, and passing his hand through the blankets, lifted Morag's nightdress, and put his palm on her belly. His hand ached with pleasure. Perhaps there was a chakra there, in his palm, amongst the bones and muscles and tendons. Like Christ's stigmata, only made of pleasure. And an added ache of joy seemed to rise out of Morag's belly into his hand. An added softness, and her belly was soft enough as it was.

'Goodnight, little Undifferentiated Consciousness,' he said.

And he tried to go to sleep. He fell into a dusky, purple-flowered doze. Everything was in order. The skip. The sand and cement. Tools. Bus fare . . . He waded waist-high through the purple wheat of a dream in which a child was hiding from him. They were playing Hide and Seek. But the child was nowhere to be seen, and as he searched and searched Peach grew anxious. Then it struck him that before he could find the child, he must remember something. Something that was vitally important, he dreamed, to his next day's work. When he remembered it, he'd see the child in the purple wheat. But the whole of him, even his sleeping body, was clenched against remembering it. For it was something dangerous. Frightening. He called and called, cooees of terror.

When the first rays of the sun passed golden through Morag's shawl, he woke, still up to his armpits in his search for this memory. What was it? He couldn't think. He dragged the piano stool into the kitchen, climbed on, and began to meditate. Six o'clock. He was late. He usually began at four. He only had two hours to still himself before he faced the day's ordeal. He breathed in deeply and gathered his consciousness into the point of pure awareness which he called the 'Pharaoh's Tomb'. Who was he? He was nothing. Where was he? He was nowhere. So there was nothing to worry about. Light from the spiritual world poured downwards. *This* was him. This light was his true being. The base of his spine began to glow. The material energies were awakening. He brought himself down into his Heart Centre, and thought of love. When he thought of love, it went. He sat as still as he could, in his Heart Centre, incapable of love by his own right. So who would love *him*? He waited for the Divine Heart to beat love into him.

43

He waited and waited, as the sun rose outside the kitchen window. But his Heart was empty. Then all at once, out of the gnawing of his Belly Centre there came a fierce red face, its fiery hair pomaded with cement dust, its nose red-veined with drink. It was Fergus O'Fury. And with him he brought the dreadful memory of the thing that Peach didn't want to remember, but had to. He brought it straight up out of the bilious, frothing 'head' of Peach's stout-black stomach.

Fergus O'Fury leered at him.

'Call yerself a builder, do ye? Don't ye remember – 'twas fifteen years ago, in Australia, and ye wit yer first whiskers growin' trew yer acne, and yer poor old Dad, tired o' supportin' yor lazy bones, made ye get a job. Do ye remember it?'

'Yes,' said Peach, humbly bowing his head.

'Put de mornin' papers in yer hand, turned ye out o' doors, 'n told ye not t' come back witout one. Six days ye go out. And six days ye come back witout even de smell of a job about ye. But on de seventh ye see dis ad, 'twas for an Assistant Handyman in a posh girls' school. Just for de holidays, like. A handyman? You? Dey wanted a skilled tradesman wit certificates. So ye went to de interview 'n told a terrible lie. Ye admitted that ye weren't a tradesman, but ye said dat you'd learnt everyting ye knew from helpin' yer old Dad about de house. T' exact and diabolical opposite of de trewt! Dis touched de heart o' de old School Bursar, a Latin scholar, who was doin' de hirin', and 'ee told ye t' report de next mornin' at eight o'clock sharp for work. Do ye remember?'

'Yes,' said Peach abjectly. 'I remember.'

Fergus chortled.

'De Head Handyman now, a walnut-coloured man turned on de late o' fifty years' experience, 'ee saw right trew ye, de minute 'ee clapped eyes on ye de next day. 'Ee knew he'd bin lumbered. But all went well for dat first mornin', wit you emptyin' bins and cleanin' de boiler. Do ye remember it?'

'Yes,' mumbled Peach, the memory growing like an ulcer in the dark.

'Den after lunch, de Head Handyman says t' ye, "Gist pop

44

into dat girls' loo and unblock de handbasin, will ye?" So off ya go. De young ladies are on holidays, of course. And ye have de jakes to yerself. And 'tis just as well, for 'tis close as a coffin in dere: two cubicles and, in de corner, de tiniest wash-hand basin ye've ever seen, wit a special bin beside it for sanctified pads. 'Tis a little triangular-shaped basin fixed into de corner o' two walls. And sure 'nough, 'tis half full of scummy water. So ye tink to yerself, "I needs a piece of wire, a coat-hanger or sometin' to get at dis." But someting tells ye dat ye oughtn't t' go to de Head Handyman and ask *him* for a wire coat-hanger. So ya wait till 'ee's up on de parapet strainin' de flag-pole, and ye plunder trew de tool-shed till ye find a long piece o' very kinky wire, in de end o' which ye make a little shepherd's crook. Den back to de kazi. And ye start fishin' down de plughole o' dis little basin. Ram de wire down, remember?, joggle it around, and pull it up, and . . . Be Jaysus . . . four strands of slimy girl's hair! Not ennut t' block even dat piss-hole sink. But 'tis a start, ye tink. Ye've found de root o' de problem, so to speak. So ye kneel dere, fishin' away – though someting – some true understandin' – makes ye keep givin' little looks o' dread out o' de door behind ye. When de Head Handyman comes in about an hour and a half later, ye've got almost a full head o' hair, lathered in decomposin' soap. And de basin's still blocked.

‘ 'Ee leans agin de door. 'Ee's a good man. 'Ee feels dat 'ee's received a slight wound, but wedder o' de understandin' or 'is flesh and blood, 'ee knows not.

‘ "Down dere – you unfasten it down dere . . ." and 'ee gives a little tweek of 's fingers and pints to below de basin. And out 'ee walks. Now you, Mr Tradesman, Mr Farder's help, ye look under the basin 'n see a great iron ring where de down-pipe jines de porcelain. Ye look at dat big rusty ring, and ye know dat ye'll never shift it wit yer bare hands. Ya have a try. 'Tis immovable. 'Tis rusted on. Yet he'd pinted at it wit a little tweek o' his fingers, as if t' say "Jest flick it around and de job will be done." But tweek it ye cannot.

45

'So 'twas wit a deepenin' dread dat ye goes back to de tool-shed and asks him for a monkey-wrench, de biggest 'ee's got. 'Ee looks incredulous, but gives you de biggest shiftin' spanner in de shed. It has a three-foot handle. For sure, ye could strip down de Harbour Bridge wit dat spanner. Do ye remember?'

'Yes, oh yes,' groaned Peach, beginning to shudder on his piano stool.

'So ye set t' work on de mighty ring under de basin, wit de mighty spanner. It takes many tries to shift de ring, and when it does shift, 'tis stiff wit rust. Dis is de first time it's been moved since de tilet was built. De ye remember de dread?'

'Yes. Yes.'

'Ye unscrews it, and half a basin o' sewagey water falls in yer lap. But dis leaves a gap – between de top o' de pipe and de bottom o' de basin, of about an eight of an inch. Too little t' get even yer piece of wire down. 'Tis time for desperate measures. Ye take de down-pipe in boat hands, and wrench it savagely to and fro. Dere's a strange bumping comes from down in de plumbing 'n little hair-line cracks scamper across de concrete floor. But ye've done it! – ye've pulled de pipe far ennut away from de basin for ya to get yer wire in. And like a mad angler ye go rootin' around again, hopin' de few extra inches will get ye to de block, which is probably in de U-bend in de pipe. But, in spite of dese structural alterations, ye only get two soggy Minty wrappers and more hair. And now ye can't tell wedder de block is clearin' or not. For de plug-hole now gives upon emptiness. And if ye switched on de tap, 'twould merely pour out into yer lap. De sense of Time itself departs from dat girls' tilet. One hour . . . two . . . three . . . ye can't tell how long ye've been in dere. Sure, fishin' is a great ting for passin' de time.'

And Fergus roared with laughter in Peach's swollen Belly Centre, undermining the foundations of his tradesman's confidence.

'When de Head Handyman, out of a farderly anxiety after ye, finally comes in, 'ee can say nuttin'. 'Ee wants to say someting, but 'ee can't. 'Ee stands for a moment surveyin' ye in de sewage of yer lies. Den 'ee eloquently bends down, and wit a flip o' his work-shone fingers, unscrews a tiny stopper dat ye hadn't seen at de bottom o' de U-bend in de pipe, and a wad o' wet offal falls on de floor, followed by a spurt o' grey water. De basin is unblocked! Den 'ee stands up and walks out, still unable t' speak. But when 'ee's got 'is safe distance from ye, 'ee calls out from the playground "Fasten it up and come back to the workshop at once." Do ye remember it?'

'Yes. Oh yes,' moaned Peach, rocking to and fro. 'Please stop.'

'So ye mop up de tilet floor, and screw de little stopper back into de U-bend. Dat leaves de down-pipe which ye have disconnected. Ye push it back into place, bringin' up a bit more concrete, line it up wit de tread under de plughole, and screw up de ring dat jines de pipe to de basin once more. Ye screw it as far as 'twill go. Den give it a little shake. Sure, it seems secure ennut. But how secure is secure agin de tide o' wrongs ye've done dis honest man? Perhaps it isn't tight ennut yet. De water might seep out and rust de sanctified bin. So ye take de mighty shiftin' spanner and fit it t' de mighty ring again . . . And begin tightenin' it more 'n more. And each turn is a wrong ye've done dis man. It takes anudder three or four turns wit de spanner. Sure, dat should do it. But will it? Who can say? Definitely not yourself. Ye've tampered wit plumbin' dat has stood sealed for tirty years. Sure ye can't, after all dat ye've done, leave dis innocent Head Handyman wit a leak under his tilet basin. Dere's only one way t' be sure – and dat's to tighten it to de very limits o' yer strent. Ye put one foot agin de wall and take de spanner in boat hands. Ye get it aroun' anudder tree times. One more wrench an' she'll move no more. But – do ye remember? – de whole strain o' yor screwin' 'tis being carried by de bottom o' dat little triangular washbasin screwed on to de two walls, and wit your final, conscience-sealing wrench de bottom o' de basin falls out – de plug-hole an' a six-inch ring o' de porcelain around it – crashes on to de floor. Sure, de basin is unblocked for good 'n all. Do ye remember, Mr Experience?'

'Oh Christ,' Peach sobbed in his belly-darkness. 'Stop it!

Stop it!' He wanted to get up and go back to bed. But Fergus hadn't finished yet.

'So dat was de last time ye masqueraded as a handy sort o' fella. Dis is de next!'

'But I'm honest. I'm conscientious. I'll do my best.'

'Honest are ye? An honest bricklayer, wit years of experience, are ye?'

'I swear, Fergus. I'll do that lady a good job if it takes me a month. If it takes me a year. If it kills me!'

'Dat', chuckled Fergus, 'it may well do!'

And he vanished.

Peach opened his eyes and was blinded by the morning sunlight. It was eight o'clock. The sun was shining full in his face. What had he done? Had he disturbed one of the Wrathful Devas? He'd read of this in books of Tibetan mysticism. He'd read of the dangers of confronting the demons of the Belly Centre without a pure heart and a clear mind. They stood as Guardians of the Threshold to the other world. The meditator who awoke them as he passed could be destroyed and driven insane, crushed like a louse on the doorstep. He climbed from the piano stool and shook himself. He walked into the bedroom still trembling.

'Well, I'll be off to work then, Morag.'

She rolled over sleepily.

'Good luck, Peach. See you tonight.'

His tools were waiting for him inside the front door. He put the saw in his shoulder-bag along with *The Esoteric Philosophy of Love and Marriage* and *The Awakening of Intelligence* which together weighed more than his sledgehammer, but which were, at this moment, more necessary to him. He put the spirit-level under his right arm, swung the pickaxe, shovel and brush up on to his left shoulder, picked up the sledgehammer with his free right hand, over two fingers of which he hooked the plastic carrier bag with his trowels, chisel, clubhammer and string, and stepped out of the door, which he closed with his foot. It was a glorious spring morning. The material world had put on its golden simplicity. He was exhausted by the time he got to the bus stop. He put his tools down. There was a twenty-yard queue. Peach stood at the back, behind two thickset women with voluminous black hold-alls from which J-cloths, the heads of mops and bottles of Harpic poked.

'I'd cut their flippin' perks off,' said the larger woman loudly, 'if I ran London Transport.'

'Three quarters of an hour! It's disgustin'.'

'My Ern always came on time, when 'ee was on the buses. An' 'ee didn't know what a perk was, not in them days. Ya could set the hall clock when Ern came. Oi! watch what yer doin' with that saw, won't ya!'

In trying to deflect the bad aura that surrounded the cleaning ladies, Peach had turned his back on them, and his saw, poking from his shoulder-bag, had taken a couple of bites at the larger woman's elbow.

'Oh, I'm dreadfully sorry,' said Peach.

She was just turning on him, massaging a few red drops out of the hardened skin, when the bus, or rather, buses, came.

'And 'ere they are at last,' said the smaller woman. 'Typical, innit! Nothink for an hour, then a whole pack of 'em – one, two, three, four . . . *five*, all up each other's bum! And full to the hilt no doubt.'

The queue broke up and made a surge for the one bus that had stopped. It was true, it was already pretty full. Elbows flew, shoulders went in, people stood on each other's feet. The larger cleaning lady winded a slow navvy with her hold-all and disappeared into the mêlée with her friend. Struggling to get his tools back on his shoulder, Peach was the last one on board.

'Upstairs. Upstairs. No room in 'ere,' screamed the conductor from somewhere on the lower deck.

On the platform, Peach unhooked his pickaxe from a man's knee and clattered upstairs, the broom-handle waving uncon-

49

trollably before him like a spear. It sounded as if he was bringing a horse on board. When he got to the top of the steps, every face in the packed upper deck was turned anxiously towards him.

The only free seat was at the front.

'No standing upstairs! Get off if you can't sit down,' shrieked the conductor.

'Excuse me,' said Peach. 'I do beg your pardon.'

And watching particularly for the axe-head and the teeth of the saw, he picked his way to his seat.

It was a long way to Camden Town. Peach wished it were endless. Anything but get off. Not through that lot again. They'd all had time to stoke their ire. He got his tools straight. And shut his eyes. Sometimes the bus must have been going east. For then the sun shone full in his face. Perhaps he wouldn't get off at all – just wait till the last stop, then sneak off with his tools and leave them in the bus shelter, dump them, abandon them to anyone who might need them and walk home to Morag. He stilled his breathing and kept his eyes closed. He still had twenty minutes before he had to make up his mind. Perhaps he could even meditate.

'Some of 'em 'll be bringin' their bleedin' beds on board next.'

The two cleaning ladies were in the seat behind him.

'They never used to let these tinkers and dossers on a London Transport bus.'

Peach tried to emanate Christic love from the back of his ears, which were glowing like rose petals, but by the time the bus reached Chalk Farm, the upper deck was waiting for the Judgement Day. The bus careened out of Adelaide Road at sixty miles an hour, leaning into the bend like a speedway motor-bike. Being now officially Full Up, it was tearing past fist-shaking bus-stops and through red lights. In spite of the conductor's threats, five people were standing huddled at the back of the upper deck. Perhaps he could jump off now and leave his tools on the bus. Would no one ring the bell?

'Excuse me,' said Peach, and rose from his seat.

He got the pickaxe and sledgehammer on to his shoulder all right but the sledge and the pick-head were grappling like locked horns, their handles knocking at the window, so that he had to hold his broom, shovel and spirit-level under the other arm, with the hand of which he groped for his clanking carrier bag. This left him no hands to hold on with. Every passenger on the upper deck was staring at him, remembering wrongs they'd suffered at the hands of cowboys.

'Excuse I.'

But as he stepped over the man next to him, the bus skidded sideways through the lights at Chalk Farm and into the centre lane of Chalk Farm Road, flinging him off balance, so that he stumbled and got his right leg jammed between the broom-handle and the spirit-level. Then, for some reason of his own, the driver slammed on the brakes, and Peach went scything down the aisle in an avalanche of ironmongery, his pick-head swathing above the heads of the terrified passengers like the helpless battle-axe of Attila the Hun, borne along by a horde of clattering barbarians. Peach turned to apologise and saw a black hold-all, upside down, swinging from the tip of the blade.

'Me bag! 'Ee's tryin' t' nick me bag!'

'I do beg—' said Peach.

A smoker at the back grabbed the hold-all, then tried to grab Peach, but was levelled by the ganger man's bubble as the bus gathered speed again, only to swerve left and brake again, pitching Peach headlong down the stairs to land on the pavement in a pile of weapons. He picked himself up. It was his stop. No one else had got off. Some kind and unknown hand had rung the bell.

It was a short walk to 26 Charmley Street. The skip was already standing outside. He put down his tools and rang the bell, still shaking. Mrs Pleasance opened the door.

'Oh Peach, what a pity. You've just missed the skip driver.

51

Still, you've got a lovely morning. And I paid the driver myself. I hope that's all right.'

'Oh, yes,' said Peach. 'Thanks very much.'

Mrs Pleasance scanned the kerb which was empty except for the skip.

'Did you come by van?'

The bus stop was just at the bottom of the street.

'I . . . ah . . . oh . . . left it round the corner,' said Peach, with an iota of truth.

'And, while we're talking about money' – Mrs Pleasance was now leading him through to the garden – 'I've got you three hundred pounds out of the bank. Is that okay to begin with?'

'Oh yes. Thanks. Thanks very much,' said Peach, stunned by the speed at which good things were happening and not knowing how to thank Mrs Pleasance enough, but she was by now showing him the tea-things in the kitchen.

'Help yourself whenever you like. The loo's upstairs.'

Peach had a cup of tea, then set to work.

The old concrete came up easily. It was only an inch or so thick – a grey skin cast over the ground, and underneath was good black earth, easy to dig. The little patio was directly outside the kitchen window, in the right-angle between the main part of the house and a kitchen extension. With the wall of the house next door on the other side, it was surrounded on three sides. Below the kitchen window was the gully into which all the down-pipes from the roof gutters ran. A foot further into the patio from this gully was an old iron manhole cover set into the level of the concrete. And as he levered up mosaics of concrete with the ganger man's pickaxe, Peach saw that this was going to be a problem. Below it was the manhole itself, of solid brickwork, probably. If his new patio ended up even fractionally higher or lower than the old one, he would have to raise or lower the whole manhole to meet it, so that the cover came in at the finished level of his paving. It must be possible to do this. But it would be tricky. He wouldn't lift the ancient cast-iron cover now, to have a look. This was a problem he hadn't foreseen, but it could wait till later.

He'd just finished lifting the concrete when the sand and cement arrived. He found some old floorboards in the front garden and laid them across the angle of the gutter to leave a space for the water to run under. He felt such a sudden rush of joy at being in charge of this moment that the eight bags of cement which the truck driver dropped on to his shoulder landed as lightly as albatrosses instantly folding their wings with a little puff of grey tail-feather. The bags were warm as birds. He stacked them on the footpath. Then it was time to drop the sand. The driver manoeuvred the back of the truck into the gutter, freed the tailboard, the tipper hoisted itself up, and a little mountain of sand rushed from the truck and re-formed itself perfectly at his feet. Peach was in ecstasy. A tiny mountain of sand as instantaneous and perfectly cast as if it had been drawn by an old Chinese watercolourist. It was very big. And it was his! He paid the driver with the money Mrs Pleasance had given him and tipped him a pound.

'Cheers, mate. What ya doin' in there?'

'A patio. Brick-paving.'

'Where ya gettin' the bricks?'

'I don't know.'

'We usually have 'em. But we've run out. We get 'em from the demolition. And if there's nothin' comin' down you can't get hold of 'em. Six months back, they were givin' them away. Two hundred quid a thousand. Now it's three hundred and fifty and you can't get 'em for love nor money. 'spect you'll find it's the same everywhere.'

'It is,' said Peach. 'I rang twelve builders' merchants and none of them had any. I only want four hundred. How long do you think it'll be before you've got some?'

'Us? Dunno. That's the way it is at the moment. Could be tomorra, could be six months. More like six months I expect. You should try gettin' 'em yourself if you only want four hundred. Just go round the demolition sites in your van.'

'I suppose that's what I'll have to do,' said Peach forlornly.

53

'Actually, I saw a house comin' down just now – round the corner from here, in Knightley Parade. You could have a look there.'

'I will,' said Peach. 'Thanks a lot.'

'Cheers, mate. See you soon.'

And the big green truck roared off.

Peach gazed sadly at his mountain of sand. If only he hadn't already broken up the old patio. Now there might be a hole there for months! Still, he would walk round to Knightley Parade after lunch. They might sell him some bricks. Perhaps he could carry them back. It wasn't all that far. Or spend a day's wages and buy a wheelbarrow. He had a cup of tea then started carrying the broken concrete out to the skip. He remembered to leave some of it out the back, for hard-core. Then he started digging out the earth and bagging it up. By lunch-time he'd made a 'show' as they said on the building sites.

Peach sat in the sun with his cup of tea. Tiny infra-muscular centres were opening up and down his back and behind his kneecaps, and even in his ankles. Centres he didn't know he had. And in the sole of each foot a huge ache, a wound-like Centre pushing the bones and tendons apart. And in the palm of either hand, under the faint hardening of his skin, a delirious softness, like a spiritual lesion opening and shutting. Much of it was exhaustion. But it was a high energy exhaustion that throbbed throughout his body. When he straightened his back and drew in a deep breath, the prana poked amongst the bones in his bum, looking for old Kundalini. But she was coiled up on a bag of cement, asleep. He became a skeleton clothed in tongues. Each tongue was a muscle speaking its tiredness and happiness. The sun beat down on his Thousand-Petalled Lotus, and each Petal secreted a jewel of sweat to adorn his forehead. And in his Heart Centre, Peach O'Hare was at peace.

Mary Pleasance had stopped her typing. She and her husband Frank came out on to the grass to have their lunch. Frank was a tall, blond-haired American with a roll of scores under his arm.

'I've made some salad, Peach. If you'd like to join us.'

They sat talking of music and books while they ate their lunch. When Peach stood up at last, he suddenly felt properly tired, as if the salad in his belly weighed more than the hundredweights of cement had in the morning. And that was the next thing to do – bring the bags of cement in while he still had some strength left. Before they got nicked, or a dog pissed on them. Peach went out to the pavement, now part of his building site.

He was just about to lift the first bag on to his shoulder, when a hearse came round the corner from Prince of Wales Road. It was black, as hearses should be. But there was something familiar about it. And something odd. Although there was a coffin in the back piled over with wreaths and garlands, and it was driving at a funereal pace, there was no following cortege. Then as it drew closer Peach saw stars, rainbows, flowers, bolts of lightning rising in multi-coloured swirls and zig-zags through the black, funereal paint, as though the hearse had been a circus trailer in its last incarnation. Could it be? Now the vehicle was carrying some mighty weight. Peach could hear the mudguards grinding against the tyres, and at every dip in the road the rear bumper bar shaved off a skin of tarmac. The walnut coffin with the brass-scrolled handles must contain a very heavy person indeed. As the hearse drew level, Peach saw a monstrous Third Eye, as big as the front bonnet on which it was painted, the pupil purple, the iris red, the white, yellow, staring up through the black spray-job, and knew who it was.

'Randy,' he called. 'Randy Braithwaite!'

Like his vehicle, the undertaker was sitting very low at the wheel, so that only his head and the white collar and black tie of his undertaker's suit were visible. But it was definitely Randy, his old friend, the genial travelling showman, juggler, monocyclist, magician and one-man street theatre, who busked all round England, the multi-coloured hearse his home, dressing room, prop box and the wings of his stage. He'd slept on

Peach's floor once, for three months, on a downer. And now he'd turned undertaker?

'Randy,' cried Peach, running beside the hearse, which was moving slowly enough to be in a real funeral. For Peach had suddenly remembered that he needed transport, any transport, and that his friend owed him a favour.

The hearse pulled reluctantly to a standstill, but the driver didn't get out. Peach walked up to the passenger door. The driver flattened himself across the seat and pushed the door open an inch. Peach put his head in. A brown arm shot from the sleeve of a white robe and dragged him bodily into the hearse.

'Randy!'

His friend, whom he'd last seen in a clown's suit, his braces covered with glitter, was now wearing a long white robe, the cowl of which, gathered round his neck, hid the fact that his undertaker's hair came down to his waist and was matted like a mudlark's nest. Round his neck was buttoned a tuxedo-bib which ended above the nipples of his bare, bony chest, and from under which half a dozen leather pouches hung, smelling of herbs, fungus, blood and bone, and the sweat of his hairy navel where they rose and fell dementedly. His robe was bound at the waist by a rope from which hung a dagger, a goblet and a bunch of dried thyme. Its skirt was stained with what Peach hoped was blackberry juice. He peered into the ferocious face. The glasses were gone, and the nose where they had once perched cockily had been broken and flattened to a hawk's hook. His contact lenses stared at Peach from a predatory height, like an eagle's. But it was definitely Randy. Peach shuddered. Lying across his lap, and the whole length of the front seat, was a gigantic crowbar.

'Randy? . . .'

'Hush,' his friend hissed at him.

Peach recognised the coffin. It was the one Randy had used for his sawing in half trick. But now it was heaped with plastic flowers. And the crowbar was the one he bent with mirrors. But now he carried it like a weapon.

'There are enemies all around . . .'

He pulled Peach flat on the seat and gave him a hard stare.

'I'm being pursued, Peach. By the police. And Somerset County Council. And . . . the demonic Forces of Reason!'

'And what's happened to the old one-man show, Randy? Where's your clown suit? And your stilts, and your monocycle, and your juggling balls? And Pecker? . . . Where's Pecker the Psychic Parrot?'

'You have to sacrifice a lot of things when you become a Druid, Peach.'

'A Druid? . . . Pecker? . . . Good God, Randy, you haven't sacrificed Pecker?'

'Oh no. Not like that. I left him in Somerset. My Quest is fraught with dangers – too great for a parrot.'

'A Druid, Randy?'

'Forget that name, Peach. I am Allwrath now, High Priest of—'

'Look, Allwrath. Would you like to come in for a cup of tea. I'm working here. A little landscaping job. I need your help.'

'I'm sorry, Peach. I can't stop. Firstly I'm on a Druidic Quest. Secondly, I'm being followed. And thirdly' – he lifted his head reverently towards the coffin in the boot – 'I can't leave God alone!'

'God?'

'Yes, Peach. There. In the boot. Come.'

Peach gave the brass-handled box a terrified look.

Keeping as low as he could, Allwrath slid through the inside window into the back of the hearse. Peach crawled after him. The Druid unceremoniously swept the flowers aside and lifted the lid of the grim-looking coffin, and Peach saw, wedged tightly into the purple velvet lining, a six-foot kerbstone.

'A kerbstone, Allwrath? . . .'

Allwrath's voice suddenly rose in incantation:

'I stood on a kerb in Glastonbury. Just by the ninety-one bus stop. I had drawn them with my juggling, a sizeable crowd pressed against the window of Woolworth's. I came to the

57

finale of the show: Pecker the Psychic Parrot Answers Your Question. You remember the routine, Peach: A volunteer comes forward. With all the usual razzmatazz, I ask him to think, just one thought, and whatever it is, Pecker, perching on my shoulder, will speak it out loud. You remember how it went, Peach – Pecker could only say one sentence. I'd trained him to it – "What a load of old codswollop." But that was what they were always thinking! This day I stood on a kerb in Glastonbury – a volunteer had come forward – Pecker scrabbling on my shoulder, waiting to speak . . . When all at once a mighty force gripped me by the ankles, a stony lightning striking upwards, a vast Earth-Thought concentrating my mind to granite. I looked at the baubles and accoutrements of my theatre lying in the hearse behind me. My six tinselled juggling balls: I saw that they were the illusionary propositions of Modern Philosophy. My monocycle: the self-circling self-centredness of Monism. My stilts: the absurd pride of Rationalism. My false bra. My magic coffin. I was surrounded by post-Cartesian abstractions.

'The force rose up my legs. It was fortunate, Peach, I was bare-footed. It would have melted my plimsolls. By its power I saw a mighty Circle of Stones rise from Glastonbury High Street. Great standing stones taller than the Post Office. An altar so high, it towered above the illusory bus that appeared to be driving through it. A Circle so vast it made Stonehenge look like a bluestone bracelet. The Power entered my mouth as Words. My voice grew as mighty as a menhir in my throat.

"Where is the Ultimate Circle?" I cried to the terrified crowd, without knowing what I was saying. "Where is my Sacred Circle? What have you done to my little ones, my dolmens and trilithons, my standing stones raised by the Giant Race?"

'No one in the crowd knew. They stood dumb and terror-stricken. On my shoulder Pecker had regressed to "Who's a pretty boy?" over and over. A true modern thinker.

' "Where have you hidden my Sacred Site?" cried the Mighty Thought that rose from my feet.

'It hung before my eyes like a ghost: the vast stone circle

that had once stood on holy ground, somewhere in England. It had been pulled down, and its stones scattered. But the mighty Thought elucidated Itself: Find that Sacred Site, rebuild the Druid Altar, call up the Powers of the Earth, and the great stones will fly from the four corners of England and take their place in the ring, and the Ultimate Circle will stand forever more!

'At the Centre of the Ring I saw a single stone, standing erect on a pyramidal altar. It was smaller than the others, only six feet high. But I could see by its pondering ponderousness that it was the most powerful stone of them all, that it was indeed God – the pineal stone of the Ultimate Circle! Then imagine my astonishment, Peach, when I looked down with my earth-eyes and saw that very same stone, God Himself, under my own feet, palmed off as a kerbstone by the County Council. In terror and awe, I leapt off Him, for fear that my flesh would melt on my bones, just as three shoppers got off the seventy-three from Taunton and walked right over him. Imagine my rage! I bellowed, Peach. I shook their impious shoulders. I bore them against the window of Woolworth's with my crowbar, so great was the strength God had given me. The crowd had dispersed. Old Bill was edging tentatively forward. I climbed with holy dread once more upon my God, and He spoke to me one last time, before I was moved on.

' "You are no longer Randolph Braithwaite. I have chosen you as my High Druid. From henceforth you will be known to all men as Allwrath. I pronounce you High Priest of the Sacred Circle. And I give you a mission: Find the Sacred Site where the Sacred Circle once stood on earth itself, before its stones were scattered by the Empiricists of the Eighteenth Century, to be used in bridges and railway stations, to be made into horse troughs, to be crushed into aggregate for the dead pavements of the modern city. The Sacred Site has been lost. Find it! And rebuild the altar you saw in your vision. Then I will awake. I will climb your altar, and call up my consort, Gaia the Goddess of the Earth, from her centuries of sleep. We will dance upon your altar. The lost stones will fly to us from the three corners of England, and dance in the Sacred Circle and with megalithic might will shatter the whole of Modern Thought. Go forth! Do it! But first, lift me from this gutter."

'I had to wait till nightfall, with Old Bill nosing around, Peach. It was brilliant midnight. Hecate window-shopped at Woolworth's. A few lonely elementals waited at the bus stop. Luckily I had my crowbar in the boot of the hearse – remember – I used to bend it with mirrors. And I had the coffin. I jemmied Him up, lay the coffin on its side and rolled God into it. See! He fits it like a glove. I'd just got Him into the back of the hearse, when round the corner comes Old Bill on his push-bike. He saw me in the moonlight, and the deed I had done, and gave chase. Luckily, there was just enough power in the old hearse to draw clear. But what a sitting duck I was in my hearse now, painted as it was with stars and rainbows and flowers. The Logicians of Oxford and Cambridge would track me down in no time. I lay low. I nipped into a little backwoods garage and got a quick respray – black as midnight, fighting logic with logic. Impossible to distinguish from an ordinary hearse. I even had this bib and tucker from the old show days. I disguised myself as an undertaker. I gave them the slip – Old Bill, Somerset County Council, the whole Fabric of Modern Thought. Since when, a wandering Druid alone and unhenged, I have been searching for the Sacred Site, by day and by night, God guiding me from the boot . . .'

'But do you think it's in North London?'

'I don't know, Peach,' muttered the Druid. 'I wouldn't have thought so myself.'

He looked searchingly at the neat rows of houses with their tidy front gardens.

'But He has led me here, so I've come.' He looked up and down Charmley Street. 'Though it's not what I would have chosen, Peach.'

'You were born just round the corner, Allwrath.'

'Was I?'

'Look Allwrath, do you remember when you slept on my floor for three months?'

'A Druid never forgets a favour, Peach.'

'Well, I need the old hearse . . . to pick up some bricks – only four hundred.'

'I'd like to help you, Peach, I really would, but any more weight in here and the old hearse will pack up.'

'Well, can't you take the stone out, I mean God, till we've got the bricks?'

'Impossible.'

'It'll only be for half an hour – less, if there're no bricks to buy. Three months is a long time to take up someone's floor, Allwrath.'

For a minute, Allwrath communed with the kerbstone.

'All right then,' he muttered.

They took one brass handle each and dragged the coffin out of the hearse, both glancing around paranoiacally. It hit the road with a crash.

'God, it's heavy, Allwrath.'

'Pure power, Peach.'

They lugged the coffin on to the pavement, through the gate, and into Mary Pleasance's empty bicycle shed.

'She'll be safe in there till we get back,' said Peach.

'*He*'ll,' said Allwrath adamantly.

When they turned the corner into Knightley Parade, they saw a cloud of dust rising from a house at the end of the street. An assortment of trucks and vans was parked and double parked outside. Not just builders' vans and brick lorries, but pantechnicons, radio-controlled plumbers, interior designers' deux chevaux with their logos on the side, garden wholesalers and second-hand timber merchants, scrap-iron dealers and totters' horse and carts. They were all jostling and shouting, like brokers at the Stock Exchange, around a large, red-haired man. It was Fergus O'Fury. He had a roll of twenty-pound notes in his hand the size of a brickbat. And the anxious dealers were trying to press more notes into it.

Two cranes, with iron balls swinging at the ends of their

cables, were lurching through the remains of a half-gutted house.

'I told ye, bricks to de front, timber to de back,' roared Fergus upwards at the gang of navvies with pickaxes who stood astride the parapet hacking off the crisp white stucco. He was answered by half a yard of brickwork that landed with a thud and a cloud of lime-dust on the doorstep, spraying them with milk and broken glass.

'Dat's better,' said Fergus contentedly.

As the masonry hit the floor it shattered into its hundred separate bricks, which were instantly snatched up and cleaned by a gang of labourers with hammers and trowels. Before they had a chance to stack the cleaned second-hand stocks, prime yellows, they were hurried along a human chain on to the backs of lorries and vans at thirty-five pence each.

'I'll have five thousand, Mr O'Fury sir,' said a small pigeon-chested man with a giant lorry. 'Here's me money.'

'Sorry, mate. Bricks is already sold down to de footin's.'

'I'll have the footin's. I'll have the footin's.'

Fergus took his money.

'Come back in an hour or two.'

A Second Empire chaise-longue came sailing out of a first-floor window.

'Wot'm I bid dere?' cried Fergus.

'Look! It's got gold fluted legs,' cried one antiques dealer.

The gilt-scrolled couch with satin bolsters hung in mid-air.

'A de la Tour,' shouted another antiques dealer. 'Eighteen . . . eighteen . . . twenty-three.'

'Wot'm I bid?' cried Fergus.

'A grand.'

'Fifteen hundred.'

'Two grand.'

The chaise-longue hit the ground. Its golden legs splayed. 'Fuck me,' they fluted as the upholstery disembowelled its springs.

'A fiver,' groaned the antiques man.

'Gone!' cried Fergus.

'But Mr O'Fury, I beg you . . . this priceless piece. If you'd only bring it down by the stairs . . .'

'Stairs is sold 'n gone already,' said Fergus. 'Dis here is a penalty contract. Dis house is coming down t'day or I get paid nuttin'.'

He looked at his watch.

'Sure, I'll be away by four. I TOLD YE, TIMBER TO DE BACK,' he roared upwards, his face turning purple with rage, as a pine dresser shattered at his feet, spraying them with slivers of Willow Pattern.

Out the back, where the garden had once been, was an inferno that reached to the first-floor windows and withered the clematis off the walls three doors down. Broken rafters, naily joists, splintered floorboards and gaping door-frames were sailing into this hell-fire. So intense was the heat that the window frames next door were turning into charcoal. But this didn't matter too much, as it was a derelict house, almost falling down by itself.

'Peach O'Hare! Me menta. Me friend in time of sorrow,' cried Fergus O'Fury putting his brickbat in his pocket to shake Peach's hand. 'Wot brings ye here den?'

Suddenly the saloon bar of the Mother Black Cap came back to Peach, and the fate of his ten-pound note.

'Bricks, Fergus. I need four hundred second-hand stocks, quite . . . desperately. I've got the money if you can spare them.'

'Spare dem? Spare dem? For de man who set me on de part t' freedom? Sure I'd tear 'em out o' de buildin' wit me own hands, if dey weren't rainin' down already.'

He waved to one of his men.

'Four hundred best yellers for me friend here. Where's yer lorry?'

Peach pointed to the hearse, where Allwrath slid lower behind his wheel.

'Four hundred best yellers in dat dere corpsemobile!'

While Fergus's men were loading the bricks, Peach told his friend something about his own job. The patio. Mary and

Frank. The depth of his foundations. And the manhole which he was coming to dread.

'Sounds fine and dandy t' me,' said Fergus. 'Nuttin' t' worry about. Ye don' get paid for worryin' in dis trade. And are ye earnin'?'

'Well enough,' said Peach.

Fergus drew him aside.

'Sure I'm doin' all right out o' dis one. All right indeed! 'Tis a little under de counter demolition job. A below de bar contract.'

He lowered his voice to a whisper.

'Yer queer fella, property speculata wot owns dis house, approaches me in de saloon bar last night, 'twas last orders I do remember, 'n 'ee presses dis bevvy o' blue notes upon me, an' yer slip o' paper wit dis address written down upon it. 'Tis a Grade One Listed buildin'. 'Tis not meant to come down at all. Do', begorrah, 'tis listin' now. Dat's why it 'twere well 't were done quick, like. Down t'day, gone t'night. Den 'ee'll build yer new flats. De Council'll scream blue murder. But 'tis a fight accompli. Asked me if I could muster de gang t' do it overnight. But sure, 'twas easy. Dey were all staggerin' around outside. Give me de address 'ee did,' and Fergus pulled out a grimy, torn-off envelope flap.

'Are you sure that's an eight, Fergus, and not a six?'

'Ah sure, 'tis an eight all right. But de ting dat amazes me, Peach, is dat dis house is full o' chattels, jinery and ironmongery, crockery and bet-linen. Must've bin such a rush job, dey didn't have time t' move dem.'

Peach and Allwrath unloaded the bricks at 26 Charmley Street, got the coffin back into the hearse and chucked the flowers on top of it.

'Some of these undertakers will stoop to anything to earn a few extra quid,' said old Mr Dibbs across the road, through his net curtain. 'Don't bury me with that lot, Maggie. I don't want to be lowered to me consummation by a bloke in a dressing-gown. I suppose the short one's 'is gravedigger. They're all moonlighters these days, cowboys the lot of 'em. All gettin' something on the side. Each man for 'imself. Good luck to you, mate,' he called feelingly to the kerbstone in the coffin, as Allwrath pulled off. 'Good luck to you, old son. You'll be lucky if ya make it to the Garden Suburb at all!'

Mary Pleasance passed the hearse as she turned the corner on her bicycle.

'What lovely bricks!'

'Yes. Best yellers,' said Peach, with a glow as golden as the pile of bricks itself.

By the time Peach got the cement and bricks into the garden and had covered the cement for the night, and stowed his tools in the shed, it was six o'clock. He was exhausted, but happy. He said goodnight to Frank and Mary and caught the 27 home. After a bath and something to eat, he sat in the kitchen with Morag.

'I can't believe my luck. Mrs Pleasance gave me an advance. I got four hundred bricks for nothing off this Irishman I know. The sand and cement came on time, and Randy Braithwaite turned up just when I needed him, only now he's called Allwrath.'

'You looked whacked. You won't be able to get up at five tomorrow to meditate. It'll kill you.'

'I'll just wake up when I wake up, do an hour, then go to work. I'm sure they won't mind if I'm late.'

'I hope all this isn't going to interfere with your meditation, Peach. Or wear you out. It's like having two jobs.'

'Well, that's the funny thing. Working today was *like* meditating – There's a pile of bricks in the street and nothing in the garden. I start taking them through. After five loads I'm knackered, because I've been breaking up concrete all morning. But I tell myself "I'll have a cup of tea after the tenth load." After the tenth load I'm even more knackered. But the pile in the garden is starting to look so big, it gives me heart for another five loads. By which time the two piles are equal, the pile in the street and the pile out the back. I'm halfway. So I say to myself "I'll do another three, just so that when I start again after my cup of tea I'll be on the home stretch." It's all in the mind, see! And when I've carried through those three I'm so close to the end I carry on till every last brick is in the garden. It's like condensing time. It's like arguing weight and number – a pile of bricks – out of existence. It takes you beyond Time and Space. It's meditation!'

'Perhaps everything's meditation.'

'Oh crikey yes! And then when I *did* have my cup of tea and I straightened my back and stretched up my arms – to greet the Divine Source again, and to ease the aching – it was as though . . . as though, just for a moment, *I* was only a body, and everything else in the world was spirit. The Divine Source greeted me bodily!'

'That sounds nice.'

'And a cup of tea never tasted better. Perhaps it's a good thing I've been led to this work, Morag. Perhaps it's a way of letting the Spirit descend deeper into Matter and—'

'You know, Peach, we'll have to start thinking about whether we want the baby born here or in a hospital. I want it here – but I don't know whether they'll let us, seeing there's no hot water.'

'We can boil up under the table like we always do.'

'I don't know if they'll go for that. A Health Visitor will come around. And there're certain standards. If the house doesn't come up to them, the doctor isn't allowed to deliver a baby there – by law. That's if we can find a doctor who'll do a home birth anyway.'

'But the place is *clean*,' said Peach.

'Yes, but I'm worried about the water. And the wiring too, if they see it.'

'But this is a squat, Morag. We can't put in new wiring even if I knew how to. We might get evicted the day the baby comes.'

'Well, that's another thing,' said Morag. 'But I do want to get it sorted out. And I do want to have it here, where the baby was conceived, and where we're used to. But you know, Peach, it's going to be a terrible upheaval.'

'I know,' said Peach happily, stroking her belly. 'The Descent of Spirit into Matter.'

The next day he didn't get in till midday. Frank opened the door with a cheerful grin. He didn't seem to mind. Peach had a cup of tea then set to work digging and humping the earth out into the skip. By that evening he'd excavated half the patio area. On Wednesday he finished the digging and rammed the hard-core in with the ganger man's sledgehammer. He'd dug the earth away around the manhole, so that it now sat up seven inches above the rest of the area, its frame and solid brickwork exposed. It would have been easy to lift the lid and see what awaited him. But Peach didn't touch it. He decided to leave the problem till he'd made a 'show'. On Thursday he started carrying through the sand, using a builder's rubbish bag. By now the local dogs had scaled his sand mountain and left their commemorative cairns. Peach blithely flipped them into the skip with his shovel. Matter, on all the rungs of its ladder, was a joy to him. The kids, too, burning over his mountain on their bikes, had turned it to a dune, with a fair stretch of desert on all sides. Peach didn't mind. Sand was a universal blessing to young and old, builders and babies. It was to be shared.

By the end of that day he had taken through the two thirds he would need for his foundation. On Friday he mixed it up with five bags of cement, and laid the foundation, taking care to leave a fall, from all three directions, into the gully under the kitchen window. He still didn't touch the manhole which now stood high and dry, its ancient iron cover smeared with cement, four inches above his new concrete. It took him all of that day to do the concreting. This was slow, but he was working in a confined space, and didn't want to splash cement up the whitewashed walls of the house. Also, he only had a small estate agent's sign which somebody had put in his skip, to mix up on. Still, he was well-pleased by the end of that day, even though he'd planned to have the whole job finished by then. Things had gone smoothly. And he was a hundred and forty pounds up, from not having to pay for Fergus's bricks. It was heady stuff, this tidal flow of large sums of money, a small wad of which, a quarter brick-end, he now carried permanently in his trouser pocket. If he finished the job by next Friday, which he should do easily, he'd still be earning more than his original twenty pounds a day.

But when he started laying the bricks the following Monday, it went even slower. He knocked up enough muck to do one third of the small area, and screeded it level with a straight-edge, as he'd seen on building sites, allowing for the falls to the gully. But the bricks were a hundred and fifty years old, and were all shapes and sizes. Some were bowed. Some were bent. Some were gnarled like old men's fingers – these Fergus had called 'rubbers'. So that when he sat them on the screed they were all at slightly different levels, and the surface looked nobbled. Although this was attractive, in a rustic sort of way, Peach was working to higher standards. He took the bricks up again and re-laid each one separately, scraping away or adding to the cement as required, checking each brick with his spirit-level, re-laying it a second, third, or fourth time till it obeyed a perfect level which existed only in his mind. In this way he came to know each brick individually: the pale, chalky ones that cut obediently when he came to the end of a course. The steel-blue ones that broke where they liked. The warty ones. The pock-marked ones. The ones with blue knuckles that took five minutes' furious chiselling then broke like eggs, showing their golden yolks, shot with purple and ochre. For there was a lot of cutting to be done. Which was something else he hadn't estimated for. There was forty-two foot of edge to the patio, half of which had to be cut for the brickwork to come up flush against the house, and he hadn't sized the courses to fit the space. That was fifty bricks to cut. And he'd only allowed for sixteen breakages. As he slowly shattered his way towards the limit of bricks he would need, Spirit began to withdraw from Matter, in some vast Cosmic Rhythm, and he found himself alone, human, swearing violently, his fingers bleeding, swinging his hammer wildly amongst a growing pile of bats.

But still, by the end of the second week, he'd got the four hundred bricks laid. And they looked nice. For he'd strung the courses along a line, as he'd seen the bricklayers do, and got the falls perfect. And the cutting looked professional. But that still left a new sill to be built under the kitchen door, for the old one had lifted with the concrete, the whole patio to be pointed, and the manhole raised, which he still hadn't touched, merely staggering his brickwork as close to the metal frame as it would go.

But Peach was happy. He was becoming friends with Frank and Mary, who, not knowing that he'd got Fergus's bricks free, were mainly worried about how little he must be earning. But, though the tide was swinging back, Peach was still a little ahead and besides, the little twelve-yard patch of golden brickwork looked truly charming. It would be a good advertisement. Where each of the bricks had been on the outside of the unfortunate house, it was black with London soot. But all the other faces, the frog, and the flat which he was using for his paving, were pristine yellow and to Peach's fanciful mind their goldenness was the goldenness of the sacred, unpolluted City of God, Jerusalem the Bride, which is, as yet, a symbolic city, but which seemed to be getting closer in these golden bricks passing through his toughening hands.

The pointing took him two days. The sill one. The clearing up one. Which left raising the manhole cover. He put this off till the very last day, the Friday of the third week, the cover, which he'd cleaned with a wire brush, sitting at an odd angle, an inch below the patio.

At last, he confronted the Unknown. He got the corner of his shovel under the ancient cast-iron cover and tried to lever it up. It was welded in with fifty years of dirt and rust, and at first only came up enough for him to claw at it with his fingernails. But there was too much weight in it. Finally he managed to jemmy it up far enough to get two fingertips into the hole. But the cover fell back and nearly chopped them off. At last, by levering and wedging the manhole open with pebbles, Peach managed to get a grip on the lid, and with one mighty heave, laboured it upwards. He leant the cover against the wall then looked down into the rectangular hole. It was three feet deep. A tangle of drains ran into it: the waste from the kitchen sink, two pipes from the bathroom upstairs, including the soil-pipe from the loo, as well as the pipe which carried the rainwater from the roof, and now also the patio, which ran into the gully, and from there cut into the manhole. All these drains disgorged upon an open pipe at the bottom which disappeared into the dark hole of the main drain, sloping downwards under the house and out into the sewers twenty feet beneath the street. Peach looked at it with a small pang of dread. The insides of the pipes had a corpse-like pallor over which the clear slime stippled. It was a subterranean world that had never seen the light of Jerusalem's golden patio. Whatever he did, he mustn't drop any cement down there.

He waited till Mary and Frank had gone out, so that none of the spaghetti junction of drains would be in use. Then he carefully laid three rubbish bags over the open drain at the bottom, taking care to wedge another bag into the mouth of the main drain. Over the bags he placed a sheet of hardboard to stand on. The manhole was already half-filled by these precautions. Now he set to work with hammer and chisel and a deepening sense of dread, cutting at the effluvial joint between the metal frame in which the cover sat and the tough cement at the top of the manhole. The frame soon came away, dripping rust. He set it to one side. He mixed up a small gauge of muck and put it on a bag. Then he cleaned the rim of the manhole. It would have to come up about an inch and a quarter to meet his bricks. The mortar he'd mixed was very strong — two to one. Using the pointing trowel, he carefully

70

laid it on around the concrete rim. Only a few gobs dropped in. They'd be caught below. He sat the iron frame on the cement. It was too high. He beat it down with his clubhammer. The mortar began to weep from the joint down the side of the manhole.

He hastily lifted the frame again and scraped off half an inch of cement. More dollops dropped on to the bags below. They'd be all right. When he sat the frame down again, it was nearly the right level, but it wobbled at two of its corners. He plastered more cement into the joint under the two low points, but ninety per cent of it slid off his trowel on to the bags below. It'd be all right. Still he pushed the next few trowel-loads into the joint with his fingers, so as to drop less. The mortar seemed to be getting wetter and wetter, so that even when he'd packed the joint with it, the frame still wobbled suspiciously. Grabbing some fragments of broken brick he leapt into the hole. The hardboard broke in half under him. But it didn't matter. There were at least four bags beneath it. He pushed slivers of brick under the corners of the frame and more cement slid down the manhole. But at last he'd got it firm and level with the paving. Not daring to look at the morass of trodden, cemented bags below him, he climbed from the hole and had lunch. Luckily Frank and Mary were still out.

After lunch he brought the paving up flush to the level frame. This was slow work as every brick had to be cut. Then he had to point them, and make a neat showpiece of a joint all round the edge of the frame. At last he was finished. With almost ceremonial care, he dropped the cover into the frame.

It didn't fit. With thirty years of rust removed, it sat up obstinately, a quarter of an inch above his perfect paving. Groaning and cursing he lifted it off, and leapt into the hole again. There was a cracking, crumpling sound under his feet which he ignored as he set to work, relevelling the frame. He could see Mary washing potatoes in the kitchen, and heard the water running under his feet. A piece of hardboard broke off and disappeared. But it was all right. It would be caught somewhere or other down there in the tangle of cement-stiffened bags.

It was dark when he finally climbed out. He dropped the cover on again. A perfect level. He pointed it by moonlight and the light from the kitchen window, where Mary and Frank were having their dinner, peering anxiously out into the darkness. He washed his trowels, shovel and spirit-level, swept up, and washed down the part of the patio where the pointing was hard. He was just about to leave when he remembered the tangle of bags and broken hardboard sitting in half a gauge of dropped muck at the bottom of the manhole. Sobbing he struggled the cover off for a third time, and, reaching down into the excremental blackness, pulled up the mashed hardboard and cement-clogged bags. He could no longer remember how many he'd put in. When he thought he'd got them all out, he cleaned out the drain at the bottom with his fingers. Thank God he'd remembered. He put the cover back on, repointed the joints that had been disturbed, washed his trowels again, and stood up. It was a pity it was too dark to see his handiwork. He'd have to wait till the morning, when he came back for his tools and his last payment.

As he walked down the street to the bus stop, a wave of happiness swept over Peach. He was knackered but exultant. His fingertips burned where he'd been prodding the cement, his back ached, his kneecaps groaned from so much wet kneeling. But a joy that was purely spiritual healed these bodily ills, and made him glow with well-being. He'd done it! He'd finished his first job! And finishing in the dark, leaving without being able to see what he'd done, made it seem as much a spiritual achievement as a physical one. As though the perfect patio he'd left behind him in the dark existed in another world, was, in fact, a golden dream, which would still be there in the morning.

The few other passengers on the late bus home stared at this slight man in his toeless plimsolls and cement-cuffed trousers with their armorial shields of wet cement on each kneecap –

smiling uncontrollably to himself in the front seat. But they didn't know what he'd just done.

Neither did he.

Peach arrived early the next morning, which was Saturday. He was looking forward to seeing his finished handiwork in sunlight. All he had to do was sweep up one more time, get paid, and take his tools home. He'd be able to afford a taxi for them.

Mary opened the front door for him.

'Hello, Peach. The patio looks absolutely lovely. Frank and I have been sitting out there admiring it. Come and have a look.'

Peach followed Mary down the short passageway. He, Mary and Frank stood in the kitchen doorway. The patio did look beautiful in the morning sunlight.

'The bricks sort of shine,' said Frank. 'The old ones are so much nicer.'

'Now, about paying you,' said Mary. 'Frank and I were just saying that . . . it's taken you . . . quite a long time . . . I mean, perhaps a little longer than you intended . . . And we've worked out, very approximately, how much you must have earned and . . . we think you should have a bit more.'

'Oh no,' said Peach aghast. 'No. I'm perfectly happy with my price, and the bricks . . .'

As he was talking, Peach noticed that *part of the patio was moving*! It was a paver's nightmare in broad daylight. The manhole cover was bobbing up and down, creating the illusion that all the bricks around it were in motion too. He glanced to see if Frank and Mary had noticed. But they were too busy haggling with him.

'Well, I'll leave you two to discuss this,' said Frank. 'I'm going up to have a quick bath.'

'Now,' said Mary, mistaking Peach's distracted look for reluctance. 'You estimated for three hundred and forty-six pounds eighty-three. Well, we thought that if we made it a round four hundred, it would be fair on both sides.'

'No, no. I can't,' said Peach, his voice quaking with guilt. 'It really was a firm quote.'

'But it would spoil our enjoyment of your work, if we thought you'd lost out, Peach.'

The manhole cover was bubbling in its frame. Mary still hadn't seen it. Peach took one nonchalant step across the patio, and stood on it. Was it guilt? Or was it the dreadful force under the lid that was now making *him* shake? But Mary didn't seem to notice it. She hadn't expected him to be this stubborn.

'Frank and I have seen how much love and care you've put into it, Peach, and it's turned out so lovely that—'

Just then the telephone rang in the front room.

'Excuse me.'

As soon as Mary was gone, Peach leapt off the cover and tore it up. This was now easy, as the force underneath was already lifting it. The three-foot deep well was brimming with a vortex of excremental waters. Grey currents from the kitchen sink tumbled over brown currents from the loo. Geysers of grey soap bore intricate turds to the surface, then sucked them down again with a plop, like brown fish in a maelstrom. The odd pea from last night's scrapings rode on the current with its fellows that had been eaten. Twists of pink toilet paper, foundering like sails, were pulled down by their brown ballast into an ocean of Harpic and toast scrapings. These were things that he ought not even to think about, let alone be looking at. Upstairs he could hear Frank's bath running, the bath which drained into this same manhole. One more cupful from the kitchen tap, and the whole maelstrom would well up and flood his golden patio, perhaps even run into the kitchen. A bathful, and it would be pouring out the front door. It was time for action. A stick! He needed a stick! Peach dropped the manhole cover back on, praying it would hold the flood back, and bolted up the garden. Behind the shed he found a bamboo cane. He ran back down the garden. But when he reached the house, Mary was standing at the kitchen window, looking out at the patio again. She smiled and waved. He waved back with the stick and pretended to be spiking the flowerbeds. He prodded deep amongst her daffodils.

The phone rang again, and Mary disappeared a second time into the front room. He tore up the manhole cover, rolled up his sleeve to the shoulder, lay face-down on the patio, and plunged his arm into the cesspool, poking around with the cane for the mouth of the main drain. Frank's bath had stopped running, and upstairs he could hear a soft splashing and some contented humming. He located the mouth of the main drain, and rammed in his cane, which snapped, adding half itself to the unnameable block further on down the pipe. Peach rolled his sleeve back over his shoulder with his clean hand, pressed himself against the patio, and plunged again with his broken cane. Down, and further down, he rammed it. But the block wouldn't move. Then he heard the ding of the phone being put down, and footsteps coming back to the kitchen. They were the footsteps of his Fate. They would find him, flat on his face on his golden handiwork, up to his armpit in his true nature. At that moment the front door-bell rang, and the footsteps stopped in the hall, then retreated down the passageway. Even as he poked, Peach heard the front door open and a flurry of happy greetings. A moment later he heard Frank pull the plug.

It was time for desperate measures.

There was another manhole at the front of the house, in the path by the front door. He'd noticed it when they'd dragged the coffin in. It would be a deeper manhole, as the drains fell in that direction, towards the street. The blockage could be anywhere under the house but pray God he could reach it from there. He heard the gurgle of the bathroom pipes. He dashed into the kitchen and up the passageway, his right arm dripping sewage to the shoulder, the shit-stick clutched in his hand. Mary was standing at the front door talking to a tall, well-dressed woman. Her broad-brimmed hat, her two-piece suit, even her handbag and shoes, were white.

'Frank's having a quick bath. We won't be a minute and then we can go,' he heard Mary say.

'Excuse I,' said Peach, handing them gently aside with his stick and plunging past.

The woman in white stepped backwards. The manhole was no more than three feet behind her.

'Careful, madam,' said Peach as he pulled it up and jumped in.

It was eight feet deep. Mary screamed as he disappeared from sight. But Peach was already at the bottom desperately plunging his stick up and down the drain. There was a whoompf like a wet mortar and one of Peach's rubbish bags shot out of the hole, horribly congealed. Then a mighty wave. Peach started to climb, but there were no handholds, and he was borne upwards by sheer terror of the brown torrent.

'Just checking the falls,' he smiled at the two ladies as he clambered from the hole, his shoes squelching, his trousers dyed in the colour of his trade, and the mighty flood passed beneath.

They kindly believed him.

A<small>FTER</small> he'd left Peach, Allwrath turned randomly into Prince of Wales Road and headed east, waiting for a vibration, a rune-right impulse, a signal from the Earth Goddess as to where to look next for the Sacred Site. Ten miles an hour was pretty much the hearse's top speed, with God in the back, so he approached the traffic lights into Kentish Town Road steadily. Though they were red, they had been red for a long time, so Allwrath didn't slacken speed.

A funeral procession consisting of an ancient hearse and twelve shiny black limousines was approaching the same traffic lights from the south. The lights were green. But they'd been green for a long time and were still some way off. In the first car of the cortege, the Reverend Briggs sat holding the lifeless hand of Mrs Nugent on one knee and an open *A–Z* on the other, scanning its dense grids, and shooting anxious glances through his driver's window at the dwindling rear-end of the hearse in which the mortal remains of Arthur Nugent, former organist of St Cecilia and the Martyrs, lay under its heap of flowers, and which had now pulled some fifty yards ahead of them. Whilst observing a token twenty-five miles an hour, the undertaker was cutting out juggernauts, pushing taxis into the kerb, and dodging from lane to lane whenever he could. The Reverend Briggs knew this undertaker from previous funerals – a passionate man of the turf, his cocky black cap more suitable for a jockey than a funeral attendant, he would be hell-bent on getting back to the parlour in time for the three o'clock at Haydock. 'Could be riding in it himself, the speed he's going, blast him,' muttered the Reverend. The driver of his own car, on the other hand, who led the procession, clearly thought it was his own funeral he was driving to, and stopped to let buses pull out and children cross the road wherever possible.

So that now, the hearse and its following column of limousines were a good sixty yards apart. It was undignified for one thing. For another, they seemed to be lost. He was sure they should have kept left up Chalk Farm Road. It was obviously a short-cut the undertaker knew. But the Garden Suburb with its waiting crematorium was nowhere to be seen on the map up which his finger wobbled, following their progress.

'Death is . . .' he told the limp hand on his other knee '. . . (the Railway Bridge – Camden Road –) . . . a progression ever . . . (Is that Hawley Road?) . . . upwards. Death is like . . .'

What was Death like? He was a kind and unsuperstitious man. It was probably like getting lost more than anything. But the Church of England is not here to spread alarm.

'. . . is like . . . a cadence . . . in one of Arthur's organ recitals . . .'

(A nice simile, though he personally prayed It wasn't quite that bad.)

'. . . so this must be Prince of Wales Road at the next lights.'

He scanned the traffic. Arthur's hearse was now seventy yards ahead of them with a jam of cars between, while his own driver had just pulled over to let a pantechnicon get in front. But there were the traffic lights coming up! Thank God! they were just turning from amber to red. The hearse would never make it through. They would be able to catch it up. The next moment his own driver had pulled up close behind the pantechnicon and nothing more was visible but a large double bed.

But Arthur's hearse had in fact put on a spurt in the final furlong and nipped through the lights at nearly fifty miles an hour just as they were turning, winning a photo-finish with the red gateposts of Hell, and Arthur, who'd always enjoyed a little plunge himself, was through, free, galloping ever onwards, faster and faster, past the winner's enclosure, up Kentish Town Road, while the stands of demon shoppers roared him on. And his vicar and loved ones waited behind the double bed, presuming him to be on the Other Side.

Allwrath was approaching the same lights from the side-street. There was a streak of black, then the lights turned green. Allwrath put his foot down. But the hearse was slow to respond. Little by little she dragged herself towards twelve miles an hour. The green light hung before him like a mirage in a desert. Just as he reached it, it changed through amber back to red. Allwrath slammed on the brakes. But the brakes were as lifeless as the accelerator, and nothing happened. And now God, in the back, was adding his weight to the momentum. Although Allwrath was pumping the brakes, the hearse continued to accelerate, reaching fifteen miles an hour as it passed through the red lights with a cresting motion, like a black swan. Allwrath slid down behind the wheel. The two streams of traffic on the high street were already pulling away. A juggernaut roaring down the inside at fifty nearly hit the Centre of the Sacred Circle. Allwrath slewed sideways across the intersection, reaching twenty, and just cutting in front of a pantechnicon as it pulled away. The next moment he'd plunged into the safety of the opposite side-street, just as the hearseless funeral began to move.

'There he goes,' cried the Reverend Briggs beating the glass behind his driver's head and pointing left, as his *A–Z* slithered to the floor. 'I knew we should have kept left at Chalk Farm Road. It's a disgrace. And keep up with him this time, man. For God knows which way he's going.'

Allwrath heaved a sigh of relief. Thank Gog, it was a quiet street lined with factories and a vandalised school. That was a close shave! He drew himself up higher in his seat, and glanced in the rear vision mirror. He paled. A strangled cry passed the Druid's lips. He pumped his lifeless accelerator. But now his hearse was feeling the dead weight of God again, and was beginning to slow. He glanced desperately over his shoulder. They'd tracked him down at last! He was being followed by twelve shining black limousines packed with rationalists in their best thinking suits!

* * *

79

3-Tooth leaned deeper into the tunnel wall. Cosmic winds in B minor blew through his fingers and away across the lunar landscape that was lit by a dying fluorescent tube. The child in the moon twitched on the end of its electric umbilicus, and sang:

'There's a red house over yonder
That's where my baby staaaaaaaaaaaays . . .'

3-Tooth glanced sideways out of his shades. Big Al was coming down the tunnel. 3-Tooth pretended not to see him. It was getting on for rush hour, the only hour of the day when the tunnel wasn't completely deserted, and he had a chance of earning some money. Big Al stopped in front of 3-Tooth and gave him a hard stare. He looked down contemptuously at the handful of coins in 3-Tooth's guitar bag. 3-Tooth pretended not to see him. He pumped his wah-wah and walked on sideways across the moon like a blind man, seeing through his shoes. Big Al sidled over to the other side of the narrow tunnel, took his guitar out, and threw his army camouflage guitar bag out into the middle of the walk-way, no more than three feet from 3-Tooth's. It was a challenge. 3-Tooth felt his blood rise, interfering with the pure flow of his inspiration, sending murky clouds scudding across the dark side of the moon. He switched up his amp with his foot and kept playing. Although Big Al was bigger than him, he wasn't frightened. For his anger at this belligerent beggar-busker was purely aesthetic.

Big Al couldn't play. Not a single chord. And it wasn't that he loved music but was slow. He was slow all right. But the reason he couldn't play was because the art of music, as he put it, was for pooftas. He was proud that he only carried this musical instrument to beg with, or to be more accurate, as a weapon. He grabbed a fistful of fretboard and his strings whirred and plonked. 3-Tooth watched sideways through his shades G major dying of asphyxiation and bruises to the throat. Though it didn't matter what frets he pressed, Big Al's guitar was out of tune anyway. He began to strum with an aggressive lack of beat. He opened his mouth and appeared to be singing. His voice came out of his nose in the drawling style of the 'talking blues'. No melody line. No key-change or cadence. Only a rambling monologue, a one-sided conversation with the opposite wall of the tunnel. Something in Big Al would not let him sing. A middle-aged tourist had turned the corner and was walking down the tunnel. Better tanned than the London weather warranted, sporting a blue blazer, and wearing his camera lightly, he peered apprehensively at the narrow gap between the two buskers. 3-Tooth turned up his amp to shield the man from Big Al's virulence. But somehow Big Al's voice bludgeoned through even that electronic wall of sound.

'Well I'm standin' by the highway . . . oowah oowah . . . and there's this cunt in a poncy blazer comin' my way . . . oowee oowee . . . smilin' like 'ee's just 'ad a meal of red hot shit . . . Oh Lord . . . Well if 'ee asked me twice . . . by this old highway . . . I'd smash 'is teeth out through 'is ear-holes . . . Oh Lord oowah . . .'

At this point the pedestrian passed Big Al, smiling in terror, not sure if he made out the words, and nervously dropped a fifty-pence piece in his bag.

'. . . Thanks a lot, fuck-face . . . Remind me t' give ya a kick in the nuts next time I see ya . . . Standin' by this highway . . .'

It was too much for 3-Tooth. It was an insult to his calling as a public musician. It was an insult to music herself. And to his guitar bag, with eighteen pence in it. Black storms of rage swirled across the moon in F sharp. The 'Red House Over Yonder' exploded.

'You piss off, Al. This is my pitch, 'n I don' want none of yor vomit on it.'

'Oh yeah, McGuire. You want a punch in the face?'

3-Tooth put down his guitar and stepped into the middle of the tunnel.

They were just getting to grips when Old Bill came round the corner. Big Al had 3-Tooth down and was kneeing him in the face. But he was on a bond of Good Behaviour, and one more affray and he'd be busking in the Scrubs. So he hastily gathered up his money, guitar and bag, and beat it towards the station.

'He attacked me,' 3-Tooth explained to the officer.

'I don't blame 'im, son, some of that music you play. Now why don't you get off out of it and leave us in peace for today.'

four

Peach brought his tools home in a taxi, and placed his earnings on the table: five brand new twenty-pound notes, five one-dimensional face bricks, Clapham blues, fresh from the kilns of Value. He spread them out one by one on the table, in a line. Like bricks new-laid on the footings of some mighty edifice, they only showed one face, they seemed flat, like the paper they were printed on. But this was an illusion: these twenty-pound notes had two, three, four – a hundred faces, a thousand dimensions, a million meanings, being, as they were, wholly symbolical. Peach wasn't a mercenary man, but when he'd earned a few more he imagined folding these twenty-pound notes into a brickbat as thick and blue as Fergus's, and feeling the pure sensual pleasure of your pocket sagging with paper. And for the first time in his life, Peach became aware of the power of the Twenty-Pound-Note-In-Itself. They weren't just pieces of paper. This power had nothing to do with actually *buying* anything with his five twenty-pound notes. It was simply there, in the paper. Was this the beginning of miserdom? He hoped not. No. He'd always been easygoing with money when he had any. But for seven years he hadn't had any. He had had no bank account and had lived on the change in his pocket, which he'd earned busking. His contribution to the housekeeping had been less than Morag's, and she earned little enough. What furniture they had, came off skips. Morag had found his trousers, shirts and coats at War On Want, at ten pence a time. That left underwear and shoes and socks, which he bought with Christmas money from his parents. Perhaps this feeling of freedom he had now, as he looked at his profits lying on the table, was simply the lifting of a burden of guilt he'd been carrying around in his pockets all these years. He certainly didn't have to climb into the 'Pharaoh's Tomb' to realise that *he was enjoying being a breadwinner*.

Morag came home and added forty pounds of her own, four tens, to the course of money on the table. She'd sold a coat. She'd woven it on her loom, that always stood under the window, wherever they lived. Now her next job, an Aztec rug, was strung on the frame.

But now the money was on the table. One hundred and forty pounds!

'Millionaires,' said Morag nervously, taking a sheet of paper out of her bag. At first she placed it on the table beside their money, but it spoilt the effect. She picked it up and gave it to Peach.

'I've made a list of things we're going to need.'

Peach felt something grow heavy in his guts. It was the breadwinner's pang at eating his own bread. He saw at once that the pleasure of being a breadwinner depended on keeping the loaves rolling in. It wasn't like Sartori, a pleasure of the Now. It would be daily bread from here on in. A skyscraper a day. Nose to the grindstone in the City of Value.

'It's still early. I thought we could go down Portobello together,' said Morag contentedly.

Peach suddenly felt tired. He didn't like the market, never had — especially on a Saturday. The pell-mell of private enterprise disoriented him. His three weeks of manual labour plus meditation, by which he'd earned his fortune, caught up on him all at once, and he felt like going to bed. But, seeing how happy Morag was, he smiled at her as brightly as he could, and read the list.

'A pram *and* a buggy?'

'Yes. They can't go in buggies till six months. They can't sit up.'

'A Moses basket *and* a cot?'

'Actually, Lucy will lend us her Moses basket, so we only need the cot.'

'New saucepans . . .'

'They've got to be sterile.'

'A blender. A plastic bath . . . A vacuum cleaner? . . .'

'They crawl around and eat things off the floor, Peach.'

'A spin-drier. A lavatory brush. Curtain material, a FRIDGE?'

'Absolutely. Babies've got delicate stomachs. We can't leave the food out on the windowsill any more.'

'But how are we going to hump it around if we get evicted?'

'We're squatters, but we're not refugees. The baby's got rights. We've got to have a fridge, Peach. Of course I'll be breast-feeding for a long while, so we don't have to buy it today. But if I see a cheap one I will.'

'Socks for me?'

'Now you're working they smell more. Haven't you noticed when you're in the lotus position, Peach, with your feet turned up . . . ? Oh, and one thing not on the list – I'm going to get one of those Tibetan dresses. I want it now, for the spring, but it will do for a maternity dress, too, in the autumn.'

It wasn't hard to picture Morag in that dress. It was the single item on her list he could visualise. She would look beautiful.

Peach looked at the rows of red and blue-red bank-notes one more time before he folded them up. The bottom courses of a mighty edifice demolished already! He smiled as jauntily as he could.

'All right. Let's go down the market.'

It was the first fine Saturday of spring. The sun beat down on the Portobello Road, and new stalls sprouted among the winter-toughened perennials, like lichen on the damp clothes many of them were selling: solo jewellers, their shops hung on a black velvet board, potters spreading their clay corms on the pavement, old ladies with trays of fudge, sprouted like fungus out of the winter's dole-queue log. The stalls which had weathered the cold months might look down their noses, but secretly they were glad to have these new growths of hope and ambition cropping up in doorways and under the railway bridge.

The fruit and veg barrows – those hardy evergreens who'd sold avocados and grapefruits under frozen bulbs in the dark months – now flowered like fruit-trees blossoming friendly offers: three Portuguese honeydews for the price of two, take two fresh pineapples and you get a hand of rotting bananas free. Of course all the fruit and most of the veg that hung on these hot-awninged trees had just come out of six months' cold storage. But so had everybody else, so no one minded. The Harpic Man, who had swaddled his stall of bathroom essentials in polythene over the winter till it shone from within like a translucent igloo, had survived. His glacier of stiff J-cloths, ice-detergent, and Vim-frost had almost frozen to a halt in January. But now the polythene was off, and his stall was melting visibly, dropping loo-deodorisers, toothbrushes and aerosols into the baskets and shopping trollies of the passers-by. A half-price lavatory brush and a pair of rubber gloves landed in Morag's bag.

Mr Darning's man-made mountain of second-hand clothes – nothing over 10 p – had stayed out all winter and suffered many wettings and occasional snowstorms. This was because it was too big to pack up. Mr Darning simply dragged his mountain-on-wheels under the arches and left it there from Saturday to Saturday. His Everest of rancid suits, vests, petticoats, long johns, ladies' hats and shirts was never stolen. In fact it often grew bigger during the week as people discarded their clothes upon it. Now, in the bright spring sun, it was smoking like a volcano, and even Morag walked by aghast, though there were undoubtedly bargains hidden in it. Once she had mined deep under Mr Darning's mountain and found a string vest with a flower on the front which turned out to be a fungus, in which lived a family of spiders who had woven most of the vest themselves.

Mr Darning was the only stallholder in the whole Portobello Road Peach felt he could relate to. He didn't seem to care whether he sold anything or not. He sat beside his stall, Saturday after Saturday, a prophet beside his own mountain, above profit and loss. Perhaps he was even meditating, like an old Tibetan yogi deep in his cave, as humanity swirled and yelled around him. God knows how he lived. His mountain of clothes only grew – it never shrank, except after a wet Saturday. Peach would have liked to talk to him. He was the Still Centre in the bustling market. But his presence was too forbidding, and he was perpetually pissed.

Everyone else was high on money and that magical moment when money changes hands. Now that was something Peach couldn't understand at all. That moment of actually *buying* something always filled him with confusion and even, some-times, a slight giddiness – as though he'd been present at some important psychic transaction, upon which his fate depended, but had somehow missed it. Of course he bought food and books but surveying his life since he'd left home, he knew it was phenomenal, the number of things he hadn't bought. Not just cars and suits and cameras, but humble, household things too. Things that everyone needed. That *he* needed. But hadn't bought – kettles, window-cleaner, inner-soles. And it wasn't miserliness. For a long time he'd thought it was because he was above worldly possessions, 'travelling light', perpetually 'on the road'. He'd spent many years living in a basement firmly believing this, and not buying anything, dreaming of India and beyond. It was true that he had got from Sydney to London. But this was only because the government had paid for it. Once in the Old Country, he'd scarcely left London, and had never been further north than Cambridge. He had, in fact, made two attempts to hitch-hike to India. At the first attempt, he'd got as far as a little country town in Belgium and settled down for a year with a family, the father of whom was a mystic and follower of Simone Weil, from whom Peach had learned much before he was deported for having no money. At the second attempt, he'd sat huddled on the Orient Express, as far as Istanbul, where he'd immediately booked into a cheap hotel, the Hotel Nassar, where he'd read 'Jerusalem' three times, and not come out for two weeks, eating in his room, playing the guitar for five and six hours at a stretch, before catching the train back to London, vowing that any future journeys he made would be spiritual. So Peach knew that his utter lack of worldly possessions wasn't a lack of worldliness. He needed security as much as anyone. And, being honest with himself, he had to trace the phenomenon back, not to 'travelling light', but to this momentary loss of reality every time he bought something more than food.

Morag, who knew about this, had taken the hundred and forty pounds in her purse and her bag was already bulging — with two brand new saucepans, four babygros, a tobacco plant, and the toilet brush and rubber gloves. And she hadn't spent ten pounds yet. It was miraculous. Now she wanted to be alone for some more serious shopping. She gave him one of the ten-pound notes.

'You go and get your socks. There's a stall down there that does three pairs of worksocks for a pound. It's an unbelievable bargain.'

He felt like a child.

He found the stall all right. How could he miss it? — a large table covered with nothing but worksocks. Beside it stood an open van, in the back of which Peach could see large boxes marked either BLUE or BROWN, and M or L, stacked to the ceiling. It was a specialist stall. Which must be why the socks were so cheap. The proprietor was a Pakistani. Sure in the knowledge of the unbeatableness of his prices, he didn't have to harangue the passers-by. He didn't have to wave his socks in the air as if they were hands of bananas about to go off. His socks were top quality. He stood serenely beside his table, almost embarrassed to have found the secret of life so easily, a large warehouse in East India Dock Road. A radio in the back of the van tintinnabulated distantly, transforming Radio One into the tambura hubbub of the Karachi kasbah. But he was safe from poverty now. This table on the Portobello Road enshrined him like a local God of Worksocks. A stream of pound coins rolled through his money belt, transmigrating inexorably into five- and ten-pound notes. Even giving change was serenely easy. There was no writing sums on the back of paper bags. A large sign above his stall said everything:

WORKSOCKS   MEDIUM   LARGE

BLUE   BROWN

FIFTY PENCE A PAIR

THREE PAIRS FOR A POUND

In spite of the sign, and the fact that Morag had already told him the price, Peach found himself asking, 'How much are the socks, please?'

The stallkeeper gave him a mystified but friendly smile. Perhaps it was a German tourist who couldn't read English?

'Fifty pence a pair, sir,' he said distinctly. 'Three pairs for a pound. What size are you – Medium or Large?'

Peach froze and found he couldn't answer.

'Either size would probably fit you, sir,' said the stallkeeper, not unpleased to have someone who actually needed help. In some ways, it would be nice to do shoes, which are more personal.

'. . . allowing for shrinkage. What colour do you prefer?'

Peach still said nothing. He wished he'd gone to Woolworth's, where no one ever tried to help you.

'Blue or Brown?' asked the stallholder, as if spelling out the sign.

'Oh . . . er . . .'

With only the slightest dash of salesmanship the man picked up a pair of blue worksocks, size Medium, and put them in Peach's hand. Peach felt them. Good, thick socks, which he indubitably needed. But although he knew they were there, *he couldn't see them*: they had become unreal. He was thinking of Morag's shopping list, each item a link in a chain which he knew, with a heavy clanking in his heart, was endless – prams, cots, fridges – each item cold as steel, till he could scarcely move or breathe. His free-wheeling spiritual days were over.

'Do you like them, sir?' asked the stallkeeper, reminding Peach of the existence of the socks.

'What . . . ?' Peach gazed at the socks. 'Oh . . . ah . . . yes. They're . . . beautiful.'

'Only fifty pence a pair, sir – three pairs for a pound,' the man reminded him politely. A real bargain! 'You won't find them anywhere cheaper than that, sir.'

'Oh, I know,' said Peach. 'It's just that . . .'

Someone leant across him and bought half a dozen pairs.

The stallkeeper zipped a tenner into his belt.

'Look. I tell you what I'll do for you,' he said testily. 'If you take another two pairs, you can have the lot for ninety pence.'

He picked two more pairs from the table, a blue to match the ones Peach already held, and a brown for variety, and put them in Peach's hands. Peach was aghast. He only needed one pair. He could wash them in the evening and dry them while he slept. Or at the most two pairs. But the man didn't seem to sell them in twos. And his freedom, that inner place where he stood above all compulsion, *chose for himself*, was being more and more thoroughly violated with every pair of socks that landed in his hands.

'No. No. Thank you. I've got a pound . . . It's just . . . I'm not sure . . .'

'You mean you've got the money.'

'No,' said Peach desperately. 'Yes. It's just that . . .'

The stallkeeper had met some hagglers in his days as a runner in the Karachi bazaar, but never such a haggler as this. It must be the English way – depreciation by condescension. Now he just wanted to get rid of him.

'Listen,' he said grimly, 'I'll tell you what I'll do for you – it'll be the talk of the market – you can have those three pairs for fifty pence!'

A small crowd gathered, attracted by the amazing offer. There was someone in here giving socks away! The stallkeeper eyed them savagely. Perhaps they were a gang, working together like three-card tricksters, sending this maniac in first to beat him down to rock bottom, then moving in, the whole gang of them, and clearing him out. Well, he wouldn't let them! He should snatch his three pairs of worksocks back, and demand his pound like an English shopkeeper. But the stallholder found he couldn't do this. Some warm breeze from the Karachi bazaar kept him at it. He would sell this young madman these socks if it killed him. With three hundred pairs on the stall, and another two thousand in the van, he couldn't afford to have their very existence called in question.

'FORTY PENCE,' he bellowed, full in Peach's face, ignoring the crowd, even though its hands were full of money. 'THREE PAIRS OF WORKSOCKS FOR THE PRICE OF ONE! Now what size are you?'

'M . . . m . . . medium,' said Peach, '. . . I think . . .'

'Yes sir. You're Medium. Of course you're Medium,' shrieked the stallholder, casting a grim professional eye on Peach's split plimsolls with the cemented toes. For a moment he turned to the crowd, beseechingly.

'Do I not know my trade? Are they not three pairs of the highest quality worksocks . . . ?'

But were they 'highest quality'? Were they not ordinary, middle-of-the-road worksocks, made in Taiwan, which would probably stiffen to nylon planks in a day on this young man's obviously sweaty feet?

'Look. I tell you what I'll do for you,' he cried almost in tears. 'THIRTY PENCE THE THREE. My last offer!'

'L . . . l . . . look. I'll just . . . run and get a . . . get my wife! . . . I'll be back in two ticks . . . I'll check with her about . . . about the colour.'

Peach tried to put the socks back on the stall.

'One . . . two . . . three . . . *four* pairs of worksocks,' gasped the stallkeeper, slapping a pair of brown socks on to the pile already trembling in Peach's hands. 'Two blue. Two brown. *Twenty-five* pence. There is nothing to ask your wife!'

The ten pounds in his pocket was already spent. It was spent twice, three times – a hundred times over. If he worked till the day he died, he would never get it back. Morag's list was endless. The material world had wound its chain around his neck, its knot an unborn baby, and was drawing it tight. Even if these four pairs of socks were just one penny, they would still be too much. He didn't have that penny, not really. And anyway, he couldn't hand over a ten-pound note at this juncture and wait for his nine pounds seventy-five change. The man would tear him limb from limb.

'Look,' he said imploringly, 'I'll . . . I'll . . . definitely have a . . . pair . . . next week! . . . I'll . . . c . . . c . . . come back next week . . . Will you be here on Saturday?'

'Not if there are any more people like you in the world,' shrieked the stallkeeper. And waving his arms, he began to push Peach away from the stall.

'Go! Go! I GIVE YOU THE SOCKS! They are my humble gift. Take them and never come back!'

Peach tried to put them down on the stall, but the man wouldn't let him. With the strength of the crazed, he pinned Peach's arms to his sides, and drove him backwards through the crowd, still clutching four pairs of socks.

Morag found him an hour later, cowering under the flyover.

'You got some socks! Four pairs! How much were they?'

But Peach couldn't tell her.

By the time Morag had finished her shopping they were both laden. Walking home up All Saints Road, they passed Arthur's Second Hand Pianos. Half a dozen upright pianos, in varying stages of decay, stood on the pavement in front of the shop. Though their embossed panels and scrolled music racks may have felt affronted by Arthur's rough handling and knock-down prices, to Peach's imagination they looked well pleased to be out of their Edwardian parlour on such a glorious day, their rotting hessian backcloths ruffling in the breeze.

''Ello Morag. Nice day, Peach,' called Arthur from the

darkness of his piano cavern above the tinny tunings of Radio One.

'Get the accumulata, did ya?' he asked, nodding at their armfuls of purchases. 'Come in 'ere, Morag. I wanna show ya somethink.'

He led them to the back of his unlit shop and stood them before the ugliest piano Peach had ever seen. A cliff of black wood that looked as if a bush-fire had been over it. The beetling eves of its lid were sharp and heavy. Its panelling was as bare as a Methodist coffin. Upon all this Protestant weight, a single gilt arm bearing a florid candelabra had been fixed at some later date. The music rack swung on two screws like a folding skeleton. Arthur opened the lid. The keys were the colour of jaundiced knife-handles. It looked as though you could cut your finger on the basalt blocks of the black notes. A great coldness emanated from the keyboard. It may only have been the back of Arthur's shop, where it was still winter, but Peach shivered. On the back of the lid was written OBERAMMERGAU PIANOS, AACHEN.

'Don't look much,' admitted Arthur, 'but this pianna is for someone wot 'as got ears. 'Ave a play, Peach.'

Arthur pulled up one of his kitchen chairs. Peach sat down at the piano and gently touched a C major chord, his thumb on middle C.

''Ear that, Morag? A lamb in wolf's cloving, that is. A 'undred knicker an' she's yours.'

'A hundred?' said Morag.

'None o' the dealers is interested 'cos it looks a bit square like. But if ya shut yer eyes an' use yer chandeliers . . .'

Arthur was right. From out of the ugly black box came a vibrant chord – loud, metallic, and yet somehow poignant. It was a chord like Roman warriors striking their swords on their shields, confirming some great oath, while their mothers wept. Such a clanging, big-boned piano must have tortured generations of children in Aachen. And yet there was something maternal in the worn ivory under his fingers. Peach played a scale himself, as jerkily as a child practising, descending chromatically into the bass. Ever-deepening echoes awoke round each string as it stepped downwards to the next. There was something both austere, and yet heart-rending, in this blackly echoing sound. It was as though this stiff-backed Lutheran upright for torturing children yearned, like a repressed child itself, to be a concert grand thundering out the Hammerklavier Sonata and the Complete Organ Works of Bach. He could hear the bottom strings tensing like the cables of a suspension bridge. He played the same C major scale, with his right hand, beginning from middle C, up into the treble. And bells clambered ever upwards, till, in the upper octaves, he was fingering the coffin of a harpsichord. It was a marvellous instrument. It would take a virtuoso to play it softly. Yet Peach knew that once he got back into practice and gave himself to it, he could make this old piano thrum. It was a pity they couldn't afford it. He moved into F major and wandered through muzzy, hesitating harmonies. He forgot about his socks, and remembered the piano he'd had at home as a child.

How it had seemed like a thing created by God's own Hands, so far was it beyond being a merely human machine. That was in the days when all he knew about God he'd learnt at Sunday School. Perhaps God had never been so real since. He remembered God-thumping middle C with both his thumbs, on that old piano back home, and setting off chromatically with both hands towards either end of the keyboard, careful to keep in time and not miss a note, so that his hands were always equidistant from middle C, which was Undeniable God, his right hand going up into the treble, his left hand going down into the bass, always a perfect interval apart. He'd imagined that when he reached the ends of the keyboard, which were two polished rosewood plateaux, simultaneously with both hands, he would somehow be able to keep going outwards in both directions, for ever, hearing the notes inside him, one incredibly high and getting higher, till even the dog couldn't hear it, one correspondingly deep, and getting deeper, till he met God on the Other Side of Him. That realm beyond the bookends of the keyboard was the Unknown, where adults meet God. But his arms had never been long enough to reach both ends at once. So he'd always made his way, slowly and chromatically, back to the God he knew, Who dwelt at middle C.

Sitting on a kitchen chair at Arthur's piano, Peach found that his hazy chordings in F major, as he remembered these things, had turned into a sort of fugue. It had a melody. Or rather, half a melody – a motif, which he hadn't thought out and which he still couldn't quite *hear* as it wound in and out of polyphonic chords, clearly defined, trim as hedges, passing into distant thickets of sevenths and ninths and groves of counterpoint, binding his fingers in thick-set knots with thorns, complex, but somehow not completely *heard*, and yearning to become that one original note, that sunlit middle C from which it had all begun. But the more he played, the further away he got from that God-note, first spoken under the trees at Sunday School, by an old spinster, when the corrugated iron roof of the church got too hot and they had their lessons outside – the unequivocal sounding-forth of God, two thumbs hitting an ivory key. Whatever fugue it was he was now playing, as unplanned as his child in Morag's belly, it was taking him higher and higher, up the keyboard, till he was an octave and a half above that original, sunny note. He looked down at it, as he remembered, as though from out of a swaying tree. It was too far to jump without breaking the melody and losing it. But Peach yearned for that one, lone sound. Then suddenly, he shut his eyes, and felt a deep breath pour down his chest as though a barrier near his heart had broken. The breath bore his hands upwards, still playing. Then all at once he was jumping, upwards, outwards, and down, down through breathless spiritual space – and had landed with both thumbs, with both feet, indeed with the whole of his being, on middle C – and a great pang of sorrow sobbed through him.

He opened his eyes, amazed. For middle C is the happiest, most open note in the scale. But he was falling down it now, as if that one note were a well of sorrow that had no bottom.

He leapt off it and played for a while in C major, little triplets in thirds, like lambs skipping in a void, yet still falling, falling. He played a childlike, two-finger chord in the bass, as a ground for them, both notes filled with sunshine and innocence, yet the chord just dragged him down, faster and faster, into a nameless, bottomless sorrow. And he heard Miss Wheeler, his Sunday School teacher, saying 'Unless ye become as little children' – to the children. And this was the bottom of sorrow. At the precise moment it got too much to bear, his hands, completely of their own accord, moved back into F, refound the little fugue tune, found that it had triplets and thirds in it, and gladly let it wander off into the thick-set sevenths and ninths, where it lost itself for a period, like a mouse in a hedge. But it also meant forgetting.

He forgot the living moltenness of the past, and remembered it again in ordinary pictures. Losing himself in F major, Peach remembered a later period: his teens. When he'd mastered a certain technique on the old piano back home and got his Fourth Grade Certificate, and was himself mastered by his own dreams, and his ambitions no longer lay in reaching both ends of the keyboard at once – but in playing Beethoven's Waldstein Sonata, an Advanced Performer's Diploma piece, of which he was as physically incapable then as he'd once been incapable of stretching his arms fourteen octaves. It was one of the most difficult pieces Beethoven ever wrote and his music teacher had refused point blank to teach him it. So Peach took the music home and learnt it alone, a closet virtuoso, neglecting the pieces she had set him. He believed anyone can do anything if they only want it enough. He was mastered by the will-to-power. If he had read Nietzsche, he would have understood that he, Peach O'Hare, was the superman Nietzsche had prophesied. His will, which had grown muscles doing twenty laps at football training, and nerves passing exams, he now turned full upon this unfortunate masterpiece, undeterred by the thickets of semiquavers and breathtaking double thirds which the wise composer had placed around it like a barbed wire fence. Surely only a virtuoso would think of crossing that technical Iron Curtain – and he would do it by the main gate – a recital at the Sydney Town Hall.

But Peach's programme was this: he would go through the sonata bar by bar. He would spend as long on each bar as it took to master it – one, two, three days, a week if need be. Virtuosos did no less. He would begin by playing each bar at one sixteenth of its proper speed. Even at one sixteenth, many of the bars were unplayable. But by playing them over and over and over, he would master each one by sheer mechanical repetition. Thus he mastered the first bar. Then the second, which he welded to the first in a lengthy two-bar performance. Then the third. At one sixteenth of its proper speed the sonata was unrecognisable as Beethoven, or indeed as music. The drumming chords of the opening clanked like a disjointed piston, doing untold damage in the compression box, and the great iron wheel of the cantabile theme could not be heard to turn. It was inconceivable that this bar belonged to one of the fastest pieces in the classical repertoire. When he'd mastered it at one sixteenth, Peach doubled the speed to about an eighth of its proper tempo, assuming that his fingers, having learnt the right mechanical postures by heart, would be able to make them twice as fast when he simply *opened up the steam*. And it worked. The marvellous arpeggio triplets that glitter up and down the keyboard, clanked up and over each other like locomotive wheels beginning to turn, and a mighty 'Chug' passed through the piece. On a good day he learned twenty or thirty bars and vague inklings that this might be the Waldstein Sonata arose in unsuspecting listeners. Up till now they'd thought they'd been listening to 'free jazz'. Couplings locked. Wheels clanked. Passengers looked out of the window. They sensed a mighty head of steam, snorting, panting, dragging them inexorably forwards, through the Adagio, which, in spite of its name, was as demanding as the Allegro con Brio they'd just suffered. They entered a dark tunnel in F minor, and passed out, on the other side of the mountain, into the Allegretto, one of Beethoven's sunniest and most difficult themes. Talking madly to himself in imitation of Glen Gould,

Peach doubled the speed, till he was playing one bar at a time, at half-speed, crashing through unplayable notes like small stations turned to a blur. At last, when he was satisfied with his performance at this pace, Peach would gird himself, and, breathless, stiff as a board, deaf as a post, play each single bar, starting from the beginning, over and over and over, *at full pace*! The piano shook. The flowers in the vase above him trembled. Getting dinner ready, his mother held her breath in the kitchen. Outside, his father looked up from his raking. The great locomotive of the Waldstein Sonata opened its throttle and swept through the open countryside, derailing continually, ploughing up fields, crashing into mountains, *but never once stopping*, each perfected bar riveted to the next one by a will of iron, though the very boiler was shuddering. But who was at the wheel? It certainly wasn't Peach. Perhaps it was Beethoven, the first Romantic, the last Classicist, his hat blown off, his cravat black with grease, shaking his fist at the Future, as he swept into it with a deafening roar. Peach had played the Waldstein Sonata from beginning to end!

He could still hear the silence that reigned after the mighty, pounding finale-chords of that first performance. It was still in his blood, thrumming like the steel frame of this big-boned piano. It had passed up the wall and stilled the picture. It had spread two or three doors in either direction, though back home the houses were far apart. It had taken two and a half years, three or four hours a day – hours he should have spent learning to drive and chasing girls, or helping his father with the raking, or even practising his scales. His parents made pained, sarcastic remarks, and reminded him of the neighbours. His father, who loved music, claimed he could locate the exact ulcer in his stomach he'd got from waiting for the great glissando passage in double octaves. But probably, wrongly, thinking that the Waldstein Sonata was better than getting girls pregnant or coming home drunk, had never physically restrained him. When that first silence had died away, Peach turned back to page one, and played it again.

And now, sitting at Arthur's piano, remembering it in F major, Peach felt that same silence stiffen through him, and yearned again for the leap down to C that would release him from these pictures, this memory machine. Was it Love – love of the Waldstein Sonata? – that had kept him at it for two and a half years? Or was it just adolescent will? Had he had something to prove, and chosen Beethoven to pick on?

His F major meanderings darkened for a moment into F minor. An unthought-of A flat clanged like a tragic bell. And for a moment, Beethoven's Adagio theme, shockingly simplified, entered his free improvising, and then was gone, like a cloud across the sun, leaving his heart beating. Yes, deep down, it had been Love. He had mutilated the Waldstein Sonata with Love. He had fought his way through discords and a locomotive beat, to the Idea of it. The Idea that comes before Creation. The Idea that exists in clangorous silence, and from which Beethoven, deaf himself, had written it down. *That* must have been an act of will! Perhaps only Will can fight its way close enough to an Idea to create it. And that is true love. Perhaps Beethoven would have understood him, and forgiven him.

And with that thought Peach found that he was suddenly back in C major. The home key! He was standing on the firm, warm earth of a simple closing chord.

Morag and Arthur were watching him appreciatively. Arthur had switched his radio off. He lifted his hands from the humming piano.

'Peach, that was beautiful,' said Morag.

'Told ya she was a good pianna,' said Arthur with a glow.

Morag's eyes were bright.

'You never told me you could play like that.'

'I was just mucking around.'

'We'll have it, Arthur,' cried Morag. 'Eighty pounds if you'll deliver it.'

'If you say so, love,' said the entrepreneur of pianos.

IT WAS a Saturday morning some weeks later. Peach stood before the kitchen window, his legs planted firmly apart, his arms stretched upwards, his body forming an X, his head flung back. The beams of the rising sun played upon his Belly Centre. John Lennon was wrong. It isn't 'above us only sky'. Each direction has its own nature. From above comes Wisdom turning into light as it approaches the denser medium of the brain. From below comes Love turning into light as it takes root between the legs. From above comes Father. From below comes Mother. The two pyramids of light pass, overlap, and coalesce in the Heart Centre, forming a multifaceted Star of David. To either side, right and left, lie all the other men and women with whom Peach shared this earth, each one a star in his or her Heart Centre. To think of loving them all, as Christ urges us, seemed hopeless. To love one or two was hard enough. Or to love even yourself in this light. Yet, having tipped his fingers above his upturned face at the height of his reach as though to create a point, an unopened crocus-tip of light, through which Wisdom could enter space, if It wished, he began to spread his arms slowly downwards, and as his arms spread like an opening crocus he made himself at least *think* of the existence of all these people, till reaching the half-way, cross position, he made himself think of loving them, and looking straight ahead, he saw them all joined in One Person, a Mighty Being descending in an ellipse of light, till his arms, aching from the gathering sense of weight, dropped further, became a cloak, a shroud, a stripped crocus, till his fingertips touched at the root of Love, between his balls and his bum, where love becomes less abstract.

The kitchen disappeared. And the birds singing outside and each individual swish in the leaves disappeared into a node of thought. His own body dropped away, and the only seeing was being. There were no images, just a million enterings. The Mighty Being engulfed him and died. And Peach stood in his own darkness, in his own kitchen. Its opacity was his opacity. Its weight was the aching in his arms. He opened his eyes, blinked in the strong light, and sighed. It seemed that the work of lighting his Inner Body till the Great Spirit could live, and not only die, in it, was endless. His inwardness was larded with a darkness that had nothing to do with shutting his eyes. He sighed more heavily. Still it was his work to do.

He climbed on to the piano stool, folded his legs, turned his palms outwards, shut his eyes, and began again. With another crucifix stretch of his arms he fostered the light downwards, down the kinked plumbline of his spine, to the Root Centre, at the very base of his spine. This was the place where he, Peach O'Hare, as a human parcel of matter, began, before matter became sexual, let alone personal. This was what his mother knew about him, but he'd long forgotten himself. Really this place ought to be roaring with light. But the descending light had condensed to a dead-weight flicker. And yet this was the beginning of him, Peach O'Hare, landscape artist, father-to-be, and self-employed meditator. He thought of Morag. He tried to imagine *her* place where light turns into dead weight, below sexuality. He thought of the bone between the folds of her bum. Love stirred him in the dark. And another fine-stretched breath's worth of light made its way down the bricklayer's line that hung with the tip of its plumb-weight touching the base of his spine. Morag! Another person! The beginning of the endless world! The tip of the lead plumb glowed, became candescent with the unwound light from his brain, and began to flicker and flare and rotate about itself, and turned into an upside-down candle, with enough breath to clearly light this dead place where he sat. It was a perfect square he saw, cast by the flame, and as white and empty as it. He knew it was the ground plan of the Holy City of Jerusalem, the four-square City of God that would one day be built on earth. The calluses on his rough hands grew warm. He could

101

feel their grain glistening with sweat. And he felt a pang of joy. For somehow or other, beyond his understanding, this Jerusalem had to be built in the real world whose sun was now tanning his face. Good to be a bricklayer then, even if you only laid sixty a day. A decent knocking-up board and he'd manage seventy-five. It was a symbolic trade.

He drew another deep breath and rolled the light's fine-drawn bricklayer's string up into the beginning of a ball, in his brain, and the heavy plumb of his attention rose from Jerusalem in the Root Centre, and joyfully swung before the second Centre, where the spirit is rooted into flesh by the sexual organs, and babies are made. This Centre burst into light of its own accord, through much use, the plumb-weight spinning imperceptibly, like a candle in a wind tunnel, gathering force. So that Peach had to steady his mind, and ask himself what love of others there was in this place. He immediately thought of Morag again. She tended to crop up in all his Centres. But next to her image was the thought of the child she carried, who was still an absolute stranger to him. Yet the thought of that unknown person hovered within the knowledge of her, like a passion-fruit seed in a mist, and his heart started beating with a love that wasn't wholly sexual.

Time to roll up the string to the Belly Centre. For now the light was burning bright. Bright enough to illuminate his whole subtle body, working upwards to his head, from whence it would carry him outside himself into the spiritual world. But now we come upon an idiosyncrasy of Peach O'Hare's, though it's a thing that perhaps he shared with a lot of modern people – he didn't care for the Belly Centre. The traditional seat of emotion, the Passion-body, the place where the astral body is umbilicalled into the physical body, the Belly Cave of Milarepa, haunt of demons and wild desires, pit of despair – it was always dark to him. And he feared it. He had the greatest difficulty feeling Morag here. In fact he would rather have kept on winding the light up past the Belly Centre altogether, give it a miss, and get on into the Heart, where he could be reasonably sure of warmth and peace and balance, when it opened. But the meditational texts said you must open all your Centres, in an orderly progression, working upwards. If one was left unopened, the repressed forces would play havoc with the subtle body and destroy its harmony. So Peach stopped at the Belly Centre and waited outside. He summoned the thought of Morag and his child again to help him.

But already within the wild and windy darkness that howled around him, he sensed the presence of a fourth person. Perhaps it was his own demonic double, his Spectre. Peach trembled. He saw a cave in a Himalayan mountainside. Snow lay on the ground, whipped and whirled by a storm. Gathering all his powers he entered the cave, with Morag and his unborn child at his side. Darkness engulfed them. The Himalayan stone surrounded them, creaking and grinding with the storm. He gasped. His guttering light went out. And fear gripped him. Then, in an instant, he saw another light, coming from the *Other Side*, from the back of the cave. A dirty, greasy candlelight. But it was no longer *his* light. A man sat monumentally meditating, wrapped in a grubby tantric robe. He looked as though he'd hewn himself from the very stone by the power of his concentration. Peach began to freeze, from the marrow outwards, till his skin goosepimpled with dread. From under his cowl, the eyes of the Tibetan were looking at him.

'I have been waiting here for you for thirty-three lifetimes. It has taken you six thousand years to climb to this Cave.'

'I'm sorry,' quavered Peach, holding Morag's hand tight.

'I am the Tibetan. Come to guide you to the Realms Below.'

A huge, squat finger appeared from the sleeve of his robe, and though the echoing voice had pronounced 'Below', pointed straight up. By the power instinct in that one finger, Peach's head rolled back, against his will, and his mouth fell open. He stared at the rocky ceiling. The booming 'Below' had goosepimpled the very stone. Was the Tibetan lost too? Or was *he* falling upside down? He wished he'd never entered this cave of horrors. He wished he'd never heard of meditation. A mighty wind groined the recesses of the cave. And only Morag holding his hand stopped him from blowing away.

'If you wish to enter all things, you must first let the dread of them excavate your bowels, and their horror tunnel your guts.'

As he brought his head back down, Peach thought he glimpsed the Tibetan's huge sleeve wiping across his white moustache. But strange to say, the moustache came off on his sleeve, into which it faded away. What ghastly magic was this? Or did this stony man grow a moustache of snow?

'Yours will be the moan between the sledgehammer and the stone – ' chanted the Guru, readjusting the robe over his great knees. 'You will fold up your bones like a tent of groans, and sleep in the dark when the sun goes Down.'

And again the great finger appeared out of its sleeve. And although the cave still echoed 'Down', again it pointed up. And again Peach's head rolled backwards and his mouth fell open, till he was staring at the stone ceiling again. But no sun could he see.

'Morag. Morag,' Peach cried aloud. 'This is the dreadful Guardian of the Threshold. He has swallowed Up and Down. Time and Space swill about in his stony stomach. He will drink me too! Oh Morag!'

But Morag had left him.

Then, as he lowered his head, Peach saw it again. The Guru wiped his monumental sleeve across his snow-white moustache, which came off on the robe where he'd wiped it. And where he'd adjusted its folds lower down, a monstrous polyp-headed bulge was showing. Peach panicked. Surely he wasn't trapped in this cave with a mad yogi performing some unspeakable tantric ritual.

'If ye wish to enter all things, ye must become one wit me. I am your Fear and your Fury. I am the graveyard in yer guts, and yer excremental tunnel. De one dat leads DOWN!'

And a third time the great forefinger emerged from its cement-cuffed sleeve and jabbed the air in an upwards direction.

'Behold, de pit!'

But Peach gathered every ounce of will-power in him and held his head firm and looked straight in front of him. Though seismic kundalini forces that shook the very mountain tried to get him in a head-lock and force his head backwards, he held himself still, and his gaze straight forwards, prepared to witness Death if need be.

Assuming himself to be unobserved, the Guru whipped out a hand, pulled up the skirts of his robe, and grabbed a creaming pint of the blackest stout Peach had ever seen, two thirds drunk. In one sweeping movement he lifted it to his lips and knocked it back, his Throat Centre working hard, then whipped the empty back under his robe. The white head of the pint left a royal moustache on his upper lip, which he wiped off with his sleeve.

'I am Debt itself. I am de Hole Universe. Me Name is Unnameable,' roared the Tibetan.

'Fergus O'Fury,' cried Peach out loud.

'Be Jaysus, young fella, you said it. I deliver ye!'

'Peach! Peach!'

Morag burst into the kitchen in her nightdress. Peach was rocking to and fro in the full lotus position on the piano stool, little spasms starting up all over him. But being used to his meditational techniques, she paid no attention to this, and shook him roughly by the knee.

'Peach,' she cried excitedly. 'Feel this!'

'The mountain's shaking, Morag . . .' shouted Peach with his eyes still shut and rocking violently, his head flung back '. . . the mountain's shaking . . . the roof's cracking . . . I'm falling head-first into the stars! . . . And past them, I think I can see . . . the Divine Source . . . if only . . .'

'Hang on a second, Peach. Feel this.'

His eyes were tight-shut, facing the ceiling. She lifted her nightdress and put his sweating hand on her belly, which was now freshly rounded.

'I think I can see the Divine Source, Morag. But the mountain's shaking.'

'Wait, Peach. Wait . . . Wait . . . NOW! – Did you feel it?'

Under his hand was another mountain-top – or rather a small, soft hill well-rooted in breathing earth. To touch it was ecstasy after the stony mountain of Fergus O'Fury, the Tibetan. It breathed and yet was still. It was an eternal hill, though it would pass away. It was Morag's belly. Suddenly, from deep down in that hill, a soft spasm bubbled to the surface and kicked his hand.

'It's the baby! It's moving, Peach. Did you feel it?'

Peach opened his eyes. He was staring at the ceiling. He tried one last time to see the Divine Source beyond the polystyrene tiles. But what was happening under his hand seemed to have come from beyond even the Divine Source. The little bubble rose to the surface again and the soft hill gave a kick. His hand melted.

'Did you feel it, Peach? It's the baby!'

'Yes,' he smiled beatifically. 'The Beyond!'

⋯→⋯━◆>●<◆━⋯+⋯

five

IT WAS a week later and Peach was mixing up a batch of cement. Beside him stood a pile of the purple face bricks known as Clapham multis. Along the foot of a low bank of earth ran an L-shaped foundation which he'd cast the day before. He was going to build a retaining wall, twelve courses high and a single brick thick. He was ecstatic. It was the first of his brickwork to go up rather than along. It was the beginning of the third dimension, and Peach was looking forward to it. The sun shone into him, expanding his self-confidence. There is nothing, the sunlight seemed to say, which intelligence, health and a good will cannot do. Aleister Crowley had pronounced: 'Do What Thou Will!', and had died a shuddering addict. He had forgotten the simple word that freed the will. The Law was: 'Love, and Do What Thou Will!'

Peach turned the mortar over and over, sprinkling it with water off his fingers, bringing it to the perfect pitch of miscability. He feathered out the stiffness with the back of his shovel. For it was a strong mix: three to one, to give the single skin of brickwork an added self-confidence. In his exuberance, he'd thrown twenty-five heaped shovels of sand and a bag and a half of cement into his mix, knocking up a gauge as big as a hill. He'd better lay the bricks quick, before it went off. But the brickwork turns out better, he'd been told, when it goes up all at once, without stopping every ten minutes to mix more mortar. He turned the cement into a fluent heap, straightened his back which was already aching, caught his breath, and looked around him.

107

To crown his joys, he was mixing up under an apple tree in the middle of Hampstead Heath – sacred ground, which he visited regularly to find peace and practise nature meditation in the middle of London. For the garden where Peach was working was in the Vale of Health, that privileged cluster of cottages and fairground caravans that borders the great pond in the middle of the Heath, and accessible to the rest of the city by only a pot-holed track. Of course, most of the cottages now belonged to film stars and successful architects, and were worth about a quarter of a million each, but there were a couple of decaying premises on the corner of the fairground which would make very nice squats. A secure squat in the Vale of Health, with his child running out on to the Heath every morning to play, and he'd be happy. He'd give up his free-wheeling philosophy and become a Zen fundamentalist. It surprised him that there were no children running around now, on such a sunny spring morning. But they'd all been driven to school long before he'd got up. Peach imagined his own child sitting in work-trousers or work-frock on his pile of cement bags, kicking the warm paper with three to one wellingtons or digging up worms with his pointing trowel. He would dig the child a worm-pit, a palace for worms, teaching it the holiness of all life and the basic principles of reincarnation. Later in the morning he would let his child mix his muck and bring him the bricks as he laid. In fact he was such a slow bricklayer that a three-year-old labourer could probably keep him going. But not today. Not with this giant gauge. That was the education he'd give his child. At tea-break he'd take it out on to the Heath to watch the bird lady magick a cloud of wings out of the sky with her twice-daily Swoop. At lunch-time he'd sit the child on his knee and tell it stories, building castles and giant's dens on the footings of a garden wall. His mortar was more than ready. It was time to lay the first brick.

Peach laid a right-angle of mortar on the corner of the foundation and set two bricks into it, making a corner of them. He checked each brick four or five times with his spirit-level to make sure it was straight both from end to end, front to back, as well as plumb. It took time, but these first bricks were all-important. The square and plumb of the whole wall would depend on them. One brick was higher than the other. He beat it down with the butt of his trowel, squeezing the mortar from beneath it till, when it was dead level, it was buried in muck. He swore, picked up both bricks and washed them in his bucket, threw away the stiff mortar, and laid them again. This time he got them right. He climbed to the top of the bank to get a view from above, to check that the bricks made a perfect right-angle. He didn't want his wall shooting off at a tangent. He'd better hurry. Being so conscientiously strong, the three to one mix was going off like lightning. He'd seen old brickies who would have used it all up by now. Brickies so quick they seemed to throw the bricks into their walls, larding the mortar along the courses as though they were pouring hot fat from a frying pan, squeezing the muck from under one brick, spinning it once on the tip of their trowel, to land on the corner of the next brick, calling out for jollop all day long, keeping the labourers running. They only checked their work with the level once or twice a morning, and their walls always came out plumb. Still, he'd pick up speed when he got this first course down. This was half bricklaying, half surveying he was doing.

Peach hurried to the other end of his foundation and laid another brick there. The mortar was already stiffening. He cursed himself for having mixed so much. He checked this brick against the two at the corner with his spirit-level balanced on a long, possibly warped, piece of wood. After three goes, he got it level. He unwound his string from its two pegs and tied each end round a brick, and stretched it from end to corner of his run. Somehow the string had got covered with cement, which made it sag in the middle. If he laid the first course along that line, it would follow a faint sag as well. He swore, and ran the crook of his finger along the burning string till it was clean, stretched it tight again, then picked up his fourth brick, and was just attempting to slap a dob of cement on its corner when he noticed that one end of his string had wound itself round his ankles. If he moved, he'd pull the whole wall with him. He was stooping, with his brick and trowel still in his hands, to untangle himself when a voice called from the house.

'Tea!'

An elderly man with a Nietzschean shock of white hair came out of the back door carrying a tray on which two thermos flasks, a milk jug, a large bowl of sugar and a plate heaped with biscuits rattled perilously. It was Peach's customer. Peach blushed to be caught in so uncraftsmanlike a position, and stood up with the string still around his ankles. He glanced yearningly at his pile of muck.

His heart was in his mouth as the old man picked his way over his fallen hammer and abandoned pickaxe. For all the alertness of his step, his movements ended in a sort of abstraction, the explanation for which lay in a hearing aid, plugged into his right ear, its wire curling down to a small microphone that hung against his shirt. It must have been a powerful microphone, for as he approached, Peach could hear it squealing feedback like a loud bird in the spring air. Just below it, and also clipped on to the outside of his shirt, was what looked like a tie-pin, which fastened a pace-maker against his chest. The old man had shown it to Peach the day before. Though he stepped buoyantly, he held his chest stiff, balancing his heart as carefully as the tray of tea things. He set it down on the pile of bricks.

'How are you getting on?' he asked, looking up into the apple tree.

'Very well,' said Peach. 'Just laying the first course.'

'Jolly good.'

The old man unloaded the tray on to the bricks, revealing under the tea things a book which he picked up reverently. It was *The Complete Paintings of Vermeer*. He opened it at a page that had been marked and held a coloured print out to the sunlight.

'This is the painting I was telling you about yesterday when you had to meet your wife. A homely thing at first glance. But it's one of the great mystical paintings of all time.'

Peach looked at the painting apprehensively. Just talking about it had cost him two hours yesterday. Now it had come into the garden just when he had a bag and a half of cement in the balance. By picking at the heel of one shoe with the toe of the other, he managed to step from his bricklaying line and come closer. Guiltily, his eyes went first to the title: 'Gentleman and Woman Drinking'. He'd never seen it before. A casement window was ajar on the left-hand side of the painting, letting in the light so directly that the top corner of the window-reveal was pure light with a plaster shadow. The lead lights and stained-glass boss of the window filled a room with such clarity that it seemed that they themselves were sources of light. Even the darkest parts of the room, under the table and the shadowed picture on the back wall, shone. The room was sumptuous but bare. The cloth on the table was a thick-piled, richly patterned rug. A lute lay across a chair with gorgonesque finials on its backrest. Sheets of music lay on the table. But the two most luminous objects in the room were a white earthenware flagon that stood on the table and a woman in a pink dress and white scarf, who sat at the table facing the window. She held a wine-glass to her lips by its round base. It was as empty and transparent as a bubble. The light, reflected from her dress, glowed in a shadow on her hand with an intimate warmth.

Over her stood a man in a brown cloak and black, wide-brimmed hat, looking down at her. His hand held the handle of the flagon on the table. Peach forgot his embarrassment over the string round his ankles and his anxiety over his mix. For something about this picture suddenly had him on tenterhooks. As though everything, everywhere, outside this moment of tangible light, was suffering. But he didn't want to see it there. Peach found himself worrying jealously whether the man and woman were about to make love when she'd finished drinking. It would be dreadful if they did. The man was

111

looking down at her longingly. His longing could be lust or it could equally be love. There was something Christ-like in his face. *Her* face, through the veil of her glass, was expressionless. Peach yearned to know her thoughts. But only one thing was certain – it was a divine blessing that the man and the woman were so locked in stillness with the chair, the table and the window. Otherwise everything would be doubt and suffering. The lute and the sheets of music were good emblems. For the painting had the immediacy of music.

The old gentleman was chuckling as he held it for Peach. He and the picture were obviously old friends who shared jokes that didn't need to be told to be enjoyed.

'Wonderful, isn't it?' he said to Peach.

Peach felt that he was required to say something. Yet the painting left him wordless.

'It's like a still-life without fruit,' he said at last, and felt a fool.

'Yes, yes,' cried the old gentleman impatiently. 'It's not a guitar.'

Peach blushed. He raised his voice.

'It's very static, I mean.'

'Of course, of course,' cried the old man even more impatiently. 'When she's drunk, he'll play. But you're missing the point. Like most people you're looking for the story in the painting rather than at the painting itself. This isn't some trivial anecdote of Hals. Look at the light! Look at the light!'

The page buckled, and Vermeer's interior light dazzled under the apple tree. Peach stared at it blankly.

'The light has such reality in the painting it has the status of a material object. It's as tangible as the table. It is no longer a medium but a Thing-in-Itself.'

Peach glanced desperately at his heap of cement.

'But is there any such thing as a Thing-in-Itself? At first glance, Vermeer seems to be saying Yes. What could be more itself than that rug? What does it need of human eyes, fingers and feet, *to be*? As Schopenhauer says . . .'

For Christ's sake, why had he mixed so much? Twenty-five

shovelfuls at, say, seven bricks a shovel – that was a hundred and seventy-five bricks from this one gauge. He looked at the three bricks he'd laid already. They'd taken him half an hour. Say ten minutes a brick. At that rate laying a hundred and seventy-five would take him – thirty hours! Till five o'clock tomorrow afternoon! And the heap of mortar already had a more rock-like look about it than it had had twenty minutes ago.

Schopenhauer seemed to be saying, and it took him half an hour, that the material cosmos has its own reality, beyond the reality that human perception gives it. If there were no eye, the sun would still be real. If there were no ear, the breeze would still sigh. If there were no hand ... Peach gave his pile of mortar a furtive kick. What had been fluent workable jollop now shed dry crumbs from a gathering hardness within. Christ Church bell struck one. If it hadn't been in a thermos, his tea, still untouched, would have been stone cold.

'But by making us look at light, Vermeer is holding our gaze at the place where matter becomes perceptual. We become aware of our own presence in the presence of those hard, external objects. For light is a medium between us. Without light there would be no table. Without *us*, there would be no chair. In other words, *There is no such thing as a Thing-in-Itself!* . . .'

Peach made a gesture of agreement at the painting with his brick. Then, as quick as lightning, he picked up his trowel and slapped a dob of mortar on the end of it. It fell off before he could reach his string. The stickiness had gone out of it.

'But how has Vermeer shown us this, eh? How has he done it?' the old man asked the fence.

But the fence was folded in upon itself, taking notes.

'How has he shown it?' he asked the apple tree, but it was shuffling the thousand pages of a ten-volume book of blossom.

'Eh?' he asked Peach.

Peach squinted at the sun. The source of all Light. A bag of cement was a room without windows, costing three pounds fifty. The brick in his hand was an instrument locked in its case, a lute that would never be played. The sun's beam across

113

his shoulders was growing heavy with heat, fine hardwood on his reddening neck. Deep within him, below the threshold of both his conscience and the old man's hearing aid, an unborn bricklayer shouted 'Piss off!' at his customer. The sun had baked all the moisture out of the crack between his two corner bricks, turning his dob of cement a weak yellow.

The old man watched him shrewdly.

'That's right,' he chuckled. 'You'd have made a good student. Yes, it's the Light again. Always come back to the source. Feel it. What's *its* source — or, I'll give you a clue — sources?'

Peach stared obediently at the painting. If it were possible to hate such a beautiful thing, he hated it. If the old man were holding up the original before him, he might perhaps have put his brick through it. Why should mere oil-marks on canvas have such power? He said nothing.

'That's right,' bellowed the old gentleman. 'The light is shining through the window on the left. But look at the palm of the woman's hand as she holds the glass. That wondrous fleshly pink *shines of itself*. The light from the window could never illuminate it so. Look, even, at the brass buttons on the back of her chair, or at the black leather itself. They are sources of light. Do have a cup of tea. I quite forgot. Try a jellied centre.'

Peach poured himself a cup of tea and ate three jellied centres. Brewed in a thermos, the tea was still scalding hot. But his mouth was as dry as if he'd just eaten a mouthful of his own Portland cement, and the strong brew simply slaked the lime on his tongue and left his mouth lined with sensitive sugar. Sparrows were singing in the tree above him. With the sugar entering his work-cleaned bloodstream, their chirrupings passed straight down into his brain, reopening the ecstatic fissure in his skull till it pulsed as it had done when he was born. He entered a state of absolute sweetness which would have been complete if he weren't adding up how much cement he'd have left if this first gauge was wasted. Not enough to finish the job — and without transport, that was a major problem. He didn't have the courage to ask the builder's merchants to deliver a single bag, not to this out-of-the-way place. They'd laugh at him. He'd mixed up enough to do a quarter of the whole job. He'd been an idiot. If he didn't lay at least four courses with this lot, he would be in real trouble. He was losing money even as he stood here. He reckoned he could just about freshen up the gauge now, by slinging on a bucket of water and mixing vigorously. Though where he'd left his shovel standing upright in the mix, it looked as though he'd now have trouble pulling it out. Perhaps he should get stuck into it now. It was the old man's fault if the job was bodged. He could keep talking if he wanted to. He could hold the book open above Peach's line. The fact that the only student in his seminar was laying bricks obviously wouldn't stop him.

'I think I'll just get back to work,' suggested Peach with a timid shout.

'Of course not. Dr Johnson was right to kick his stone. The outer world *is* real, though not a Thing-in-Itself. The light from the window confirms that reality. We'll call it the Outer World. But everything that exists is also created, moment by moment, from *within* itself, from its Idea. For if you weren't seeing Ideas, I would be holding up to you a pageful of utterly meaningless marks. So, there are two worlds: the Outer and the Inner. And the question now arises *Which one is Real?*'

'Perhaps they're both real,' said Peach lamely.

'No,' cried the old man passionately. 'They're *both* real!'

He was right. It was Peach's own vision. A real world – apple blossom, sparrows, mortar – lit by union with the eternal patterns of Thought pulsing outwards from the jellied centre of the brain. To stand in the midst of a world of Spirit! To mix cement and lay bricks in it. And, sharing the eternal patterns of Thought, he and the old man were one. *They* were the two worlds in Vermeer's painting. A sparrow landed on Peach's hill of cement mistaking it for a boulder, and when it flew off, it left no claw marks where it had stood. A profound anxiety, that began in his ankles and rose up the backs of his legs, making them grip the air as if it were solid, that froze his genitals and grabbed at his heart, rose into his brain and overwhelmed Peach. He'd have to hire a van to get a new bag of cement and lose half the profits of his job plus a morning's work. It wasn't the money he minded so much as a loss of faith in his workmanship and his ability to see the job through. Perhaps he could still go for it. Perhaps he could at least lay the brick he still held in his hand. They seemed to have reached a quietus.

He stepped towards his pile of cement.

'So the question is,' yelled the old man almost desperately, rubbing the clip of his pace-maker like a chrome fetish. 'Where does our mystic world originate? From Outer or Inner? From Everything or Nothing?'

' "Nothing will come of nothing," ' quoted Peach humbly, not so much to add to the argument as to show that he was still listening.

The old man's hearing aid screeched. He stopped talking and scanned Peach's face.

'WHAT?' he roared.

' "NOTHING WILL COME OF NOTHING," ' Peach roared back, smiling vigorously and wishing he'd never spoken.

The hearing aid screeched louder. The old man turned it up.

'NOTHING WILL COME OF WHAT?' he shouted.

The closeness of the ear-splitting microphone to the old man's pace-maker made Peach shudder. Perhaps the microphone could short-circuit the pace-maker if he pushed it too far. He wished he could drop it. A loud shout might kill the old man.

' "NOTHING!" ' he bellowed back with a terrified smile.

With a loud crack, the microphone cut out, and the old gentleman smiled broadly.

'Oh,' he said. 'Oh yes! Yes indeed! "Nothing will come of nothing." Fine line, eh? Marvellous line. King Lear, Act One, Scene One, Line . . . eighty-nine I think it is. In the Grove

116

Edition. Utterly to the point, Peach. Shakespeare and Vermeer have a lot in common. There's a tremendous scene in *Timon of Athens* . . .'

Peach submitted himself to this possibly endless trial. It was an initiatory test. He stood stock still, squirming in his cement-stiff plimsolls, and tried to forget about his cement. He hoped that when he was this man's age he would be as passionate and alive as him, even if he were bedecked with life- and sense-supporting machines. For the old gentleman, like some Tibetan yogi, was the living proof of his own doctrines – from Vermeer's mystical realism to Shakespeare's humanised cosmos. For it was, in spite of its impediments, the old man's *body*, traumatised and unsteady, that most fully expressed the lightness and grace of his spirit.

'Well . . . time for lunch,' he said happily. 'I'll let you get on.'

And gathering up the tea things, he went in. He had been talking for two and a quarter hours.

'Afternoon tea at three,' he called from the house.

Peach looked at his gauge of muck. He worked his shovel free and struck it with the flat. The pile clanged. He tried adding water. But it just ran off, like a stream down a mountainside. So he broke up his mortar with his sledge-hammer, and shovelled the boulders into rubbish bags. Then he went for a walk on the Heath. Leaving three bricks shining in the sun, perfectly straight.

That Saturday morning Peach was awoken by a knocking at the front door. He went down to open it. Three men in suits were standing on the doorstep. The man in the front, the one in sunglasses, was easing the ring on his fourth finger. The man next to him was holding a leather tape-measure. The big man at the back was the sporting type. You'd need a wheel-barrow to shift the muscles Peach could feel flexing under the flowing checks of his suit.

117

'I'm the landlord,' said the man in sunglasses. 'This is my house.'

Peach quaked, but heard himself saying, 'It's funny I haven't seen you living in it then.'

'Let me correct myself, squire,' said the landlord. 'It's not a house at all. It's a little investment. An' now I'm gonna draw. This is my surveyor. And this is a friend. Now excuse me, I'd like t' come in.'

Peach stood aside. As he passed, the surveyor said to him, 'We won't be long. I've just got to do a quick measure-up, and check if there's any dry rot.'

The landlord beat on the door of the ground-floor room where Peach and Morag's friend Martha, a middle-aged woman who was once a regular tenant, lived. She came out.

'Hello, Mr Stag. Long time no see.'

'Year and a half. Bin away. And I ain't had no rent off you in that time.'

'As I told you a year and a half ago, Mr Stag, I'll start paying the rent the minute you fix the Ascot. That was when your men came with the corrugated iron for upstairs, if you remember.'

'P'raps I'll let the arrears pass then, Mrs Brown, seeing as how I'm givin' you notice to be out this Friday. And who's this?'

'The . . . the occupier . . . of the top floor,' said Peach shakily.

'Squwattas, Malc,' said the landlord's friend.

'They're friends of mine, Mr Stag. I'm blowed if I want to live alone in a boarded-up house.'

The surveyor finished measuring Martha's room, and they all went up to the middle floor. This room belonged to a mostly out-of-work actor called Alf, who'd gone to Australia in the autumn, but planned to come back. It was almost bare. There was a mattress and a heap of clothes in one corner. And Peach and Morag's spin-drier and pram in the other corner. The surveyor took a hammer from his briefcase and began to sound the floorboards.

'Dry rot here, Mr Stag. Definitely.'

'Let's see if it's in the brickwork,' said the landlord's friend, and kicked the wall by the fire so savagely that a lump of plaster fell off. He then gouged the toe of his shoe into the hole, through two inches of rotten plaster.

'Well, that's everything I need to see in here,' said the surveyor hurriedly, as the landlord's friend wiped his shoe on the mattress.

'Let's see the top floor.'

Peach suddenly remembered that Morag was asleep. He ran upstairs ahead of them. The curtains were drawn. The room was dim and smelled of dream. When the three men came in, she was barely awake, her Tibetan dress crumpled, her hair wild. The landlord switched on the light. And the surveyor began to measure. He looked embarrassed.

'Look,' said Peach to the landlord. 'Now that we've met, perhaps we can come to some arrangement—'

'You must be joking, guvnor. You crash into my house. Pull down the corrugated iron I put up. Change the locks. Then you tell me you want to come to some arrangement. The only arrangement I want with you is – Out!'

With the mattresses lying side by side on the floor, there was not much room for five people to stand in. With an apologetic look, the surveyor ran his tape along the open bed that was still warm where Morag had been sleeping. The landlord's friend was crushed against the door, and obviously felt left out. With one stride, he stepped across the bed, his foot sinking between the mattresses and forcing them apart. He began to examine the loom by the window.

'What's this then – a loom?'

'Yes,' said Morag. 'It's mine.'

'What's this yer weaving – a rug?'

'That's right.'

'Very nice. Very nice.'

He began to browse through Peach's books. The landlord was in the kitchen. The surveyor was measuring the chimney breast.

'. . . *The Tibetan Book of the Dead*? . . . *The Awakening of Intelligence* . . . *The Christ Impulse* . . . *The Tayo of Sex*? – Fuck me! Catch an eyeful of the pictures in this one, Malc. Jesus! there's a bird here's got six knockers! – '

He leered at Morag. Peach flushed with anger and blushed with shame. In truth, his interest in the Tao of Sex was no different from the landlord's friend's. But he spoke, instead, to the landlord, who'd come back from the kitchen.

'I'm afraid if you want us to go, Mr Stag, you'll have to get an eviction order.'

'Is that so, guvnor? You know as well as me that gettin' an eviction order is a lotta hassle for me. Now, if I was to say to you, amicable like, that me and me friends were comin' back tonight t' start the guttin' – I think we'd find yer and yer missus gone, wouldn't we?'

'NO!'

It was Morag who answered him. Her voice was vibrant and dark with the anger of interrupted dreams. With her crumpled dress and tousled hair, she looked more than a match for the landlord's friend.

'Well, we'll just have t' wait 'n see then, Miss,' said the landlord.

'I'm finished, Mr Stag,' said the surveyor, quickly shutting his briefcase.

'Let's go then,' said the landlord. 'But we'll be back t'night, all right?'

Peach and Morag listened to their footsteps descending the stairs.

'It may be his house, but it's our home, the dirty pigs,' said Morag.

'The surveyor's left his tape behind,' said Peach.

'Chuck it out the window,' cried Morag.

'No. I'll run down with it.'

Halfway down the stairs he met the surveyor coming up. He gave him the tape.

'Look. Don't let Stag frighten you – too much,' he whispered, glancing down the stairs. 'He may come back tonight, or he may not. If he does, I wouldn't try fighting him if I were you. Because then he could come down really heavily on you – with the law as well as his friends, I mean.'

'I wasn't really thinking of that,' said Peach, already trembling.

'But it may be bluff. He's making up his mind whether to sell the house or convert it into a hotel. If he sells it, he'll try and get you out straightaway. And I'd go if I were you. But if he goes for the hotel, you'll be safe for a couple of months, while he applies for planning permission, and I'm drawing up the specs. All right?'

'Yes,' said Peach. 'Thanks a lot.'

All that afternoon Peach and Morag spent both bedecking the house with signs that they hadn't gone – fresh milk on the windowsill, a new blanket hung across Alf's window – and busily packing up their few possessions – slinging books and crockery into boxes – in case they had to go. They worked in a fever, speaking little. Morag pulled the half-finished rug off her loom and folded it up. Peach wondered what they would do with their cot and spin-drier, if they suddenly found themselves on the street. He guiltily pictured the little foetus swilling around with anxiety in Morag's stomach. Every time a car parked outside, they stopped dead, and crouched by the window, listening. At half-past six there was a loud banging at the front door. They held their breaths and waited, but the knocking only got louder and more impatient. Peach tried to still himself as he walked down the stairs towards the violent banging, trembling from head to toe. He opened the door.

Arthur was standing on the doorstep. The big black piano was halfway up the steps behind him.

' 'Evenin', Peach. Where do ya want 'er?'

'Oh . . . um . . . Hello, Arthur . . .'

How could he explain that the piano might no longer have a home? It was three quarters of the way up the steps,

121

shuddering the old yorkstone treads as Arthur's men humped it from below.

'Oh . . . Come in,' said Peach. 'We're at the top, I'm afraid.'

'Fuck me,' said Arthur when he saw their flight of wood-wormy stairs, that shot straight upwards from just behind the door, at a cliff-like angle.

'She'll never go round that first bend, mate. I can tell ya that from 'ere,' said Arthur pointing at a corkscrew bend in the narrow stairs as the piano juddered in the door behind him.

'What shall I do? Where shall I put it?' asked Peach.

'Dunno,' said Arthur.

Even crashed against the first step, the back end of the piano poked out of the door. There was no way of shutting it now. The landlord and his thugs could squeeze straight through.

'P'raps if ya strip 'er down, take out the 'ammers and the panellin', you know, and then saw off the banisters all the way up to the top – she might go up then.'

'But we're about to be evicted,' said Peach.

'Yeah?' said Arthur. 'That's no good. P'raps ya can stick it in this room 'ere, for the time bein'.'

He pointed at Martha's door.

'But someone lives in there,' said Peach.

'Well, if they're bein' evicted it don't really matter, do it?'

So Peach knocked at Martha's door, and asked if he could leave the piano in her room till he could think what to do with it. After all, it might only be there a few hours. She said yes. And Arthur's men pushed it into her single room. The cooker stood in one corner, the sink in another. Her bed was in a third corner, and with the door taking up the fourth, the only place for the piano was in the middle of the room, in front of the window, where, like Beethoven's great black Hammer-klavier itself, it blocked out most of the light.

The old gentleman's job dragged on, while the old gentleman discoursed on Plato, the necessary madness of geniuses (with which Peach strongly disagreed, but couldn't make himself heard), the relativity of perception, celibacy, the National Health Service, the immanence of God, and the fear of Death. Before his growing deafness and his heart attack, he had been a professor at London University. Now the years of dammed-up lectures and unheard seminars poured forth, while his blue eyes scoured Peach's smiling, nodding face for the deeper signs of understanding. He quoted long passages of his beloved Shakespeare by heart, and brought more prints of Vermeer out into the sunlight of this endless tea-break, to illustrate the nature of space. Peach had never drunk so much tea in his life, or eaten so many sugared biscuits. Nor had he ever learnt so much from a single human being in his long years of primary, secondary and tertiary education. Every day he shovelled heaps of stiff cement into his rubbish bags. And if he cast sideways glances at his string, waiting tautly between two patient brick-ends, and at his trowel going grey in the sun, it was not out of impatience to get finished quick and so improve his daily rate of pay, which was dwindling on a curve approaching zero – it was more out of a bricklayer's hurt pride, and anxiety that the old gentleman would think him an impostor.

But at last, after two and a half weeks, the three-foot retaining wall was finished. Peach shovelled the earth back in behind it, and planted an area of roses. Then he made a brick path which led, down two steps, to a sunken paved area for storing firewood. This took a week and a half, during which the old man discussed Goethe, the Blitz, and Wordsworth's walking tours. Peach erected trellis around the fences of the cottage garden. And so came to the last item on his quote: pruning the apple tree which stood in the centre of the tiny plot.

It was a shapely tree, but had one large bough, about eight feet above the ground, which set off in the direction of the house at a right-angle from the trunk, like a policeman directing traffic, where it blocked out the light and clawed at the gutters. When he'd set off to find work on the first morning of his fatherhood, Peach had seen himself as a garden-builder rather than a garden*er* – and certainly not as a tree-surgeon. He had intended to go no deeper into the realm of living things, about which he knew less than bricklaying, than turfing and planting Woolworth's roses. But the old gentleman had wanted his tree pruned, and Peach had not dared risk losing the job for the sake of refusing this one small item. And he did have a saw amongst his mysterious collection of tools. But he didn't have a ladder. He admitted this to the old gentleman, who fetched an aluminium stepladder from indoors. It was a tiny little ladder, which he used for reaching the highest bookshelves in his library. When Peach had slid the extension to its full length, it was eight feet tall – just high enough to reach the branch.

'Do be careful,' said the old gentleman as Peach climbed up.

'Where do you want me to cut it?' he shouted down at him.

The old man's hearing aid squealed. Peach shuddered. He must be careful not to shout too loudly, in case the spine-chilling feedback from the old man's microphone interrupted the pace-maker under his shirt.

He didn't want to kill anybody.

'Halfway out,' the old man shouted back. 'I want to shape it upwards from there. About where you are will do.'

Peach began to saw, congratulating himself on the fact that his ladder was resting against the bough, *inside* the cutting-point. He wasn't cutting away his own support – one of the basics of tree surgery.

'. . . Wordsworth had a great bow-saw at Dove Cottage . . .' went on the old man, shaping his lecture to the matter in hand. '. . . Cut all his own wood, as I still do. When Coleridge came to visit, Wordsworth got poor old Samuel Taylor on the other end of it, and they'd saw great boles whilst discussing Poetic Theory. Of course by that time, Coleridge was reading Schelling and getting himself tangled up in German Metaphysics . . .'

It was a thick bough. As Peach sawed, the feet of his ladder began to sink into the clay of the flowerbed, till the top of the ladder no longer showed above the bough. Still, that didn't

124

matter too much – the bough was about six inches thick so there was plenty of wood to support it.

'Don't you think you should thin out some of the foliage first?' the old man shouted up at him. 'I leave it completely to you, of course. But it might take off some of the weight.'

Peach surveyed the dense foliage. From the ground it had looked shapely and light, and as if he could hold it with one hand when it fell. But up here it was a solid mass plucking at his elbow as he sawed. Perhaps the old gentleman was right. It did look heavy. He'd just have to drop his saw and catch it with both hands when it started to go. His heart was beating. Luckily his feet were only three feet off the ground.

'I think it'll be all right,' he called down.

'Jolly good . . . So Coleridge laboured at his *magnum opus* for twenty-three years, poor chap, befuddled by opium half the time and by German Metaphysics the other half. Now if he'd have trusted his original intuitions . . .'

The ganger man's saw was rusty. And the fresh juice of the apple bough seemed to be rusting it more even as it cut. For at every stroke it wedged tight, and it took all his strength to draw it back. And Peach's strength was sapping. He was swaying to and fro on the little aluminium ladder like a sailor in a storm, as he fought to keep the saw going and the ladder's feet sank deeper into the clay by the minute. But there was still a good three inches of bough to hold up the top of the ladder. He sawed on. Would the branch never start to drop?

'Take it easy,' his old teacher cried up. 'Have a rest, Peach. Come down and have a cup of tea, and we'll discuss the last chapter of the *Biographia*.'

But Peach couldn't stop, not even for Coleridge's Theory of Reality. If he stopped, he'd never start again. He was sweating fiercely and shaking even more than the little aluminium ladder. Odd words '. . . Ontological . . . Kubla . . . poor Samuel Taylor . . .' ran like beads of sweat into his echoing ears, and trickled into his eyes, blinding him. He drove the rusty saw back and forth. It bowed and twanged at him, but he kept it tearing at the apple tree's flesh. Would it never give?

'. . . you see, the view Coleridge is striving for is ultimately a Hindu one, but being a European, he simply didn't have the equipment to formulate it . . . Steady there. Take care. Watch out!'

The bough had started to give. The thin cut was opening into a mighty, groaning rent. And, strange to say, the great bush of foliage suddenly, as it came swinging downwards, doubled its weight. Leaves, leaves, leaves, in rustling hundred-weights, went rushing past Peach's terrified face. Who would have thought there would have been so many leaves? But worse still, the bough, against which his ladder rested by its top desperate inch, relieved of the vast weight, suddenly surged upwards, leaving Peach's ladder leaning on nothing but air. Luckily the ladder was footed so deeply in the clay that he only began to fall slowly.

'Steady there,' cried the old man. 'Watch out. I'll get it!'

Thinking it was the falling bough which was bringing Peach down, he ran beneath the avalanche of leaves and attempted to catch it. The last thing Peach saw as he stood on air, two and a half feet above the ground, was the old gentleman, momentarily taking the weight with upstretched arms, then as slowly and as stately as the crashing bough itself, keeling over backwards and disappearing under several tons of twigs and foliage, his hearing aid squeaking like a startled bird.

'Oh my God,' thought Peach as he hit the ground himself. 'I've killed him!'

He tore at the tangled branches and smothering leaves, but could see nothing.

'I've killed him! Oh God, I've killed him,' he whimpered to himself.

Then, from far below, he heard a faint voice calling upwards with stoical detachment,

'Are you all right, Peach? Steady! Are you there?'

A LLWRATH's lichen biscuits had run out days ago. The skin
of mushroom mead on the seat beside him was empty.
His stomach growled hungrily. It was getting louder than the
hearse's ailing engine. And yet he didn't dare stop to get food,
even if he'd had any money. For, like the centipede tail of a
meandering nightmare, the twelve black limousines were still
following him, keeping a respectful twenty feet from his rear
bumper, tracking him by day and by night, impossible to
throw off at nine miles an hour. And if he stopped and nipped
into a shop with his crowbar, the demoniac Rationalists would
leap from their limousines and snatch God from the hearse,
and argue him back to a kerbstone. He could see the three-
piece syllogisms, cut from the cloth of darkness, that they
wore. Yet he must eat!

At a traffic light in Aldgate East, Allwrath fumbled amongst
the pouches on his chest, and found the Unopened One. He
tore it open. It contained magic roots, dug by moonlight from
Glastonbury back gardens. Their power was unknown. They
were reserved, by Druid lore, for a High Priest's ultimate, and
deadliest, initiation – the passage through the Forest of
Modern Thought. He held them in his sweating palm as the
lights were changing to orange. Dried earth-fingers that held
gnarled secrets! Scrawny knots of fibre still clutching Glastonbury clay! It was sacrilegious to use them merely to satisfy
hunger. And yet if he didn't eat soon, he'd pass out at the
wheel. He jammed the handful in his mouth as the lights
turned green and the hearse climbed into first.

He entered the Deadly Forest of Modern Thought. Descartes
and Hume, in visions twelve feet high, lay on the bonnets of
cars disguised as naked girls. Above him stone trees towered,
their glass leaves fiendishly disguised as windows. Charles

Darwin and Dale Carnegie swung from branch to branch. Lurid fungi grew round the stumps, with their names written on them in scientific jargon: British Home Stores, Dolcis, Our Price Records. Some of the trees must have been carnivorous, for they were eating people and their shopping trollies whole, and hanging their shoes and records up in their glass boles to digest. Scudding through traffic lights at nine miles an hour and skilfully avoiding hills, Allwrath drove on, questing, the black cortege forever cogitating in his rear vision mirror.

The Reverend Briggs grew anxious, that first afternoon after Arthur's Requiem Service, as the hours passed and they still hadn't reached the Garden Suburb. By nightfall he was worried. The hearse was turning up one-way streets, winding down back alleys, and weaving through the railway arches of Camden Town. He distrusted the undertaker, who was probably being paid an hourly rate, and would want time and a half for burying in the dark. He'd honked at him and ttied to wave him down, but he wouldn't stop. And it would be most unseemly if the cortege overtook the hearse and forced it into the kerb. The mourners in the back seat with him were complaining of hunger. Mrs Nugent was asleep on his shoulder, her stomach protesting as she ate a dream meal. Mr McGrundle was telling him, over and over, in a tetchy whine, that he wanted to go home for his supper. Mr Sykes sat with his head slumped against the window staring into the darkness as if he'd just died himself, and the odd shut café which they passed were the Platonic idea of Food in heaven. The Reverend Briggs hadn't eaten since breakfast himself. But he wouldn't turn back. He'd come to bury Arthur, and bury him he would. He wouldn't leave him to the mercy of that undertaker. Probably slip him in a skip and resell his plot.

As chance would have it, each limousine was carrying a large hamper in its boot, prepared by the Women's Auxiliary for after the burial. It seemed most indecorous, to think of breaking into it before they'd buried Arthur. But by the early

hours of the next day, he noticed mourners slipping out at
lights, grabbing food from the boot, and returning to their
seats. By the following morning the Reverend Briggs had done
the same, said grace, and was distributing legs of chicken, cake
and port amongst his parishioners. It was most unseemly for
Mr McGrundle to be swigging from the bottle. He had a swig
himself, to show that everything was comme il faut, and
passed it on to the bereaved. He wasn't a superstitious man.
There was some logical explanation for this temporary re-
routeing of reality.

Allwrath entered the Heart of the Deadly Forest. He passed a
Pool over which the great trees bowed in an arch, their
branches locked together with iron nuts, like two rows of steel
oaks bent in a permanent storm of glass. Ghastly iron serpents
slid from the River to drink up and vomit out the strange,
man-sized insects that swirled in the vortex of the Pool.
LIVERPOOL STREET STATION read the sign. But the language was unknown to him. He drove up Ludgate Hill. On
the top a gigantic, perfectly round boulder, badly chocked by
hollow stumps, wobbled on the point of rolling down and
crushing the pedestrians in Farringdon Street. Two stone men
stood on the swaying stumps waving wildly for the people to
get out of the way. But no one seemed to hear them except
Allwrath. He swung hard right and slewed into St Paul's
Roundabout, as the gigantic boulder swept past. He drove on.
The roots were high in fibre and almost impossible to swallow.
A little fungal juice and diluted clay trickled down his throat.
Four days later, turning right at County Hall, Allwrath found
that he was still chewing the same mouthful, his chin propped
on the timeless rotation of the steering wheel. But miraculously, as well as sustaining him, the roots had the power to
keep him awake night and day. He forgot what sleep was.
Whereas the Rationalists, he saw, in his mirror, were taking
shifts at the wheel. He crossed a bridge. High in a dead tree-
trunk a one-eyed owl sat staring at him. It was obviously

trying to hypnotise him and slip some insane message made of numbers and two slowly moving hands into the depths of his consciousness. But Allwrath stared it out, hooted back at it, and drove past into timelessness.

In the coffin behind him slept the God who would fell this Forest of Illusion. Allwrath longed for the open moors, for a bed of moss, and a barrow to lay his head on. But he knew that God had led him purposely to the Forest. He was leading him to the Sacred Site, where Allwrath, His High Priest, would perform the Last Ritual, God would awake and call up His Consort, Gaia, Lady of the Earth, and They would dance together on the Altar of the Ultimate Circle and renew the human race through the power of the Earth!

3-Tooth stood under a tree in Hyde Park with his amp switched up. The black box was the centre of a sixty-yard circle of howling loneliness. Strollers, lovers, hurrying businessmen, joggers with earphones, hit the circumference of the circle and shot off at tangents to all corners of the park. It was like the 'Seventy-One Free Concert, except no one wanted to listen. His guitar bag was empty for the third day running. 3-Tooth realised, with a pang, how much his living had depended on the menace of a lone figure in a narrow tunnel, and the impossibility of crossing Edgware Road above ground. For Big Al was crucifying him. Since their fight, Big Al had declared himself Lord of the Tunnels, and Keeper of the Schedule of Pitches, and 3-Tooth wasn't on it. It was guerilla war, and Big Al was built like King Kong. He'd ferreted 3-Tooth out of the spacious tunnel under the V and A, which is long enough for two or three buskers to play simultaneously. He'd bagged him in the back walk-way of Platform 5, Oxford Circus, and beaten his head against a hamburger advertisement. He'd even hounded him out of the leaky Isle of Dogs tunnel. There wasn't a hole in London for him to creep into. But worst of all was his eviction from the Edgware Road Underpass. That was his home. He'd worked it for years.

Looked at square, it was Criminal Trespass and Grievous Bodily Harm. But 3-Tooth wouldn't be complainin' to no lawman.

His fingers wobbled like tracer bullets on strings out of the screaming sun, cool, deadly, a hundred per cent strike rate, their target a chaos of bass thunder. Perhaps he should give up buskin'. Get a steady trade like Peach. Peach looked pretty happy. Perhaps Jimi wasn't gonna come down an' play his guitar. Maybe he was into sitar music or somethin', up there in Nirvana. Maybe he was just dead. 3-Tooth looked up at the cliff of hotels beyond the trees that rimmed the park, and caught his breath.

There was Jimi struttin' across the roof of the Cumberland Hotel. He sneered down on 3-Tooth from that high stage. Behind him the shades-grey summer clouds were piled like amps.

'Stay with me, 3-Tooth. I'm comin' down. Ya can't have no Resurrection without no Crucifixion.'

'But it's me who's bein' crucified, man.'

'Drugs. Sex. Fame. They crucify ya too, 3-Tooth.'

'Let me try 'em, man.'

'There's a New Age in Rock 'n Roll comin', 3-Tooth. First group ever fronted by a spirit.'

'Just me an' you, man?'

'First gig's already booked.'

six

B Y SOME magical quality of poetic density, Fergus's tiny ad, which he'd written for Peach after ten pints, pouring his inspiration into a verbal structure limited by the change in his pocket, and which only ran for a week before it went out of print, kept bringing in the work for Peach as the weeks went by, the days grew longer, and Morag's belly grew bigger. The Classified Section of the *Camden Clarinet* must have carried the authority of Holy Writ. Folks must have cut the one-inch-by-three rectangle of newsprint out of their papers and pasted it into their wedding albums, or slipped it into a plastic leaf of their wallets with their credit cards and photos of their children. They must have had it framed and hung in the loo, or araldited it to their mantelpieces. For the little Classified haiku brought in yorkstone steps, barbed wire bin compounds, ponds, waterfalls, broken bottles on the tops of walls, turfing and even planting roses – none of which Peach refused, being, as he was, incapable of denying people's needs, whether he was able to fulfil them or not. Living as he did in a squat with a hole in the roof, sockets that spat and an exploding Ascot, he'd never before seen such a torrent of urgent household needs. He almost felled a sixty-foot plane tree next to a conservatory, but was underpriced by an alcoholic Scotsman with an axe, anxious to get back to Glasgow for a funeral. He made the meagrest of profits. And actually lost money on the broken bottles, which he felt served him right. But the epigrammatic word EXPERIENCED in Fergus's ad slowly took on a deepening truth.

One day Peach got a message to see a job for Messrs Burns Arkwright, 7 Golden Brick Yard, EC4. He looked up the address in his *A–Z*. It was a little courtyard off Fleet Street. Peach was puzzled. He advertised as a gardener, and this was the heart of the City. As his bus fought its way round Piccadilly Circus, he began to feel uneasy. Who were these Messrs Burns Arkwright? And what was their garden? As his bus waited patiently in the Strand, his unease grew. The buildings were becoming monumental. Massive gods and goddesses sat around on the cornices of banks. Their tridents and shields were weapons of economic war, in which he'd been born wounded. His bus got snarled for ten minutes in a savage ruck of traffic outside the Law Courts. A police paddywagon was backing into the great Gothic loading bay, with a delivery of convicts. Peach shivered. His bus crawled past elegant Wren churches camped on traffic islands like mad old ladies. He could have got out and walked to Golden Brick Yard. It would have been quicker. But a gathering dread made him stay on.

Beyond the dome of St Paul's, he could see the shining skyscrapers of the City proper, the ultimate Place of Power, the sacred grove of high glass, deep vaults and high-speed lifts, that enchanted ordinary folk with the sheer presence of Wealth, and turned the money in their pockets to stone. It was a long way from Hampstead and the burgeoning Heath. Was he to build the Garden even here? What did Messrs Burns Arkwright want? Perhaps it was a bit of trellis run up a wall, to coax climbers from tubs. Or maybe a window box.

Golden Brick Yard was an elegant Georgian courtyard. A low arch led off the bustling footpath of Fleet Street into this haven of more dignified money-making. Its flags were of tanned yorkstone smoothed by two hundred years of expensive footwear. It was one of those out-of-the-way City courtyards where you could still hear Dr Johnson's weighty step. Like a doctor's grave, stone finger, it took the pulse of Fleet Street rambustioning past beyond the sandwich bar on the corner. The right-hand side of the Yard was lined with old buildings converted into offices. Yorkstone steps led up to oak doors, left, not open, but ajar, as if My Lord were still within, doing his business in bed amidst the dream-natter of telex machines. It was a pity that the left-hand side of the Yard had been demolished to build the thirteen-storey Mortlake Concern Building, but 'a man who is tired of London is tired of Life.' It rose above the older roofs like a glass and aluminium sycamore in a grove of oaks.

Looking up the row of identical steps, Peach saw one flight that stood out. It was not yorkstone, but cast concrete. Whereas the other steps were shallow, with a stately upwards sweep, these began virtually under the entrance and rose precipitously up three fifteen-inch risers. Nor did they go up straight. They converged on the doorstep from three sides like an Incan pyramid of scabby ready-mix. Peach stood before it, a primitive stone doctor with his sewing-tape. The brass name-plate on the classical architrave read 7, BURNS ARK-WRIGHT, SOLICITORS AND COMMISSIONERS FOR OATHS. He suddenly felt guilty. Guilty to be standing amidst this ancient craftsmanship — finely-mitred door mouldings, well-cut lead, cigarette-paper joints in the paving — masquer-ading as a builder. And this ton and a half of many-angled concrete was to be his punishment. Peach walked up the steps.

Though the tall oak doors were ajar, Peach knocked. No one came, so he waited. A barrister pushed past him and went in. Peach followed in the slipstream of his gown. Behind the outer doors was an enormous doormat, then a pair of plate-glass doors which had already swallowed the barrister up. Peach wiped his feet, pushed through the glass doors and entered a hallway tiled in marble. Paintings hung on the walls above two empty umbrella stands and a spitoon. It could have been the hallway of any luxurious home. Two doors framed in stucco pilasters stood, one on either side of the hall. The plate on one said Office, on the other, Reception. Peach hesitated. Reception, with its associations of dinner/dance, was obviously meant for clients to wait in. Peach didn't feel as though he were being received. Whereas Office suggested work, and he'd come to work. So he chose the Office. He knocked, and when no one answered, pushed open the panelled door. He stepped into a wall of fluorescent light and the busy silence of word-processors. Half a dozen smart young women stopped what they were doing and stared at him. A young man sitting cross-legged on a table laughed frankly at Peach, as though letting him into a joke of which he might be the butt. One typewriter continued to gossip noiselessly. A telex printer purred sexily in its ear.

'I've come to see about the steps.'

The young people looked at each other quizzically. Peach seemed to have stepped into some secret so dazzling he couldn't see it; some heady concoction of work and flirtation. He had walked into a computerised passion pit with his news of steps.

'Try Reception. Ask for Mr Phillips.'

Peach crossed to Reception, knocked boldly and went straight in. He stepped into a lamplit dimness. He could barely make out the festoons of plaster on the high ceilings. The little light that came in from the Yard was well guarded by tall curtains of royal blue velvet, belted with regal gold cords. Paintings of dead solicitors hung in the shadows. A gas log-fire stood in the marble fireplace, turned on low. It seemed that little in Reception had changed since the house was built. Except that along one wall was a leather counter, behind which a telephonist and receptionist worked.

'I've come to see about the steps.'

Peach was asked to wait. He sat in one of the armchairs that were dotted around the room. He picked up a copy of *Country Life* and leafed through it. He became aware that someone was looking at him. He glanced round uneasily. It was an old woman, dressed in black. Peach smiled at her frank examination of him, from his face to his shoes. She didn't smile back, but just kept staring. Peach returned her stare. Her aquiline face was all perpendiculars of distaste around fierce blue eyes. The aristocratic cast of her nose was of a down-curving, Roman rather than Teutonic, kind, the fine marble sneer of its bridge opening, as it descended, to nostrils of disgust as big as

135

a horse's. Peach took all this in in an instant, before her stare forced him to look away. But he made himself look back again. There is in every face some point of unawareness, which is the outlet for its humanity, but he couldn't find this point anywhere on the old woman's face. Conscious superiority in every last crease and wrinkle had erased it. Even her wide upper lip showed no common weakness. It braced itself horizontally, taking the strain of the downwards movement of the rest of her face, a pearl of permanent distaste sewn into its underside like an acid drop. Peach looked away again. There were snobs in Australia, people who dismissed one at first sight. But there was always something personal in their dislike. Whereas this look he had only seen in England. The hydraulics of disdain in the old woman's face bore down upon his class, his breeding, his very bloodstock, leaving no room for personal defiance.

'Lady de Sage.'

An elderly man in a pinstripe suit, perhaps Mr Arkwright himself, walked over to the old woman.

'I'm so sorry to have kept you waiting.'

He gave her a gentle pat on the shoulder as he helped her from her chair. She walked past Peach as though he'd suddenly become extinct. But where her black heels had entered the carpet, its deep pile breathed condescendingly at him, after she was gone.

Mr Phillips came down shortly after and they went outside and stood before the concrete steps. He was a young man, no older than Peach, perhaps a Junior Partner, his smile brimful of intelligence and charm.

'Shocking, aren't they! Did they have cowboys in the eighteenth century?'

'They were built since then.'

'I know. But for God's sake why? So. You can see what we want. These steps demolished and new ones built, in old yorkstone, to match our neighbours. And it must be done over a weekend. You'll appreciate why.'

Peach could appreciate. The steps were three foot nine high. Without them no one could get into or out of the office.

'You must start on the Saturday morning, as early as you like, and be swept up and out of here before we open on Monday. It's the only condition attached to the job.'

Peach examined the steps. The concrete looked as though it had had it. Half a day to demolish it – say two hours. Then three days to build the new steps – say two. Plus clearing up and shifting the rubbish without a van. There was about four or five days' work in these steps, but he reckoned he could fit them into two days if he started early and worked late. He could charge whatever he wanted. A hundred pounds for two days' work! His heart beat. He remembered heroic yarns he'd heard on the building sites – working on Benzedrine under flood-lamps for vast wages. Oil-riggers hanging over the waves, twenty hours at a time, welding joints to a hundredth of a mil accuracy in high winds, falling into the sea with huge bank-rolls in their pockets. He measured up the steps. He'd have to hire a stone-cutter to do the fancy triangulated joints he envisioned, for such a price, at each of the six corners. He could have the stone, sand and cement delivered by the Garden Centre. He'd put the rubbish in a couple of plastic bin-liners and give it to the garbage men.

'That will be two hundred and ninety-three pounds sixty-three pence.'

'Fine. When can you start?'

'I'll do it this weekend.'

It was the following Monday morning, a quarter to nine. Peach stood in front of a hump of concrete and a little pile of chippings. He'd spent the weekend raining blows on the concrete steps with his fifteen-pound hammer. Fifteen pounds is a lot to get over your shoulder a thousand, two thousand, times. And then the bone-juddering jolt as the sledge bounces off, leaving no trace of itself on the concrete. You get to know a piece of concrete when you break it up. It is an intimate act.

As blow after blow falls, you get to know its weak spots and its tough spots, its rhythm of resistance, the manias of the man who cast it, and finally, where it will last for ever and where it will start to go. But this piece of concrete didn't want to make Peach's acquaintance. It was tough all over, and didn't seem to like him. Two thousand blows at fifteen pounds a shot – that's eighteen tons of hammering, though it felt like more. He should have hired a pneumatic drill and compressor. But that would have cost him more than he was earning. And even they might not have broken it. As it was, without them he'd managed to break off the corners of the old steps and wear down the treads to a hump of hardness just low enough to get his new steps in, and for no one to be able to reach the doormat.

The night before he'd searched the skips around Fleet Street collecting splintered floorboards and nail-studded two by two from which he'd knocked up a ramp, reaching from the footpath to the doorstep, for the first secretaries, barristers and clients of another Monday's litigation. Perhaps the litigation would be against him. He was trembling with guilt and anxiety. He was also frightened of the machine he was holding in his hands. It was a stone-cutter: a two-stroke motor with handles and a twelve-inch masonry disk axled to its side. The disk was black, and thicker than he had expected. He'd got it from a hire shop and lost the instruction sheet. And worse, they'd given him the wheel and the machine separately, and he'd fitted the wheel on the axle himself, without instructions, and there was always the chance it would fly off – at twelve thousand revs per minute, as the disk itself informed him. He'd seen big navvies, skilled labourers, handling these machines gingerly. They ate through asphalt as if it were flesh. One slip, and his guitar-playing, perhaps even his walking, days would be over.

Before him lay a long slab of yorkstone with a yellow crayon-line down its length, and a forty-five degree angle drawn at one end. This was his first tread. He would have to cut right through the three-inch thick stone, to make the lip of the step smooth and square. He placed the machine on the slab, held it steady with his foot, and pulled the rip-cord starter. The engine clanked heavily, gave half a turn, then went dead. Ten, eleven, twelve times he pulled it. Though it was only ten to nine, he was already exhausted from his weekend's demolishing, and wondered whether, when he finally got the stone-cutter going, he'd have the strength to hold it steady. At last the engine choked, grunted, ground its teeth, then howled to life. He had Gog Magog, the demon of Saxon myth, in his hands. The uproar was astonishing. He pushed in the choke, squeezed the trigger that released the wheel, and a vortex of instant death whirled itself into invisibility a foot from his toes. He was just about to set it, spinning, upon the line he'd drawn on the slab, when a figure in a pinstripe suit came round the corner from Fleet Street. It was the elderly man he'd seen in Reception last week, five minutes early for work, perhaps deliberately, so he could spend a few minutes admiring the new steps. He stopped some way from the stone-cutter's howling void and surveyed the ramp and the hump and heap of chippings beneath it.

Peach switched off the machine and pulled down his dust-mask.

'Good morning,' he said. 'Afraid I had a bit of trouble with the demolition. I'll be finished by . . .'

He looked at the old solicitor's face.

'. . . tonight.'

'You said you'd be finished by yesterday.'

'That concrete!' smiled Peach.

'Hm. Well, never mind. That thing won't make too much dust, will it?' said Mr Arkwright, nodding at the stone-cutter.

'Oh no,' said Peach.

It was the first time he'd thought of this. The hire shop had given him a free dust-mask along with the instructions, so he'd put it on.

'Good,' said the old man, and walked up the ramp.

Halfway up, the floorboards, which still had a lot of give in them, began to bow up and down, even though the old man

139

was moving at a snail's pace. He stopped dead, swinging his arms for balance. When the bowing had stopped, and had become a heavy sag in the ramp, he shuffled, more slowly still, to the safety of the doormat. Here he turned around and surveyed the three foot nine drop below him, the yorkstones scattered around the Yard, and the young man in the dust-mask.

'My God!' he said, and retreated into his office.

Peach had got the stone-cutter going again, and was just about to touch the stone with the whirring wheel, when the clock struck nine, though Peach couldn't hear it, and a little rush-hour of secretaries, tea ladies and men in suits filled Golden Brick Yard and bounced up his ramp. One or two of the younger men climbed up the hump, swung a leg over the sill and clambered waggishly up, as though they were on a school assault course. Peach switched off his machine, and stood aside, smiling paranoiacally through his dust-mask, even bowing a little in his anxiety, like a doorman welcoming them into his private Hell.

After half an hour there was a lull in the comings and goings. Peach had spent that time mixing a gauge of strong muck, spreading it out on four bags beside the ramp. When he had cut the first stone, he'd be ready to lay it at once. He pulled his dust-mask back on. It was getting soggy. It was a little wad of gauze in a flexile aluminium frame, and it seemed to be trying to get inside his mouth and suffocate him. Perhaps he didn't need to wear it. Still, there might be a little dust and there was no point damaging his lungs as well as his ears. He looked up and down the Yard. No one in sight. He started the stone-cutter. He picked it up gingerly, opened the throttle, and, keeping the wheel as far as possible from his genitals, walked stiff-legged to the slab. He sighted along the line and set the spinning wheel upon the stone.

Everything disappeared in whiteness. Somewhere far below him he could just make out the black spinning eye of Gog Magog carving through the stone. Buildings, passers-by, the oak doors above him, his pile of chippings – everything vanished. He was alone in a white cloud like Lama Govinda. Occasionally, when the machine bucked, little stone fireflies buzzed off into the whiteness seeking out the eyes of anyone foolish enough still to be watching. White dust filled his ears, softening the roar. The white cloud passed through the gauze of his dust-mask, which he'd half-swallowed in his last desperate gasp for air, and was now masticating like a chalky cud. He became one with the white cloud. He breathed it, ate it, drank it, smelt it, and heard its silence like roaring talcum powder. He was turning to disembodied stone. Tomorrow he would shit a white pebble, if he was lucky. He could stand it no more. A frightened Girl Friday hurrying past saw a white figure stagger from the cloud waving what looked like a circular saw at her and trying to spit out a length of white stocking. She'd seen *Chainsaw in Ward Thirteen*. She'd read *Dr Anti-Christ*. She screamed and ran for the safety of her office.

The dust took almost ten minutes to clear. Peach looked around. The Yard was empty. Everything was white. The tanned paving stones were white, as if it was Christmas. Two conifers in terracotta urns flanking an entrance three doors up were winter-white. The windows of Burns Arkwright were grimed with what looked like white soot. And fine white shadows sat in the mouldings of the oak-panelled doors. Peach slapped his thigh and a little white avalanche fell from his trousers. He was just about to sweep the dust from the slab to have a look at his cut, when he heard a throat being slowly and deliberately cleared directly behind him. He spun round. It was the old woman he'd seen in Reception, and now her look of universal distaste had turned almost personal. A faint flexing of her nostrils might have been enough to put him in his place, if her nostrils hadn't been rimmed with dust, so that when she sniffed at him, she puffed out a little cloud of the ghostly powder. Her black suit was off-white. But still a deeply-engrained superiority would not permit her to scream 'Fuck you!' The naked, staring dislike under her ghastly white rouge, however, let him know that, since he, with his cursed machine, had made it personal, he would personally pay for this. She swept the dust from her skirt with little, downwards karate strokes, looked through him as if he were no longer there and stepped towards the ramp. She was halfway across when Mr Arkwright appeared on the doorstep.

'What's going on here? Lady de Sage! My God! Here, let me help you.'

He leaned forward and took the old woman's arm.

'Good God, young man.'

'I'm dreadfully sorry,' said Peach. 'I didn't realise. I don't have . . .'

He looked at the dozen or so stones scattered about the Yard, all with lines drawn on them.

'. . . too much cutting left to do.'

'If there's any more of this dust or noise, I'm calling the police.'

It was a man wearing a commissionaire's uniform standing beside him. The manager of the sandwich bar was shouting at Mr Arkwright.

'If I lose any of my customers . . .'

Peach spat out his dust-mask to explain.

'I'm dreadfully—'

'I'm dreadfully sorry', bellowed Mr Arkwright to his neighbours, 'for any inconvenience. The steps will be finished by this evening . . .'

He looked angrily down at Peach.

'. . . I assure you.'

When they were gone, Peach fell to his knees, and began the bottom step. By cutting a four-inch channel into the pavement with his hammer and chisel, he was able to use some thinner slabs for risers, without having to cut them the sixteen-foot length of the bottom step. He chased out the ancient yorkstone and picked out the lime-bed beneath it till he came to something solid. Then he laid the risers in place, like a six-inch stone frame round the hump of indomitable concrete. He worked as quickly as he could but the lunch-hour rush was already pouring through the courtyard when he bedded the first tread, kneeling before it like a Stone Age witch doctor kneeling before his altar. He had to kneel, for the windows of the ganger man's spirit-level were clogged with prehistoric cement, and the little bubble of spirit wavering behind him was almost as unseeable as that other wavering bubble, the human spirit. Dead level! Peach's heart leapt. He looked up, in adoration and gratitude to have the hundredweight sack of anxiety lifted for a moment from his neck. A young man was standing on the doorstep far above him, smiling down.

'I say. That looks jolly nice.'

'Thanks,' said Peach.

And it did. Gog Magog had cut the stone to a forty-five degree angle at the corner, as neat as a line drawn on paper. Where the forty-five degree corner of the return abutted it, the joint would be no more than a quarter of an inch thick, running down to a perfect triangle, elegantly pointed in the spirit of Wren.

The young man, who wore a pinstripe suit, blue shirt, bright red tie and shining black shoes, smiled at Peach. Perhaps, for a moment, he too had a vision of the master stonemason in his Enlightenment Yard, an apron of white dust over his jeans, a level at his feet, its bubble perfectly centred, a gauge of muck on four stiff bags, slow saws, more patient than Time itself, mitring stone, and the ground for fifty yards around as white as Reason.

'Yes. Jolly nice.'

He wished he could think of something to say to this nameless Vitruvian craftsman. They were probably about the same age. He would have liked to put his arm round his shoulder with a grip that bound the classes together, and sweep him off to the wine bar for a spot of lunch. Over a glass or two, democratically, they would hold Johnsonian discourse, till they'd found the common ground between cutting stone and corporation tax.

'Yes. It's going to be . . . jolly nice.'

'Thanks,' said Peach, looking to the sky for a topic of conversation. But he could see none.

'Well, I'm off.'

A shuffling client was blocking Peach's ramp, so, in the instant, the young solicitor made a decision — an instinctive act of comradeship, expressing the fact that they were both young, vigorous men, stone-cutter and word-cutter, but essentially human. He jumped. He wouldn't slide down the ramp of privilege. He leapt into the void where human beings meet. He jumped towards Peach's building site, confident he would land on common ground. He didn't mind getting his shoes dirty. But halfway out into mid-air above the hump of concrete, the young solicitor realised that there was nowhere for him to land. He was hurtling towards Peach, who stood stock-still smiling at him like a madman. All around Peach, for about six feet in every direction, was a batch of cement, about nine inches deep, and it was a good twelve feet to the pavement beyond, where he could break his ankle on a sliver of yorkstone. The young solicitor whirled his arms, kicked his legs, grabbed Peach's shoulder for support, and landed on the stone he'd just laid. Brushing the dust off his jacket, he picked his way into the Yard where he turned and surveyed the step. It had sunk an inch where he'd landed, and two of the risers had fallen out.

'Yes. Jolly nice. Well . . . I'm off.'

He skipped off down the Yard oblivious.

All that afternoon Peach laid and relaid the bottom step. Most of the people who went in and out risked the bridge. But some of them preferred to walk over the top of him and climb the hump. It was like working in the shoe department of Harrods, till Peach scarcely needed a spirit level. He could see the stones rising and falling with his naked eye. But he didn't complain. Golden Brick Yard was white with his guilt and his building site was spreading of its own accord in all directions. It was even walking up into the marble hallway of Burns Arkwright. The smaller pieces of rubble were running under the shoes of the pedestrians in Fleet Street, pursued by a thirty-foot cement stain where the telephonist had kicked over his bucket. But worst of all was the rubbish. It seemed that once you initiated a heap in these dignified alleys, garbage flew in from all directions. He'd been so engrossed in his work that he hadn't seen the filing-cabinet drawers, cascading print-out, slipped on top of his own neat little pile of chippings. He was stuffing the paper back in the drawers when the manager of the sandwich bar emerged with two sacks of scraps, which he slung on top, in Peach's face, with a satisfied look. One sack split and chicken legs dropped into an open drawer to be filed under 'Fetor'. Now a tourist was emptying a container of curry over the whole lot. Two or three bags for the garbage men? He had half a skip load already. Peach groaned inwardly. He'd have to hire a van from *Time Out* to move this lot, and half his earnings would be gone. He put his dust-mask in his mouth and ripped Gog Magog to life, and the tourist hurried off.

A great loneliness, as enveloping as the two-stroke roar, whirled around him, and echoed outwards in ever-growing circles, followed by a white cloud. When the disk flew off and took his kneecap, no one would show their face in the Yard for ten minutes, and then they'd probably just walk right past, or even over, him, mistaking him, in his whiteness, for a bleeding stone. In the midst of so many people, he was totally alone. He had become invisible. A spirit has more body!

When Lady de Sage emerged later that afternoon and saw Peach struggling with the last slab of the bottom step, it took all of her good-breeding to maintain the haughty silence that said more than any words. She stepped to the head of the bridge escorted by Mr Arkwright, who was still apologising. Something like eight hundred people had been up and down those three floorboards battened by woodwormy two-by-two. The bridge groaned, and the quiet beginning of a splitting sound, which had been gnawing at Peach's ear all afternoon, got louder. The two old people edged downwards. Lady de Sage wondered when she would snap. In these modern times a vast fortune was nothing but a curse, a stream of endless irritations. Cooks who leave. Chauffeurs who search out traffic jams. Spiteful shop-girls. The streets a mockery of drills and rubble. Even one's family law-firm unable to negotiate a flight of steps.

At that moment, the bridge began to sag. The insolent young man was asking her not to step on his stones! She skidded a little in the mortar. Mr Arkwright leapt on to Peach's completed steps and assisted her from below. Peach ran to help her too. He ought really to take her in his arms and carry her over his sea of cement and broken stone. But just to hold her rigid elbow was chilling enough. She looked down at him as he helped her past this gauge, hating him for making her need his help. If she did finally snap it would be at this demented young man with the white hair and terrified grin. And by God he'd know it! She shook him off, and Mr Arkwright accompanied her sheepishly down the Yard. As she walked away from him, Peach saw his own hands, in three to one cement, still gripping, as if in terror, the black elbow of her suit.

It was nine o'clock and darkness had come without his noticing it. The office had closed. The cleaning ladies had come and gone. But Peach worked on. The oak doors were ajar, letting out a fillet of light for him to work by. At ten o'clock, Mr Phillips, who had been watching him all day from an upstairs window, like an anxious foreman, went home, locking up behind him. He gave Peach a fierce smile. Peach worked on by the light of the street-lamp. By eleven he had the risers of the second step in place and benched in. He could do no more. He was exhausted. He made an attempt to clear up his site. Then he hid his tools and Gog Magog under the bags of sand, careless of who stole them. His knees were stiff. His hands were raw with cement. He'd worked so hectically he'd scarcely felt them all day. But now, as the cold bit, he stood at the bus stop, his hands royally bedecked with the rings and seals of his workmanship – great ruby sores he couldn't take off, weeping signets of scab fluid, round lapis lazuli bruises, jet scimitars under his nails, bracelets of grazes round his wrists – the Maha Raja of Pain.

* * *

146

Allwrath's sick engine sipped petrol as if it were some ghastly medicine. It choked on teaspoonfuls like a rebellious child. It coughed and spat. Now it was running on the mere smell of it. At a steady eight miles an hour, he'd been getting a hundred and ninety to the gallon. But his last gallon was running out. The reluctant coughs were turning to a death-rattle somewhere in the carburettor. The Rationalists behind him had developed a fiendish system of stopping for petrol in shifts, while always keeping their main cortege on his tail. And so they followed him like a black twelve-part syllogism, two or three propositions at a time dropping off into service stations to top up their cynicism. Whereas he, all by himself, the conclusion that comes before all logic, dared not stop. The Druid lost speed. A heavy clanking began to shake the engine. And here he was, manoeuvring round the back streets of Golders Green, far from help. In this part of the Deadly Forest, the petrified trees had been cut back to lonely two-storey stumps, on which the pebble dash broke out like a poisonous rash. There was not a human being in sight, only parked cars.

Then, turning into Rockleigh Avenue, his engine cut out altogether, and he was coasting helplessly towards a small rise, when he saw Bertrand Russell standing outside number 8, watering the garden – a million droplets of logical positives, 'Newton's particles of light', spraying out of his hose and scything down the petunias. Fear clutched Allwrath's heart, and he slid lower behind his wheel. But just as he drew opposite the house, the old philosopher went indoors, thoughtfully removing his wellingtons, and leaving the hose sprinkling on the lawn. His garage door was open. Allwrath peered in, and saw his Chariot of Mental War – a 1986 Mercedes. The old rationalist had thought out the history of human thought, but he'd forgotten to take the keys out of his fuel-cap. Allwrath seized his chance. Muttering an ancient courage-rune, he pulled into the kerb, grabbed his crowbar, and leapt out of the hearse. He ran up the drive and disappeared into the garage. He opened the Mercedes' fuel-tank, unscrewed the end of the hose from the tap, and plunged it deep into the philosopher's petrol. Then he ran back out on to the lawn, tore the nozzle from the hose, and dragged the end of the hose out to the hearse's empty fuel-tank. Then, risking his sanity, and the very tissue of his brain, he sucked the stream of logical positives, the arching syllogisms, the glittering floricide, he sucked The History of Western Philosophy, out of the hose, fiendishly disguised as water. He spat it out, and sucked and sucked again, till he tasted good clean petrol, which he siphoned into his own tank, glaring in triumph at the funeral cortege, daring it to come any closer. But the line of black cars had pulled over discreetly. And not one modern thinker stepped out.

The Reverend Briggs was growing confused. Was it two weeks now, or fourteen, since they'd left the church? He thought he recognised the back streets of Golders Green, which was nearer the Garden Suburb than last week, but he didn't know which route to take from here. And now the hearse was bearing westward again, and his *A–Z* was open at Epping Forest. If this took much longer, he would have to halve the sandwich ration again. Though God knows, their food was approaching zero, like a curve in calculus. Soon he would be halving crumbs. And to be drinking port, even in sips, on such a light stomach, was unwise. Even he, a plump and vigorous man in the prime of life, was feeling light-headed. This morning he'd caught himself holding a scrap of sandwich up to the light and talking to it. That was understandable enough, under the circumstances, except he'd heard the words 'This Is My Body', muttered with a fervency that could only be called Popish. Perhaps he'd only meant it in the sense of 'What You Eat Today Walks and Talks Tomorrow'. But it had sounded as if he were trying to coax some Higher Goodness into the bread for which his guts were writhing. Now God was a reasonable man, and would never pretend He was a piece of bread. Yet now, like some God-sotted Benedictine, he found that one mouthful of the blessed port got him mystically drunk. Perhaps Christ *was* in the wine. And when the Reverend Briggs caught

148

himself transubstantiating an almond slice on the sly, he feared for his sanity. Perhaps the Divine *did* interfere in the orderly, rational running of things. He wished It wouldn't, but how else could he explain what he was seeing with his own eyes? Perhaps there were kinks in reality, which in heathen times were called miracles.

For the back of the head that was driving Arthur's hearse looked different. The black jockey's cap had changed into what looked like a white towel, or cowl. The undertaker always wore a black, skin-tight suit, flecked with cigarette ash. But his brown hands were now gripping the steering wheel from out of white fulsome sleeves, as of a gown. Good God! Could it be? Drawing level at a slow corner he glimpsed leather pouches hanging from the man's neck, of the type used by the Saints of the Early Church to carry the eucharist around in, their only food. Please let it not be, O Lord. The Reverend Briggs stared at the back of Allwrath's head, as they turned into Rockleigh Avenue. This undertaker was the last man to merit it . . . But had *he* been transubstantiated, like the Bread, into a Blessed Martyr of the Primitive Church, driving at a skilful eight miles an hour, winding them back through the streets of this material London into the visionary Jerusalem, where they would see God face to face, and Arthur would step from his coffin, before he'd been buried? A white sweat broke out on the vicar's wine-red forehead. It was the last thing on earth he wanted. So much for a quiet diocese in his waning years. So much for his prize marrows at the Autumn Fete – bolted! But if it was a miracle, he was the first man to have seen it. And, as John the Baptist to this Divine Being, he might end up Archbishop of Canterbury. Blood of the Madonna!

The hearse had drawn to a stand-still outside number 8. The Reverend Briggs waved his cavalcade over. Then the door of the hearse flew open, and out leapt – not a Blessed Saint or a Martyr, but – Good God Almighty – the Good Shepherd Himself! There was no mistaking His long white robe and Shepherd's hood. And in His hand he held a mighty crook. His hair was long and matted, his eyes fierce with Revelation, lenses to contact the Unwatchable Light. And on His belt there

149

hung the Holy Grail and a Devouring Sword. It was Jesus Christ come back to earth. The Reverend Briggs fell to his knees, gripping the glove-box.

'Behold!' he commanded his parishioners in a ringing voice.

A hose was sprinkling in the garden of number 8. The Good Shepherd strode up the drive and disappeared into the garage, no doubt to turn up the tap. For, the next instant, He strode back down the garden, stepping through the spray, tore the nozzle from the hose, which He dragged to His hearse, took a good long drink, and thrust it into the petrol tank of His own Blessed Vehicle!

An excess of light giddied the Reverend Briggs. It was a Holy Moment. It was the first Vision of his clerical life. And it brought words with it – disconnected phrases from the New Testament – about a certain marriage, somewhere – Cana, was it? – ecstasy made memory stumble – where the wine ran out, and . . .

With a full tank of water, the hearse moved slowly off.

The Reverend Briggs's mouth fell open. He turned and leered at his flock over the top of the seat, in his effort to put the Amazing Light into words.

'Dearly Beloved. For God so loves the World, He gives His Only Begotten Son – Follow Him quick! – for a new Ministry upon Earth – O, All Things Bright And Beautiful! – He hath tuned His Mercies to the Modern World, its horrors of pollution, its imminent oil shortage. Behold, we are Guests at His Mystic Nuptials, His first Miracle, HIS TURNING OF WATER INTO PETROL!'

3-Tooth stood in a forty-yard circle of screaming music and deserted grass. The rest of the park was littered with bodies.

Jimi had never given 3-Tooth such a rush. Pure inspiration flowed from the amp, into his fingers, up his arm, along his shoulder, and up his spine into his brain. On each string, above every fret, an astral diamond vibrated, turning to a diamond-tip of pain as he pressed it down and bent the string from one side of the fret-board to the other, till jewels of sound stretched forth like chewing gum from his amp. A silver-spangled presence shone in the tree under which he played, its quicksilver light catching his shades so obliquely, they turned to mirrors in which he could see his own eyeballs. The Cumberland Hotel was invisible. In each silvery-black pupil stood a tiny figure, arms and legs stretched to the circumference. Perhaps it was his, 3-Tooth's, ego, his pride, vanity and worldly ambition, about to jump once and for all into the outer darkness of his shades. Perhaps, if he kept this rush going, he would be enlightened. Or perhaps it was Jimi, signalling from a star.

'I'm with ya, man,' cried 3-Tooth ecstatically. 'I won't let this one go!'

Someone entered the forty-yard circle, whose centre was his empty guitar-bag. Someone was coming towards him over the sun-browned grass. Throughout the rest of the park the grass had been trodden to dust. But inside his forty-yard faery circle, it was so long that it was going to seed. And now someone was walking on it towards him, through the terrifying wall of sound.

If it was Jimi Hendrix, come to him at last, 3-Tooth dared not look at him. The wattage of the vision might kill him.

'I'd die, to play with ya, man,' 3-Tooth cried, staring straight upwards.

As the figure came towards him, bending lasciviously to and fro, head cropping the grass one moment, then flung backwards the next so that its black hair stood a yard in the air, 3-Tooth caught a reflection of tight black leather pants and his heart stopped. Taking his life in both hands, he looked down.

It wasn't the greatest guitarist in the History of the Universe. But it was the next best thing – a thirteen-year-old vagabond-chick, black leather jeans and a fishnet vest, studs and icons on her black leather jacket, dancing orgasmically a foot from his face, on his empty guitar-bag. She was the best thing that had ever dropped in it. She was mouthing at him through the uproar of his music.

'Far out, man.'

He showed her three ecstatic teeth.

'Hendrix, baby.'

'Who else.'

She was his soulmate, his dancing Kali, made flesh. She was his other, black half. She was dancing up against him, gyrating her hips around his, so close that the silver buttons of their trousers gnashed their teeth. She understood him. She was the Cosmic Groupie, coming for him from a black hole. Her shades were two pits of desire. The moment had come to throw his guitar aside and gyrate with her into the rhododendrons. 3-Tooth kept playing. She wanted him, and he wanted her. He hit a marvellous E7 riff, descending from the treble. In truth, he daren't stop. If he did he might lose Jimi for ever. For a moment he wondered if, if he got his amp into the bushes with his foot, they wouldn't be able to do it without stopping. But it wouldn't be right. Jimi had brought him this high. It was Jimi who had turned her on. He couldn't abandon him now. He hoped she'd understand. He hoped she could hang on for a few hours, till the inspiration had taken its natural course. 3-Tooth kept playing, pouring himself bodily into the big, red guitar.

She *did* understand. She threw back her head and let out a bloodcurdling yell.

'If all the hippies – cut off their hair –

I don't mind – I don't care! – '

Her body quivered from the feet upwards. For a moment 3-Tooth thought she'd stepped in his amp and been electrocuted. She toppled backwards and flung herself a yard across the grass, then rolled a yard back, till she came to rest, shuddering, panting, but replete, in his guitar-bag. She lay there looking into the sky and breathing deeply. Then she rolled over and went to sleep. 3-Tooth smiled benignly, glad to have been of some service to her. And like the Cosmic Male himself, like a star in the Night's endless gig, he kept on playing. When he'd finished, he'd wake her up, and they'd get down to it in the flesh.

But when, still grooving, he looked down two hours later, she was gone. 3-Tooth's voice cracked as he sang. His guitar-bag had never looked so empty. He kept playing, but there was a sob in it. His wah-wah was out of control. He played on and on, dutifully, till at last the inspiration drained from him, and he stood in his own resounding silence. Five hours had passed. He would never see her again. At this very minute she was off seeking orgasms on the other side of the Universe. 3-Tooth slumped against the tree and took off his shades. When he spoke into the blinding light, his voice was as gravelly as Jimi's.

'Sometimes, man, I wonder why ya don' let me get a steady job, and a mortgage, and a – wife. P'raps I could join up with Peach.'

It took Peach three more days to finish the steps. As they rose higher, fewer and fewer people bothered about the ramp, and simply chose to walk over him as he worked. It was like building a down elevator in stone. If he added together the number of separate times he'd built the steps, they'd reach to the first-floor window. He'd had two warnings from the police and a physical assault from the commissionaire three doors up. The commissionaire was a big man, in full dress uniform, in the flower of his rage, and if Peach hadn't forgotten his Buddhist scruples and picked up his sledgehammer he might well have been laid out on one of his own slabs. Mr Arkwright and the Senior Partners smiled more grimly as each day passed. But it was the old lady, Lady de Sage, he feared most. She was, the young solicitor informed him, writing her Will, and so she came in every day, for it was a long and complex document. And each day she stared at Peach's labours with a more concentrated malignancy.

It was Thursday when he finished. Every tread was in place and firm, a gentle sweep, a royal succession of yorkstones up to the cement-stained sill. The pointing was neat, the corners square and he'd be away before Lady de Sage came out. Not that she would find anything to sniff at now. Except for the rubbish of course. The heap now stood seven feet high, more than a skip-load, two or three vanfuls, all his earnings. But in his relief at the thought of getting away, Peach didn't mind too much. Someone had added a three-legged chair during the night over which skeins of flaccid spaghetti, donated by the Bistro in Fleet Street, lolled and palely sunbathed. There were plenty of beer cans too, and polystyrene containers blowing around. Mr Phillips had asked him a dozen times when he would move it. Now it was pay-time, they stood together in front of the heap.

'The steps are beautiful, Peach,' said Mr Phillips smiling bleakly. 'But we really can't pay you till that rubbish's gone.'

So, after six days' suffering, he was going to have to blow all his earnings on a van, and go home empty-handed.

'I don't know how you're going to move it. But if it's not gone by tonight, we may well think of suing you.'

He gave Peach a granite smile. Peach felt tears rising.

'Of course, Mr Phillips. I'll just nip round . . . and move it now.'

Peach plunged down the Yard. He had no money on him. It would take him two hours to get to the bank and back. And by the time he'd bought *Time Out*, found a call-box, and phoned round for a van, it might well be . . . too late. Far from spending all his earnings on the rubbish, he might well find himself paying for having worked here. Their meagre savings would be gone. The baby was three months closer and he was back where he had started.

In the entranceway into Fleet Street, with his back to Peach, stood Fergus O'Fury. He was making the sign of the cross above the roaring traffic, as though he had just blessed it. The Red Sea of cars, which a minute before had been snarled to a stand-still, parted miraculously, and the tail of a semi-trailer

154

surged up on to the pavement beside him, braking an inch from the Bistro's side-walk tables, upon which two abandoned glasses of red stood trembling. Fergus O'Fury shook his head sadly at the treachery of wine-drinkers. He was a beer-drinking man himself, and he would never desert a pint. He made the sign of the cross over one of the glasses and muttered,

'Dis is My Blood.'

He knocked it back in one swallow. He smiled at the empty glass. Sure, 'twasn't all dat bad, a working man's blood!

'Hello Fergus, how are you?'

Peach had felt so low he'd thought of slipping past behind Fergus's back.

'Peach O'Hare! Me young friend. Me menta.'

Fergus looked yearningly at the second glass.

'Drink dis,' he cried forcing it into Peach's hand before temptation found him. ''Tis my Blood.'

Peach knew enough about drinking with Fergus not to refuse. He shut his eyes and swallowed the wine dutifully. It was a fine red. It slipped along the reaches of his blood like another, subtler blood. Like a grape, half earth, half light, his head, which for six days had been crushed in the wine-press of guilt and anxiety, burst open in a warm pulse of well-being. For a moment, he forgot about the rubbish.

'Wot brings ye to dis neck o' de woods?' said Fergus.

'Steps,' said Peach solemnly. 'I've just built some steps up this Yard.'

And he jerked his head up Golden Brick Yard.

'Let me have a look at dem den,' said Fergus. 'Let's see me young ganger's workmanship.'

They walked up Golden Brick Yard, leaving the semi-trailer, still half on the pavement, to the mercy of the traffic.

'Very nice,' said Fergus as they stood in front of Peach's steps. 'Very nice indeed! Wot ye doin' wit all dat rubbish den?'

Tears filled Peach's eyes.

'I don't know. I haven't a clue. I've got no van and they're going to sue me if it's not gone by tonight.'

'Are dey den?' said Fergus. He scratched his head. 'Den I

155

tink I can help ye. Sure 'twould be a terrible ting if I couldn't help de man who gave me a start. Ye follow me!'

He led Peach back down Golden Brick Yard and twenty yards up Fleet Street to the corner of Chancery Lane. On the opposite corner was a construction site. Yellow hoarding blocked off the pavement. A golden crane towered upwards beyond the hoarding. Labourers with brushes and shovels stood in the road cleaning off the clay dropped by the lorries coming and going through the gates. Two ready-mix lorries, their drums turning, waited by a vast cement stain on the road for a hopper so newly painted it may have been made of sheet gold. The labourers who swung the hopper into position under the concrete shute wore clean new donkey jackets with cuffs of wet cement and epaulettes of fresh-dug clay. Their helmets were new-minted from the Argos, without a scratch or a dent in the yellow plastic. Above the hoarding on a twelve-foot podium of scaffolding a sign was mounted, on which were painted, in blood-red, nine-foot-high letters, the words O FURY. The letter O was blacked in, so that it looked like the entrance to a tunnel. Fergus led Peach to a gap in the hoarding. They stood on the lip of a pit. A steep ramp of hard-core descended into a vast well shored with steel ribs below the pavement of Fleet Street. They saw the foot of the crane, set in a block of concrete as big as a house. Lengths of new steel tube were being piled into the subsoil, down which section after section of bit-shaft, knuckled together, wound into the earth, bringing up pats of crushed bed-rock and gules of black clay, which were knocked into the backs of lorries.

Peach and Fergus walked down the ramp. They climbed over pits of cast concrete, and picked their way through great rib-cages of reinforcing rods, as though they were walking in the guts of an awakening dinosaur. Carpenters were casing them in shuttering. And tonight they would be fossils.

'What are you doing here, Fergus?' asked Peach.

Fergus hunted through his trouser pockets, sieving through the change, and pulled out the back of a soiled envelope. He showed it to Peach. Lengthways, up the envelope, was a pencil drawing of a very tall building indeed. Between two crumpled arrows, one pointing to the top, the other to the bottom, was written 300 FEET.

'Sure, 'tis a big job. A man can't be always pullin' tings down. It can't be all holes in dis life, me young fella. He has t' put something up every now and den. Do', purely for meself, I prefer holes.'

'You're not just doing demolition and excavations any more?'

Fergus scowled at the drawing.

'Sure, dis ting now, 'twill be a sort o' excavation in de sky. 'Twill be a demolition o' dis air here. Dat's how I look at it. Lyin' on de footpart and lookin' strite up – as sometimes happens, be Jaysus, to a drinkin' man 'twill be a great hole in de air, shored in wit glass 'n air-conditionin'.'

They were standing in the corner of the pit beside a pile of skips, stacked one inside the other. Each skip was painted yellow, with O FURY stencilled on the side in black and red. They looked brand new. Fergus was standing with his head flung back, making the sign of the cross straight upwards. Not to God but to a tiny, terrified face pressed to the window of the crane-driver's cabin three hundred feet above. It was the face of his cousin, Fingal O'Fury, from County Clare. The only crane Cousin Fingal had seen back home was the little hand-turned jib on the back of the local tow-truck. Believing this to be the archetype of all cranes, he'd written to his cousin Fergus, who'd come on good times in London, asking for a job as a crane-driver, overtime if possible. Watching him climb the three-hundred-foot ladder to the cab had been like watching Hillary climb Everest, lashed only to a rosary. Once he'd reached the safety of the cab, he'd refused to come down, and had craned his dinners up in the hopper. He'd been on duty for a week now. He'd papered over three of the cab's four windows with the pictures of naked women so beloved of mechanical men – 'So's not . . .' he told his Catholic conscience '. . . t' have t' look into de terrible abyss.'

'Dat's what I like t' see,' said Fergus, when his cousin hadn't come down after three days. '. . . a man dat loves 'is work. Do' I should've given 'im de eye test before I gave 'im de job,' he was heard to say when Fingal lowered a hopper of concrete on to a traffic island in Temple Lane.

At night, rocked by loneliness and shaken by gusts of starry desire, the crane's tiny cab swayed to and fro and the great jib rose and fell.

Now Fergus was signalling fiercely upwards. The cable came spinning down, trailing four chains like slovenly baboon arms. At the end of each chain was a ring, which Fergus hung over the four bollards at each corner of the top skip. Then he wound his forefinger above his head. The chains snapped taut, and the empty skip rose in the air, shaking itself free of the skips below. Straight up it went. One hundred. Two hundred. Two hundred and fifty feet, for Fergus kept winding his finger above his head. Then he made a sweeping gesture of absolution with his right hand, and the skip went swinging out over Fleet Street. Peach and Fergus walked beneath it, Fergus still signalling to his cousin, as the skip circled towards Golden Brick Yard.

Peach had vague premonitions that this might not be a strictly legal, let alone safe, way of removing rubbish. But perhaps it *was* Fergus's blood he'd drunk from that wine-glass. For Fergus's thick finger waving above it, seemed to have woken some Godlike buoyancy in the wine which even now lifted up his heart. Everything would be all right. And besides, Fergus had taken over.

Rolling out along the jib of the crane, the skip went sailing past the Daily Horror Building, high above the steeple of St Dunstan-in-the-Fleet, planed in over the roof of the Mortlake Concern Building, weaving round the air-conditioning vents, till it stopped, two hundred and ninety feet above Peach's tiny building site in Golden Brick Yard. Fergus stood on the pavement in Fleet Street, by the entrance to the Yard, where he could see both his cousin's cabin, and Peach, standing by his steps.

'I'll stand here 'n dog it down,' said Fergus. 'You signal to me how 'ee's doin' comin' down, 'n tell me when 'tis full. And remember, if it lands on yer foot – dis means Up.'

And Fergus swivelled his forefinger high above his head.

Peach looked up at the bottom of the skip as it came swinging down between the buildings, waving his arms wildly to Fergus in Fleet Street. With a fierce 'Above!', Fergus was stopping any pedestrians from turning into the Yard. The commissionaire stepped from his door to speak to Peach about the rubbish, looked up, and stepped quickly back into his office.

'Take care,' cried Peach.

Fergus sent his cousin a full Catechism of holy crane-driving signs, so precise that the skip coiled and drifted down the canyon of windows, without touching a thing. Mr Arkwright looked out of the window of his fifth-floor office and knew that the last week had been too much for him. He glanced at Lady de Sage to see if she had seen the apparition too. But the old woman was signing her Will with a grim look on her face. The skip scraped gently down the fourth- and third-floor windows of the Mortlake Concern Tower, bending towards the glass like a goldfish looking out from its tank. It swung timelessly across towards the Doric portico of Burns Arkwright, skimming in past the second- and first-floor windows, Peach waving it towards the other side of the Yard, till at last he could reach it, and pushing the huge weight into the backwards swing of its pendulum, guided it away from the oak doors, down his steps, the skip gathering momentum, till it seemed it would take out the Mortlake Concern's fire-doors and swing right through its foyer back out into Chancery Lane. But with a convulsion of Fergus's hand, a sudden thumbs-up to his Maker, the skip plummeted the last six inches and landed at the foot of his steps like a canary settling on a branch. For a moment the great chains coiled slackly around the Yard, and then went still. Peach began slinging the rubbish in the skip.

'Make it quick dere,' called Fergus. 'Here comes Old Bill.'

Rubble, chippings, fillets of stone sauteed in red wine with fish-lungs and Coke tins, flew into the skip. One whiskery old man – 'I'm only looking for a job, guv' – nearly went in too. A frozen bag of cement. Half-eaten hamburgers in telephone book buns. Mashed potato dollops of mortar stiffened into company reports. And at the very bottom, a rat reading a telex from President Reagan. Peach threw the telex in the skip. But, remembering Reincarnation, let the rat go. It scuffled smugly down Golden Brick Yard.

'Soon to be Lord Mayor of London,' it hissed at the sandwich bar cat.

The rubbish was gone. Peach swept up and washed away the stain. He would just give his steps one last, loving sweep. For after all the suffering, his pride in his work was still intact. Then he was free! Finished! Away! He picked up the bottom end of the ramp and rested it on the edge of the skip, the better to sweep underneath.

Upstairs in Mr Arkwright's office, Lady de Sage watched the Senior Partner countersign her Will. He was the son of a plumber. She should have taken her family's business elsewhere the minute they made him a partner. It made her shudder to see that fat, smooth hand, that was made for groping up drains, spread out complacently on her Will. She had grown up in a world where the only houses she knew had tradesmen's entrances and servants' stairs. Where the lower orders carried out their operations subliminally, one rung below children, being neither heard nor seen. But now these people burst upon one's reserve with their drilling noises, their traffic jams, their radios, their paint smell in one's bedroom, or popped up like ill-mannered children in new suits, calling themselves doctors or solicitors. It might look very efficient with its computers and high-speed lifts, but she knew that it was anarchy. She felt giddy. She looked at Mr Arkwright's hand sitting on her Will like an excremental frog on a pile of invoices. It was mere anarchy! And with the malice of his class, he secretly welcomed it. It was anarchy running amok in the form of, in the form of . . . a young man covered in white dust, raising cement-wet hands to touch her. And Mr Ark-wright had called him in!

'Get your hand off my Will!'

'Lady de Sage?'

'Don't you touch it!'

She grabbed the Will and tried to tear it in two. But it was thick and the paper good quality, and it merely buckled. She squeezed it furiously into a ball.

'Lady de Sage!'

Several pages slid out and dropped to the floor. Lady de Sage went down on her hands and knees and gathered them up.

'I won't have you – touching my Last Wishes.'

'My dear Lady . . . The last week has been a trial for us both. The regrettable delay with the steps—'

It was as if he'd dropped a match in a pool of paraffin.

'You hired him! You imbecile!'

'Lady de Sage. Please . . . Many people find it a strain when they come to make their Last—'

'You wanted me to break my leg, didn't you? Wait till I get hold of that assassin you've got on your doorstep!'

She backed towards the door as if, the moment she turned her back on him, he'd lay her out with a length of two-inch gas pipe.

'I'll take my Will elsewhere. I'll ring Lord Lasenby. I'll put a stop to your little games,' she shouted, reaching the vestibule.

'Lady de Sage. Please . . .'

The lift door entombed her from his sight. He saw the red light on the indicator begin to descend. He raced for the stairs. Crimson-faced and breathless, Mr Arkwright reached the ground floor and ran from the stairwell just as Lady de Sage had pinned one of his Juniors to the hallway wall.

'I intend to live, do you hear me? You are not going to get rid of me so easily.'

She saw Mr Arkwright running towards her. She shook the squashed up Will at him as if it were a primitive missile.

'Lady de Sage. Please. Come upstairs. A little glass of—'

But she was already pushing her way backwards through the glass doors, shouting so loudly that Mr Arkwright could hear her as he hastened forward on the other side.

'Anarchists! Animals!'

Her old shoes found the doorstep and the head of Peach's ramp. The black heels, already ruined by cement, mounted the floorboards by heart. They could walk down this ramp backwards and blindfold, they had been subjected to it so often. For all her wealth, her life had been a bridge of nails, down which she'd made her imperious way, fending off the greed of the world. She backed along it.

'Where's that maniac they disguised as a builder? Well, I've a few things to tell him! I've got friends in the Highway Department.'

It was strange, but the bridge across which she was backing felt as though it were taking her up rather than down. No doubt it was another of life's little ironies.

'Lady de Sage! For God's sake! The ramp!' cried her solicitor through the plate-glass doors. But she didn't hear him.

'I've still got the Will! I'll live for ever! Where's that wretched cowboy?'

And shrieking like a harpy she disappeared into Peach's skip.

'Oh my God!' cried Peach.

'Lady de Sage,' yelled Mr Arkwright, rushing to the door.

But Peach had already leapt into the skip.

The old woman had sunk head first into a depth of curried sand and manila folders. Her body was pinned against the side of the skip by a dead palm tree and its pot. Peach frantically pulled her free and dragged her upright. She seemed to be unconscious, or else . . . Around her neck was wound thirty feet of tape from a disembowelled cassette. Peach tore at the tangled tape. The old lady began to gurgle. Peach struggled with the festoons of plastic ribbon, lifting them above his head and winding them round and round, to free her. Standing in Fleet Street, Fergus O'Fury gave his cousin the Athanasian blessing, and the great chains uncoiled across the courtyard, snapped tight, and the skip began to rise from the ground.

'Lady de Sage,' cried her legal adviser, scratching at the container as it pulled clear of him.

Lady de Sage lay dead in the arms of . . . ?

She opened her eyes. She was flying swiftly and smoothly up and over the Mortlake Concern Building in the arms of a Heavenly Spirit with cement on his face. The smoke and screech of Hell lay far below her – a narrow crevasse where demonic bugs swarmed blowing their horns. Her own sins lay all around her, in the form of fungoid milk-cartons filled with chippings and lumps of yorkstone dripping red wine. The sand of despair was in her shoes. Her past wrath curry-stained her dress. But she had been forgiven! Her chariot flew without wings or angelic horses, through pure silence. Celestial indeed! On the inside her chariot was steel, to remind her of her past hard-heartedness. But on the outside it was solid gold, the gold of her heavenly reward, with, she saw – leaning over the rim like an excited child and reading upside down – the words O FAIRY written in red on the side.

'O FAIRY CHARIOT OF GOD,' cried Lady de Sage, bracing her legs and stretching her wrinkled, newborn arms upwards in the joint symbol of acceptance and benediction, while the Heavenly Spirit held her tight by the belt.

'O FAIRY CHARIOT OF GOD! BEAR ME FOREVER UPWARDS!'

The skip sank on to one of Fergus's skip lorries. The old lady saw what had happened. But a change had been wrought in her in the sky above the City. She stepped down from the container with shining eyes, shook Peach's hand, and walked off down Fleet Street, nodding at the passers-by.

PEACH turned the corner on his last lap home. Their house stood at the bottom of the cul-de-sac facing up the street. He relaxed. There was no corrugated iron in the windows. No lead pipes flying out of the door. The pink curtains were fluttering reassuringly in Martha's ground-floor window. The black shadow behind them was his piano. His heart sank. Damn Morag for having made him buy it. Eighty pounds and it had become a black shadow over his life. He had nightmares about it. Its weight was his inertia. Its immovability was the mental block that had all his life stopped him from coming to grips with the real world, from picking it up by even one corner. It depressed him like its own four castors sinking into Martha's lino. And he hadn't played it once. All that hard-earned money to buy a silent box of resonant guilt. It had been in her room for three weeks now, and he'd still made no effort to move it. She'd said he could keep it there as long as he liked. But this only made him feel worse. For Martha lived crowded into one room and the only place for the piano was there in front of her window. She had to keep the light on all day.

Peach walked along the pavement, skirting the oil stain by the kitchen entrance to the Kentucky Fried Chicken. He plodded home with Colonel Sanders' secret seasoning on his shoes. The chains of reasons that bound him from moving it were long and tangled: to get the piano up to his room he would have to take down the banisters from the ground floor to the top of the house. That would be easy enough. A few blows with the sledge would do it. Then pay Arthur God knows how much to hump it up. Then once it was up, Peach would be morally bound to put the banisters back, to show he wasn't a vandal. But this was a job for a skilled carpenter. And

164

having got the piano up and the banisters back, even as he sat down to strike the first chord, Mr Stag might bang on the door with his friend and, like Rudolf Steiner's occultist meditating himself into the past, Peach would have to go through the whole process backwards, after which he'd be wandering the streets with a spin-drier, cot, pregnant wife and upright piano.

Peach surveyed the front door as he put his key in the lock. It would be a good idea if he gave it a lick of paint. Lilac blue, the colour of forgiveness, or the saffron of the Buddha's robe would give it a lift. It would be a declaration to Mr Stag that they were still in residence. But also subtly hint that they were respectful borrowers, and even maintainers, of his property, not fire-lighting dossers. The old door could certainly do with a coat of paint. It was rotten round the hinges and looked as if it would fall off the next time it was slammed. Even as he turned the key, Peach breathed the familiar draught of damp from the hallway which, in his free-wheeling days, fresh from the middle-class dryness of Australia, had seemed the smell of life itself, as though the house exhaled Reality like Chopin's lung. But now, with Alf's room filling with homeless furniture, and new responsibilities crowding round him, it depressed Peach to feel that, after the black oceans of Morag's womb filling its lungs, this would be their baby's first breath of home. Admittedly, their room was at the top of the house. But this was rising damp, and seemed to be climbing up the drain-pipes.

Peach opened the door, looked up the stairs, and decided that his guilt over the piano had unhinged him. For there it was, or appeared to be, reared on one end, at the twist in the stairs, about three feet above his head and hurtling straight at him. Peach whimpered and jumped sideways and even as he did so realised that he wasn't hallucinating. It *was* his piano. He stared at it aghast. It was standing on one end on a brick that wedged it to the lip of the step, with its other end swung upwards and jammed into the plaster on the underside of the next flight of stairs. Peach pushed against Martha's open door and fell into her room.

A man lay on Martha's bed gasping and shuddering. It was Tiger Burns, Martha's new boyfriend. His face was as florid as his Hawaiian shirt. His large eyes, usually so fierce-full of energy, had swollen with the emptiness that filled them.

'Orright,' he spluttered.

Tiger Burns was an Action Painter and Abstract Sculptor. A big man in his early fifties, he hung around squats collecting colour for his paintings when he wasn't drinking with the stevedores down at Tilbury. Morag said he was serious about Martha. But Peach suspected he was trying to muscle in on Alf's room. He'd offered to paint the loo. Now he seemed unable to breathe. His chest was jumping under his shirt.

It was amazing how quickly they'd all become accustomed to having his piano in Martha's room. Even Martha had got used to it. Three weeks it had stood there like the Edwardian Spirit of the Front Parlour returned to its kingdom. The nicotined cornice had welcomed it. The collapsed rose above the light flex had looked down on it with approval. Now it was gone, the room looked empty, transient once more, like a lath and plaster tent.

Martha was standing at the wash basin wringing out a shirt. Seeing Peach, she rushed at him then swerved towards the man on the bed.

'Fuck you,' she screamed at him. 'Fuck your bloody piano.'

'But you said—'

'Fuck what I said. It's your fault.'

'He didn't do it . . . by himself?'

He heard someone run up the front steps, a key turn in the door, and a young man whom Peach didn't know burst into the room. He was white and trembling. In his hand was a paper bag from the chemist's.

'I got smelling salts.'

'Oh Jesus,' moaned Martha.

'Orright in a minute,' dribbled Tiger.

'I had to jam a brick under it,' the young man explained to Peach. 'Otherwise it would have fallen on him.'

'But how am I going to get it down?' asked Peach.

166

If she weren't sponging Tiger's forehead, Martha may well have scratched out his eyes.

Peach sat on the doorstep waiting for Morag to come home. She might not be able to get upstairs at all. He'd managed to climb round the piano on the outside of the banisters himself, but in her condition it might not be safe.

She arrived at last and he showed her the piano. She was a vigorous woman and game for anything, but hanging on the outside of the banister beside the trembling piano they had an argument – she accusing him of putting things off till they got intolerable, he blaming her for having made him buy the piano in the first place.

She squeezed their child indignantly between the piano and the bend in the stairs, and they were up. But it would certainly put the dampers on going out.

⋯⇀━━◖➤●◄◗━━⇀⋯

seven

SUMMER'S Wheel rolled through them all. It rolled through every man, woman and child in London, making them wish they were elsewhere. It rolled through every building, through every aluminium casement and woodwormy sash. It rolled through darkened brick, and the brick remembered its first, Sumerian baking, when it was a wet ingot of clay lying on the banks of the Euphrates. The common bricks, roughly lime-cast in the innards of church walls and chimney-stacks, and untouched by damp or soot, were still awaiting the building of Jerusalem, when each would turn its face outwards from a golden wall and see perfect men and women. 'The golden bricklayers are coming,' they whispered in their beds of lime and horsehair, feeling the great Wheel of This and No Other Summer roll through them. It rolled through three million tons of steel and reinforced concrete, and the Stock Exchange expanded two millimetres. The great Wheel of Summer rolled across England bringing a heat-wave and thunderstorms. It rolled the wakeful Spirit of the Earth asleep at last, and her dreams appeared on trees and in flowerbeds.

The hub of the Wheel was a mighty Heart Centre that shone above everything, expanding by day and by night. Every morning it ovulated a distinct and separate sun and set it rolling forth. Every night it received it back. It shone through all things. It had touched the moon in Morag's womb, and stilled it. That was in the damp spring. It had sent that little moon-sun rolling forth like a wheel, and now Morag's belly was groaning with its weight. At its hub stood a Perfect Human Being, arms and legs outstretched like spokes. The hub was its Heart. The child stood in that perfection, rolling outwards towards the soiled and blistered city.

'From now on I will begin and end at the Heart Centre,' said Peach to himself, remembering Fergus O'Fury in the Belly Centre. He climbed on to the piano stool.

'The Base of the Spine is an unbuilt city. The Sexual Centre is an unbuilt body. The Belly is a cave of terrors. The Brain is a tent-city, perpetually nomadic. The Forehead is a nail of light driven into a black wall. The Throat is a closed book. Where can I find Love, if not in my own Heart?'

He closed his eyes. It seemed that all his consciousness pulsed in his chest, in a ring of light where his heart was. His brain was still. And the net of his nerves, which his brain trawled through his flesh and bones, catching him in his body, was still. It seemed that his Heart could see. Taking care not to wake his brain with its million and one preoccupations, which took up ninety-nine per cent of his life, but which he wanted to keep from this sacred moment, Peach awoke the thought in his Heart, without words, simply knowing what he meant:

'I am joined to all human beings.'

It was easy to do, for it was the thought his Heart wanted to think most. Still careful not to awaken his brain, and its million and one other thoughts, he poured himself into this 'I am joined to all human beings', amazed that it could exist outside the ferment of his brain. Was this, then, spirit? The more of himself he gave to 'I am joined to all human beings', the lonelier and more stupid he felt, and his brain threatened to spring to life with its million and one excuses. The loneliness and stupidity spread outwards from him in black concentric rings which became the very force-field that had created the darkness of outer space, and the bright pang in the stars. And although the cushion of his piano stool was hot, and the sun was drilling a hole through the front of his shirt, Peach sat in the darkness of night, watching his own isolation move out

169

beyond the stars. 'I am joined to all human beings' bubbled somewhere behind his brain, needing words as much as his brain needed oxygen. But he denied it them. He kept it a spiritual thought in the quaking stillness. Though it seemed hopeless. And now the ring of blue-black light in his Heart seemed like nothing but an optical trick, an illusion.

When all at once, a great force from beyond him, some great intelligence that was not frightened by these endless, cold concentric rings, entered – not him, Peach O'Hare, landscape artist and father-to-be, nor his poor brain bubbling under his skull – but entered the thought itself: 'I am joined to all human beings', as though that thought, to which he'd tried so hard to give himself, was a withered scabbard into which the vast intelligence plunged itself momentarily, from beyond the universe, and entered space like a blue, coruscating sword. And for a moment he *was* joined to all human beings.

The wavering ring of blue-black light in his Heart collapsed inwards, as though his Heart were a vacuum. But as it fell inwards, the blue light formed a T-shape, which Peach knew to be the hilt of that spiritual sword, struggling to withdraw from matter and become a Cross. And this was the great Intelligence withdrawing from his thought, for he couldn't bear it for more than an instant. And as the blue light struggled to love, it became, just for an instant, before his very eyes, the outstretched arms and head of *someone else*, struggling, with what was left of the great force in him, to be a man or a woman, and not an all-devouring sword. Then, as if a sword had just been withdrawn from his brain itself, everything went black, and Peach was left in total darkness, clutching the piano stool to stop himself from falling, while his brain instantly formulated its first natural thought: 'Jesus, have I had a fit?', his heart beating in terror, while, almost unnoticed, a faint blue light stayed by him, lapped around him, healingly.

Summer's Wheel rolled Allwrath round the North Circular at seven miles per hour. It was three months since he had begun eating the sacred roots, and he still had half a pouchful left. Hunger gnawed him but he shuddered at the thought of another mouthful. Rather a strand of asbestos than another life-laden fibre! His tongue felt like an ear of fungus sick to death of his stomach's grumbling. His hunger seemed to have passed into the hearse's front axle, for the old vehicle, scudding along at eight miles an hour, kept slewing kerbwards *of its own accord*, every time he passed a Pizza Express or a McDonalds. It had mounted the pavement outside a Wimpy Bar, and the Druid had wrestled with the Demons of Utilitarianism to get it back on the road. For Allwrath knew that if he walked through the glass leaves of one of these man-eating trees, he would be eaten alive and masticated by a plastic, polyp-shaped table, while God lay abandoned in the hearse outside. He tried to swallow another root. But his mouth only filled with hungry bile. He gnawed his steering wheel and drove on. He dared not stop, for the twelve black limousines were still hot on his tail.

Turning into Holloway Road, he was passed by a twenty-ton articulated lorry. Along the length of its trailer was a picture of six gigantic fish fingers, each one twelve feet high. Standing proud in their batter, they were, in the Druid's Third Eye, six breadcrumbed menhirs in a fish Stonehenge. On the top corner of the trailer was written their name: THIRD EYE FISH. By the Brain-stone of the Ultimate Circle, by the Eye of Brainhenge, here was an earth-revelation come to succour him at last. He'd never seen fish fingers that size before. Six megaliths of fish! He'd eat the lot! He read the runes below the brand name: INTRODUCTORY OFFER: FREE BAP WITH EVERY PACKET. Must be the Pictish script, for it meant nothing to him. But he understood the picture below it – a perfectly round bap six feet high and as white as limestone. He'd have that too! Allwrath put his foot down, but the heavily-laden lorry soon pulled out of sight.

Nevertheless, he came upon it, half an hour later, parked outside Sainsbury's. The driver was inside, making a delivery. The trailer was locked. Allwrath pumped his brake.

171

'Slow down! Slow down!' the Reverend Briggs signalled to the cars behind him mouthing, over the noise of the traffic, the word 'Miracle!'

Allwrath leant into the boot of the hearse, pulled his crowbar from beside the coffin, leapt from the hearse and glared at the funeral cortege, which had also pulled over.

The Reverend Briggs saw the giant picture, and caught his breath. He put his finger to his lips and whispered in awe:

'The Miraculous Draught of Fishes!'

'Fish fingers, sir,' his driver pointed out.

'Fish fingers. Fish fingers. The Lord is walking, driving, in the modern world.'

Allwrath rammed his crowbar through the hinge of the trailer door and wrenched it savagely to and fro. He could already feel the fish fingers, golden brown and hot, warming his stomach. The door was thick and heavy like the door of a fridge. He should really ask the Druid who was driving, but he couldn't wait. Must be some advanced sect, transporting edible megaliths in giant, six-wheeled earth-ovens. He'd climb the first trilithon and eat his way down from the cap-stone. He worked the crowbar to and fro. The hinge buckled, the lock sprang, and the door fell off. A great coldness, wreathed in mist, struck him. And with the coldness came a terrible emptiness. The Rationalists had got here before him! He saw an icy cavern, fifteen feet high and twenty-five feet deep. And there lay the mighty Ring of Fish – its menhirs shrunken to the size of fingers, spilling from a small cardboard box, frozen stiff. SIX FISH FINGERS, read the little coffin. But there were only two left. They'd probably used the others for lintels in cow-sheds and railway sleepers. Scattered round the floor of the van were five baps, shrunk from six-foot spheres, heavy as limestone, to little globes of frozen dough you could hold in one hand. Still, they were better than nothing. They'd melt. Rather than leave them to the mercy of Empiricism, Allwrath swept the fish fingers and baps into the skirt of his robe and carried them back to the hearse.

'Two fish fingers and some buns,' said the driver of the first limousine as they pulled out into the traffic behind the hearse. 'That's no miracle.'

The Reverend Briggs was beaming at his flock.

'But soon they will be FEEDING THE FIVE THOUSAND!'

Summer's Wheel kept 3-Tooth hanging around outside McDonalds, his amp under his arm, his guitar clutched to his belly. The walking bass of deep hunger trod through his gastric juices for a couple of bars then died away.

'I gotta eat, man.'

Jimi was leaning nonchalantly on his shoulder, making it sag.

'I gotta have a burger, man.'

'Well, walk right in and have a burger, 3-Tooth.'

'No money, man.'

'Ya don' need money if ya got charisma, 3-Tooth. All the world's a stage.'

'No charisma neither, man.'

3-Tooth looked through the doors at the distant counter. Fluorescent chips. Neon burgers. A plastic teat dispensing Coke. His taste-buds had been fitted out in salivating formica.

'Ya've give me an idea, Jimi.'

He pushed through the doors, lugged his guitar and amp down the aisle, and stood at the back of the longest queue. By the time he reached the counter he was ready to pass out.

'Big Mac, baby. Large fries. Maxi Coke.'

'That'll be two forty-six, please.'

The girl fetched his order and rang up the bill. His meal stood on the counter looking just like it did in the picture.

'That'll be two forty-six, please.'

'One moment, baby.'

3-Tooth pretended to go through his pockets. With his amp under his arm and his guitar between his legs it took him five minutes to reach his back zip-up. The girl gave him a rock-hard look. She'd seen this act before.

'Sorry 'bout this, baby. Seem to be a bit short.'

The queue behind him was getting angry.

'Look, tell ya what I'll do for ya, baby. How about I play for me dinner? I'll entertain these good people here while they're waitin' for their burger.'

He turned and faced the disbelieving queue behind him, switched up his amp, and played a riff that struck top E like a fork of lightning, and shuddered down the G string like it was a copper rod, to short-circuit the bass in A flat.

Outside on the main road, a lorry driver slammed his brakes, thinking he'd hit a cow.

'And the wind . . . howls . . . MAAAAAAAAAARY . . .'

'They're diggin' it, 3-Tooth,' whispered Jimi as the queue stood open-mouthed. 'Take 'em up, man.'

3-Tooth went down on one knee and began biting chords up and down the fret-board, short-circuiting his fillings, tottered, and leapt from his knees towards the stainless steel stage of the counter, narrowly failed to clear it, and cracked his forehead on the till where his two forty-six was still rung up. The girl hadn't seen this act before.

When he woke up in the alley out the back, he tasted blood and smelt smoke. But the blood was his own. And so was the smoke where the A string had scorched him. Jimi was nowhere to be seen.

eight

Summer's Wheel kept the work rolling in for Peach, so that he never had to renew his ad. Now he got jobs by reference, by word of mouth, or simply over the garden wall, sometimes working his way up one street from garden to garden. He put his hands to the Wheel, and his palms grew smooth with calluses. As his work improved, the swarm of sores on his hands vanished like flies in winter, leaving him with newborn knuckles. Bending over the mighty Wheel as it passed through the earth, his back grew browner than his chest, distinguishing his tan from the hedonist's, and he got a red neck. A little money came rolling in as well. 'It's made round to go round,' his Dad used to say in the days when a penny was as big as the rising sun. But now the Queen's coinage was far up in its midday zenith, and a pound coin didn't roll all that far. But Peach didn't mind. He felt that Summer's Wheel was turning him, both spiritually and physically, into one of Blake's 'golden builders': '. . . What are these Golden Builders doing? . . . is that mild Zion's hill's most ancient promontory, near mournful, ever-weeping Paddington? . . .'

In ever-together Hampstead, down by Fleet Road, Peach was building a brick shed on to the side of a house. It was a very small shed – about the size of a confessional box, four foot by four foot floorspace, eight feet high, with a corrugated roof of transparent PVC, to let the sky in and absolve the lawnmower of its manifold sins and wickedness. It was only a shed, with a narrow, creosoted door, but it was being built of second-hand yellow stocks, with ornamental courses of red engineering bricks, to match the fine large house. Its two bottom courses and its three coping courses were of this red engineering brick, both for ornamental effect, and to keep damp out of the walls. Peach had designed the door himself. And to keep it in proportion with the tiny frontage, had made the frame only one foot six inches wide. It was only when he was bricking up around it that he realised how big the lawnmower was, and that it might not get through it.

But Peach loved this little brick shed, and loved building it. He'd even added quarter-brick rebates at its two front corners, also of his own design, and at no extra cost to the customer, to give the shed a touch of English Perpendicular. The days were shortening. The Wheel was rolling him towards autumn and the birth of his child. And winter lay beyond. And as the single skin of brickwork rose round the skeletal door-frame, battened upright from the house wall, the door of his shed became the Gateless Gate, the Narrow Door, in which it was impossible to stand front on, into the darkness of Death, where the spiritual world came shining down through a PVC roof. As he wobbled on top of his customer's stepladder, bricking across its tiny wooden lintel on a quarter-inch iron, he imagined to himself the steep Gothic arch of the vestry door, into which Blake steps at the beginning of 'Jerusalem', with that strange disk-like lamp in his hand, into total darkness.

Peach was a slow bricklayer, who, after his morning medi- tation, got in about ten. And the days were getting shorter. Each night he would finally look up from his pointing to find the golden wall on which he was working vanished in the dark. The pointing had to be finished by touch, and spiritual insight. Then he had to find his tools, which were lying around wherever he'd dropped them during his frantic labours. And when he'd found them, he had to wash them. The water in his bucket was now as cold as the coming winter, and in his numb hands, his tools turned into prehistoric instruments – adzes, axes and flint shovels clogged with Stone Age cement; if he

176

didn't persevere some gnawing superstition told him they would all fossilise, and he would end up casting caves. Finally he wound his string, mortar-stiff and burning, into a ball, and, for the first time that day, looked up, and – his shed was gone! It had vanished! The night had swallowed it up, as though it too had stepped through Blake's vestry-door. He might as well have stayed in bed! Or spent the day meditating!

Then he looked again and, by the skin of his eyes, he saw – a building made of thought! Its bricks were memories aching in the palms of his hands. Its walls were dreams locked in his bones. Its door was a hole his heart would fear in his sleep. Its plumb vertical corners could be seen only by the still spirit-bubble in his brain. But they were plumb. One after the other, its horizontal courses had been rolled up into a ball of consciousness, like his string, by which he could now faintly see them again, out there in the nothingness. His vision expanded an eighth of an inch, and he saw the auras of two golden corners, an eighth of an inch beyond his own quarter-brick rebates, glowing in the darkness. And he knew they were the corners of *his* house, his own self-build, in Jerusalem, the holy City of God.

Then he covered the cement, put his tools in his roofless shed, and changed into his street clothes. Now he stood a moment, his arms outstretched blessing this garden, his customers, and his shed. Then, sticking to the material darkness in which this Spiritual City can be seen – as house lights came on all around him – Peach cut through the bustle of South End Green, and stepped into the even deeper darkness of Hampstead Heath, like Jude the Obscure, the dreaming stonemason, mental tools on his shoulder, and a rock of exhaustion on his back. Each night he walked to Golders Green, always following the same path.

Peach knew Hampstead Heath well. For seven years he'd used it for walking meditation and daydreaming. Following impulses that sprang from the stones and bushes themselves, he had plunged down thorn-tunnels known only to perverts and through silver-birch glades known only to lovers. But the

177

lovers and perverts only came out in good weather, of which there wasn't all that much – whereas Peach had been faithful to Hampstead Heath in rain, thunder and snow. He had wound his way through sapling screens into little untrodden pockets of eternity, where the grass had been flattened by courting angels. He had done the circuit a thousand times, turning pebbles in the path into Present Instants, on which he trod with all his weight now on one foot, now on the other, while Past and Future crashed through the undergrowth.

And by such years of loving attention, Peach had come to discover that Hampstead Heath had a spine. It was a living organism, in which a spine had formed. This was the path along the central ridge. It ran from the playground at the foot of Parliament Hill, up over the Hill, along the ridge, past the top gate of Ken Wood, through the trees, across the disused hockey field, over Hampstead Way, through the sinister swamps and leaf-bogs of the East Heath, around the blackest, stillest pond of all, and out on to North End Road, which ran down to Golders Green. Perhaps it had been a ley-line in prehistoric times. It ran essentially from south to north. From the top of the ridge you could see the skyscrapers and domes of the City, to the south. Down there Mr Phillips's steps stretched out for the night, exhausted. To the east were the spires of Highgate – at the foot of the hill, St Anne's delicate sandstone rocket – he'd built a pergola next door to that, and at the top of the hill, St Michael's, like an ivory and brick net-mender's needle – he'd put up a retaining wall of concrete gravel-boards just below there. To the west lay Hampstead, from Christ Church in the north, whose spire rang the quarter hours with a faithful bell – he'd lifted a yorkstone patio in that direction – to the Royal Free Hospital at the bottom of the hill, like a Great White Witch's Den of fluorescent healing, the church beside it, St Stephen's, a derelict battleship – that was where he was building his shed.

Yes, Peach believed that a ley, a line of power, ran through Hampstead Heath from south to north, which was the direction he took each night on his way home from work. The line didn't coincide with the present paths, but usually fell ten to twenty feet to the right of them. And along that straight and invisible path the grass hadn't grown summer or winter all the years that Peach had trodden it. Along other parts of the line, there was just a faint thinning of the turf and whitening of the clay beneath, which became an earthy glimmer, even on moonless nights, as though the spine of the Heath was indeed rising along this long-vanished spiritual bricklayer's line. Sometimes Peach even wondered if Christ's own feet hadn't trodden this path 'in ancient times', going home to Golders Green, turning the clay as white as his pierced feet.

Hampstead Heath was, in some sort of way, sacred to Peach. It wasn't just the smell of earth, stone, moss and wood. It wasn't just the solitary beauty of the trees. It was something more human – as though this most humanized piece of 'nature', plonk in the middle of Entuthon Benython, as Blake called the material London, this most loved and protected piece of earth, were beginning to take on a human form. This became apparent at night when the lovers and joggers, and most of the perverts, were gone, and the great white spine of its middle path rose through the clay and grass, and Peach, walking in pitch blackness, wasn't sure whether the light to see it by came from it or him. Perhaps one day, in the distant future, a whole man, who was at present just a backbone, a great white Cerne Giant, would rise up out of the Heath, fully erect, standing on Gospel Oak, carrying Hendon on his head, and walk straight up into the stars.

Along the spine-path of Hampstead Heath, as along all human spines, there were places of power, there were Centres. By the playground at the bottom of the Heath, to the south, he stopped and thought of his unborn child, whom he would bring here and push on the swings and coloured roundabouts. Even with the children gone and the gates locked, the asphalt still rang with their absent power, making the worn ecstasy-machines glow. This was the Place of Childhood. From the high ridge beyond Parliament Hill, he could see the lights of the City. At this Centre he stood with his arms crucifixate, if no one was watching, and willed that all the massive energy that was rearing up the material City of London should pass over into spiritual building – sheds, pergolas, crazy-paving . . . This was the Place of Creation. Where the path from Highgate to Hampstead crossed the spinal path, he raised his arms again and prayed to the Crucified Christ, whose crucifixion was, on some other dimension, still taking place, and came closer to men and women at points where paths crossed. This was the Place of Sorrow. By the gate at the top of Ken Wood, he stopped between two mighty tree-trunks and thought of Rudolf Steiner, Krishnamurti and William Blake, and drew their presence nearer. This was the Place of Teachers.

At the top of the hockey field, he stopped and thought of Morag, his earthly and his spiritual bride, and re-enacted their marriage – which hadn't actually been enacted in a church or registry office – by walking between two great beech trees, one of them a single trunk like a mighty lightning rod symbolising their separateness and individuality, the other a double trunk shaped like an eighty-foot-high tuning fork, which symbolised their jointness. This was the Place of Union. Then across Hampstead Way and through the sinister, unkept East Heath to the Heath's last spinal Centre – the still, black pond which signified Death. Here he always forced himself to stop, though this part of the Heath gave him the creeps and was the one most haunted by bikies and bovver boys. Like Death itself, the stagnant pond changed its colours more radically than the heath which surrounded it. In spring it was covered with green cress, as smooth and perfect as a bowling green, almost tempting you to walk on it. In summer it was a broth of chestnut pollen, a golden gruel. In autumn it was carpeted with leaves and on one moonlit night, practising his Tibetan Lung-gom walking at tremendous speed, eyes fixed on the moon and navigating by psychic instinct alone, Peach had mistaken one of his guide-trees, and walked up to his knees into Death's Pond, and gone home with frogs in his shoes. In winter, of course, it froze over. But always beneath its covering you could sense the deep black stillness. Peach loved this pond in spite of its spooky setting. He felt as if the Wheel of Time

180

had been cast in it, along with the branches and an old bicycle basket, and was rotting happily down there. He stood on the edge of it, flung back his head, and gave himself trustingly to whatever sense of annihilation a living organism is capable of. And the Divine Source always looked downwards at him through the waterlogged branches that overhung the stagnant pond, the Place of Death. Then he turned, one spiral, to wind the moment into his Heart, and off home. *That* was the moment he would bring home from work for his child when it was born. That would be his wage and his real gift.

It was a pitch-black, chilly night. Peach turned from the Place of Union, his heart beating, and plunged back into darkness. Though the stars were out he couldn't see a yard in front of him, for there was no moon. A faint frost crinkled the dry leaves of last autumn under his feet. He climbed the bank, slipped through the fluorescent unreality of Hampstead Way, weaving between two unseeing streams of headlights, and slid down the bank back into darkness. Before him was a chaotic pattern of trees and bogs. Dead branches lay on the ground. He stepped through them judiciously. Once he'd walked full-speed into a spider's web. But he knew his way almost without looking. He was heading for Death's Pond where he would stand on a particular spot, where the bank slipped level into the mud of the shallows. He would bend back his head, take one deep breath, and, for an instant, stop. From the ventricles of his beating heart to the thoughts pounding in his brain, he would stop dead. And let the Great Descent of Otherness strike him alive, bearing thoughts that would only wake later that night, in the depths of meditation. His heart trembled at it, but it was the most salutary act on Earth. For an instant the whole night would become a bottomless pond over which he hung by his feet. And God, who was always above him, would become Christ, the ancient pike, breaking the surface and fixing his brain in its jaws.

Peach was winding his way from tree to tree when he heard a sound coming from the blackness ahead of him. It was a human sound. And on a dark night, far from company, a human sound is the most menacing sound of all. He stopped and listened. Someone was whistling, over in the direction of Death's Pond. It was a jazzy whistle with accomplished trills and bluesy harmonies. Someone was embroidering a popular tune. But he couldn't make it out. Peach set off again, treading more quietly on the dry leaves. 'Probably someone whistling to keep their courage up . . .' Peach found himself earnestly wishing that whoever it was would be gone by the time he reached the pond. Though they had as much right to be here as he did. He sank into some squelchy leaf-mould, straddled a branch, and refound his way. He was getting closer to the whistling, which grew louder and louder. The unseen whistler was hotting up the tune now with Thelonius Monk bird-calls, till Peach could almost see the great Adam's apple working. And suddenly, for no reason, he became afraid of this man. He pushed on through the darkness. By now, whoever it was must have heard the crashing leaves of Peach's approach, yet the whistling betrayed no apprehension. Peach's guts turned over. The only people who came out on the Heath on nights like this were mystics and psychopaths. He'd always fancied he was safe, alone in the dark, and his chances of being mugged were less than in certain streets, but it only took one unlucky encounter and he could be lying beside Death's Pond with his throat slit. Of course, he could always slip by, veer to the right of the pond, over the ridge, and beat it towards North End Road. But that meant bypassing the Sacred Spot, and surrendering the most potent moment of his walk. And, deeper, it would betray his fear, which might be the very trigger that released the brutality he could hear beneath this jazzy warbling, and set a dark, silent figure crashing through the scrub behind him.

The next moment Peach recognised the tune and caught his breath. He knew the words – 'This is the dawning of the Age of Aquarius, the Age of Aquariuuuuuuus . . .' God. It was probably some old freak, long-crazed by acid. The next moment, he saw the figure in front of him, standing where he usually stood to greet the Divine Source. And Peach saw Death in a human body: a body so thick and heavy it seemed a living opacity superimposed on the night. Six feet tall, wide shoulders, hands in pockets, legs apart, boots planted firmly in the mud. He was looking straight at Peach and hadn't stopped whistling. He might be welcoming the Age of Aquarius, but the cold whistle keened round his Adam's apple like a blade. If there were forces of Spiritual Love pulsing through the universe, then there were also dark beings, celebrants of matter, dragging Divine Humanity down into matter's rot-hole. Peach stopped dead and stood face to face with a God of 'cold obstruction', possibly with a knife in his pocket. He clung to the one straw's chance that it was just a night-stroller like himself, and walked up to the tall, black figure.

'Nice clear evening,' he remarked, and heard his voice shake.

The whistling stopped.

'Don't I know dat voice?' said a powerful voice that Peach also knew.

'Fergus O'Fury?'

'De very same. 'Tis Peach O'Hare, is it not?'

'Yes. Yes. What on earth are you doing here?'

'Sure I'm lookin' for de rileway.'

After a flush of relief, Peach felt his fear unexpectedly return. Perhaps he was drunk and the danger in him was rising to the surface. There was something in the way he spoke the word 'rileway' that chilled Peach's heart.

'You're a long way out,' he said hastily. 'The nearest tube's Golders Green. But it's almost a mile down the hill, in that direction.'

'No, I'm tryin' t' find de new rileway. De one dat runs trew dis pond.'

He spoke like a Daemon of Matter, raising a railway across Hampstead Heath where Peach was raising a human spine. He waved his arm vaguely along Peach's ley-line, in the direction of Hendon Central.

'There's no railway line here, Fergus. Are you okay?'

'Sure dere's no rileway line here. But there will be. For I'm buildin' it.'

Peach was outraged.

'You can't build a railway across Hampstead Heath.'

'Who said anything about buildin' over it? Sure 'twill run more stritely *under* it.'

'An underground line?'

'I'm an excavatin', man, Peach. 'Tis me greatest hole. 'N if I'm not trown by dese trees, dis pond is directly over us. For we've had a nip of seepage hereabouts.'

But Peach could not still the helpless outrage or the churn of terror in him. Every time he walked across the Heath, into the bodiless Depths, he would remember the underground rattling somewhere under his feet, the fluorescent, aluminium tube sucking the marrow out of his sacred earth. And if he was robbed of his nightly pilgrimage, his spiritual life would lose, not only a heart-stilling peace, but its very backbone.

'How deep are you going?'

'Hundred, hundred and fifty foot, someting like dat.'

Fergus bent back his head as if to check the line of his railway by the stars. And Peach, standing beside him, took the opportunity to fling back his own head and search desperately for the Divine Source in the night above.

'Sure, dat's a fine piece of excavatin',' said Fergus, staring past the Plough.

He pulled a scrap of grimy envelope from his pocket and thrust it in front of Peach's nose in the starlight. Peach saw a wavering pencil line running up and down crinkles in the paper, and disappearing into a large black stain, round like the bottom of a glass, which may have been this very pond, and emerging the other side of it, and carrying on to the gluey edge of the flap. A cross at one end of the line read CAMDEN TOWN. A cross at the other end, HENDON CENTRAL. Along the line were another three crosses, marked JACK STRAW'S CASTLE, SPANIARDS, and HARE AND HOUNDS.

'I'm sure 'tis directly under our boots. For dat's Hampstead Station just down dere, is it not?'

Fergus pointed in the direction of Golders Green.

'No, no,' said Peach, pointing in the opposite direction. 'That's Hampstead back there. About a mile.'

'Be Jaysus,' cried Fergus, turning the envelope round and round. 'Flippin' engineers. Give ye a sketch, tink dey're Jose Picasso. Dey don't have t' read de fockin' ting. Over dere?'

'Yes,' said Peach.

'Well, come wit me, den, 'n I'll show ye such a hole as ye won't see till yer lyin' in yer own!'

Fergus chuckled, and gobbed in Death's Pond, which opened an eye of concentric wrinkles, took them in, and, rippling outwards, shut again. Peach stood stock still. The black pond had opened. He had entered. And it had shut again. Though he still stood dry on its bank. But he was dead. His will had gone. Fergus was crashing away through the undergrowth in the direction Peach had pointed a moment before. But now he was lost.

'Come on den.'

Rather than be left in the dark, Peach followed him.

He rustled through the leaves in a dream. He had already entered the Earth. This darkness was the Darkness under the Earth. The twigs that caught at his face were nerves swaying on the ends of mighty roots. But now he knew that the Earth had many strata, and he might well go down for ever and ever. When they emerged into the street-lights by Jack Straw's Castle, Peach's dream only deepened. And, under street-lamps and pub signs, they descended a still lower tunnel of reality. They walked silently down Heath Street till they saw the London Transport logo, glowing above Hampstead Station, a blue and red ferry-light at the end of a dream jetty. They went in, and Fergus led Peach through the ticket barrier and down the spiral stair to the platforms far below. They walked along the northbound platform, where a train to Colindale was advertised on the ancient indicator. The living waited in Limbo. But he was being shipped along this promontory of

185

soiled fluorescence towards the bottomless tunnels of Eternity. He would never see Morag again. He had missed his child in the passage between life and the Beyond, like two trains passing at a station, the doors of one only opening when the other's doors had closed. He was inexpressibly sad. The air smelled of burnt hair.

He waited with the big fellow by a plywood door at the end of the tiled beach. On the door was stencilled O FURY. So this was it. He had missed out on Heaven. Heaven was just the daydream of living men. Only the underworld was real. And God's own fury. The big man opened the door and Peach descended a precipitous shaft, on steps of scaffold board, clutching a scaffold pole rail, bare bulbs above his head. He thought he would descend for ever. Yet gradually, from below, came a roar which grew louder the further he went down. The ultimate nature of Matter is self-destruction. And here, with the pulse of Spirit gone, he heard the Earth gnawing her own vitals. He shuddered. Fergus descended ahead of him.

They stepped out of the shaft into a long, low cavern, passing from right to left. On the wall opposite there was a life-size portrait of the Pope. Peach wasn't surprised to see him here. His hand was raised in blessing, the forefinger pointing upwards at a crack above his head in the concrete ceiling of the tunnel. Peach saw the look of terror in the Pontiff's beaming face, as a train rumbled somewhere overhead and a little rubble shook from the crack. Two soiled white snakes throbbed on the floor of the tunnel. One was glutted with the sewagey weeping of the Earth, with underground lakes and pockets of ooze, which it defecated in Camden Town. The other was gorged with ready-mixed concrete which it regurgitated forwards into the darkness towards Hendon. Beyond the snakes, a flatworm bearing clay and broken bed-rock on its back, turned endlessly upon rollers, yearning for freedom, but drawn, for its eternal punishment, into a rattling uroborus.

'Sure 'tis a fine sight, is it not?' said Fergus rubbing his hands together.

Peach pressed himself in terror against the side of the cavern.

186

For two steel whips had been riveted to the cavern floor, beyond the Worm, up which a fleet of tiny barques was trundling like sadistic thoughts on iron wheels, bearing objects of torment for the minds of the dead. On the first barque a crate of gelignite came bumping past. On the second, sixty crates of stout and a harp. On the third barque, a whale's rib of perfectly curved steel. On the fourth was a coffin and a statue of the Madonna of the Rocks. The fifth barque was empty.

'Come along den. Jump.'

But Peach still pressed himself against the wall in terror of the wheels, and the big man had to drag him bodily on board as the barque clanked past. Now they rode royally up the intestine of the Earth. Fergus waved to dead men in donkey jackets, who tipped their livid yellow helmets to him as he passed. They stared straight through Peach as he clung to the tail-gate of the barque. In a ventilator shaft a dozen pairs of reeking socks hung on a string. Peach peered into the shaft. He saw row upon row of iron bedsteads and soiled mattresses. Deathly snores and pallid toe-twitchings fought their way like signs of life after a blanket bombing, from the colossi wound in grey bedspreads who slept on them. Under one pillow Peach glimpsed a box of eggs and a jar of honey. Under one of the mattresses, a pack of cards, a plate and a knife. Then as his eyes grew accustomed to the gloom, they made out pictures of naked women in grotesque postures, their genitals censored by a black hole that may have been Fergus's logo. The pin-ups fluttered on the walls of the shaft like vultures above the smoking rubble of men.

'Who are they?' asked Peach.

'De night shift,' said Fergus.

They trundled on. Dotted like ulcers of darkness in the Earth's colon, low safety niches were set into the tunnel wall for workmen to step into when the trains came past. In each of these sat a priest, head leant despairingly against the already-blackened concrete, absolution shawl as grey as powdered flint. Penitent navvies knelt on the blue-metal outside

187

the niches, telling the beads of their rosaries to clay balls with their work-soiled fingers, telling and retelling their sins now that they were dead and past mending them. The names of hideous acts clanked past like freight trucks. Impure thoughts coupled into long trains. But what sin could a man commit down here where the brain is dead? And where Fergus had banned newspapers, radios and teles, and so scrambled their sense of time they were tunnelling a fortnight ahead of pay-day.

They rounded another bend and came upon a public bar as long as the platform of an underground station. The drinkers leant abjectly on the counter as though millions of feet were already walking over them into the tube of the Future. Except for the clanking of the barques and the rattling of the rollers, the bar was dead silent. The barmen walked up and down the counter shovelling empties into skips, kicking awake those dreamers who had fallen asleep in their pint. The tunnel-like walls of this long bar were tiled with mirrors in which had been etched portraits of legendary pints garlanded in Botticelli froth, and brawls from the Mabinogion. Her long gut lined with mirrors, the Earth saw that her despair was human. Down the whole length of the bar, gigantic bottles were bolted to the wall, spirits bound upside down in Hell, their heads jammed in measuring plungers. As round as the full moon and as disconnected, the platform clock had already been installed. It hung above the carousers' heads at an eternal 10.59 – Last Orders!

They passed out of the bar as abruptly as they had entered. The tunnel grew narrow and dark, the lights sporadic. The roar that had accompanied them the whole way grew terrifyingly loud. Its source lay ahead of them, and high above it, screaming like the cry of a cut worm amplified unbearably. Men in masks gazed into little icy-blue infernos, their private Hells. They entered a low space under the Earth's rusting ribs, lit by arc-lamps swaying like flowers, in which navvies lifted shadow shovels to split his head open. And then Peach saw the Earth's Heart. It was Matter gnawing itself endlessly. It was the steel the Earth gave up returned to torment its ore in the shape of a gigantic digging machine. A Heart the size of a locomotive, roaring loud enough to power the globe. And there, like Anxiety spiralling out of itself to gouge itself, was a vast drill-bit shaped like an awl, as high as the tunnel, turning its endless screw into black Matter, which is nothing but Despair. It must have been Hardened Despair, for the spiral sent back mashed flint and powdered diamond, which dropped on to the Worm's back as it yearned southwards.

Fergus lifted Peach from the barque as it trundled round a hundred and eighty-degree turn and set off back towards Camden Town. Then he jumped down himself. They stood behind the monstrous machine. A corpse was strapped to the driver's seat, spinning a wheel. But whether he was actually steering the digger, or his arms were simply swinging to the jolts and jars, Peach couldn't tell.

'Keep it strite,' roared Fergus and the corpse paled.

'How do you know what's straight?' asked Peach, trying to make conversation. For Fergus, who was rubbing his hands together and affectionately kicking the engine's tread, seemed bent on making a social occasion of it.

'Strite's strite. Hendon Central's dat way.' And he pointed at the black rock through which the bit was turning.

'But don't you have surveyors?'

'Surveyors t' fock. Quibblin' ye about shiftin' strata 'n de like. Dey don't know what dey're talkin' about.'

'But what about instruments?'

'De only instrument I got's up here.' Fergus tapped his reddened forehead. Then he roared at the driver, 'Ye're sheerin' left. Keep it strite!'

''Tis gettin' rough, Mr O'Fury.'

The driver's voice was not human. He shouted above the din in a fleshy whisper, as though his tongue hung in a bottle of formaldehyde.

All at once the drill hit something solid. The engine gave an earth-shuddering lurch backwards, and Peach thought he was going to be crushed. Lumps of clay and little pebbles were falling on his head. The machine surged forward, and hit the solid thing, forcing the drill-bit at it, till the screw-shaft itself began to shudder and bow, lifting the whole machine off the ground and spiralling off a foot of the tunnel roof. Peach saw fragments of molten drill-bit being passed back down its own corkscrew, to drop on the Worm that winced like burnt rubber. The digger sunk back.

'Strite,' roared Fergus. 'Keep it goin'.'

The digger heaved itself forwards again, but was driven back a third time.

'We've 'it someting solid, Mr O'Fury,' whispered the driver.

'Don't you lecture me about solid,' Fergus screamed at him. 'Dere ain't no solid in dis Eart I haven't been trew. Pick up yer shovels dere, 'n get up here.'

A crowd of navvies grey with the dust that was cascading from the tunnel roof, gathered round the machine.

'Switch dat ting off.'

When the digger stopped, the silence under the Earth boomed.

''Tis some monstrous ting, Mr O'Fury,' ventured the driver.

The clay boots of the navvies shuffled anxiously. Peach's terror had left him inert.

'Sure 'tis only Satan's bum,' said Fergus sarcastically.

'Satan's arsehole, Satan's arsehole, Satan's arsehole . . .' whispered the navvies, digging their shovels into the clay on which they stood. And Peach found himself shouting amongst them. Their voices scuttled back down the tunnel like the skeletons of mice rolled over and over by their own breath. Workmen came from further down the tunnel to look.

'Let's have a look at it den. You men dere!'

Peach found that he had a shovel in his hands. He was pushed forward in the press of navvies. They scraped and beat at the adamantine thing that had repulsed the machine, and exposed a concrete wall.

'Wot de fock,' roared Fergus. He walked up to the wall as if he were going to lay one on it. He took this concrete face as a personal insult.

The navvies cleaned off the clay. The wall filled the radius of their tunnel. They looked longingly at the well-cast concrete.

'P'haps we should leave it alone, Mr O'Fury,' whispered the driver. ''Tis a monstrous big pale bum!'

Peach too found himself staring in terror at the concrete wall.

Fergus kicked it.

'Get dem kangos up. Fetch de gelignite. We're goin' t' blast it.'

'Mr O'Fury—'

'My holes are strite!'

Six corpses with kangos came forward and began drilling at the wall. Time stood still. Peach himself forgot whether it was day or night above him. Inch by inch the bits sunk into the concrete, till at last they'd made six six-foot cavities. These were packed with gelignite. Meanwhile the digger and other machinery had been withdrawn round the last corner. The charges were wired. All the navvies had disappeared. The explosives men unwound their cable, and they too disappeared. Only Fergus remained at the wall, and Peach, who was too frightened to leave him. Fergus was still staring belligerently at the concrete face, as though his eyes alone could drill through it and see what was on the other side. He seemed to have forgotten about the dynamite. He kicked aside tangled cable as he paced up and down the wall. Peach's heart thumped. He'd only been having a quiet walk home across the Heath, and now he was standing a hundred and fifty feet under the ground in front of a loaded wall. And the worst of it was that, being dead, he should have had no fear of a wall exploding in his face. But he did. It was a dread beyond a living man's fear of death. The wall was Time. And the explosion, when it ripped his face off, would last for ever. He hated Fergus O'Fury for dragging him into this fight. He hated his ignorant belligerence, the self-glorifying brawn in his head. Fergus spat at the concrete, but it said nothing. He rammed a protruding stick of gelignite in with his fist, but the wall did not react. Fergus smiled, the sickening smile of the victor.

191

'C'm on.'

Peach followed him back round the bend. There was a moment's complete silence. Then a terrific WHOOOMPF.

They waited for the dust to clear, then peered round the bend. The charge had blown a narrow hole, six feet high and three feet wide, through the wall. The dead navvies stared at it in terror and wouldn't budge, even when Fergus bellowed at them. So Fergus walked the hundred feet up to the wall by himself. For a moment Peach wavered, between the company of the terrified dead and the living ignoramus, then hurried after Fergus. They stood before the hole. Its mouth was large enough for a man to walk into. But they stopped dead. For though they were deep underground, a chink of light shone through from the other side.

'Wot t' fock's dat?' Fergus asked Peach. 'Ye don't tink de Prince o' Darkness shites light?'

Peach stared helplessly.

Fergus spat nonchalantly at the concrete and pushed his way in. Peach followed. The hole got narrower. The light was coming from about twelve feet in front of them now. As the hole closed around them, Fergus had to shoulder aside lumps of concrete and bend back twisted rods. Soon he was digging with his bare hands, passing the rubble back to Peach. Although the explosion had only opened a gap as big as a thumbnail in the far side of the wall, it had loosened the concrete enough for them to dig up to it. At last they were lying on their bellies an inch from the chink.

''Tis not hot light,' said Fergus hopefully. 'Ye have a look den.'

Through the chink ahead of them they could see what looked like a room. There were three layers of lead behind the wall which Fergus tore aside with his teeth.

'Must be havin' trouble wit de damp,' the big man muttered.

He butted with his head. The wall collapsed inwards, and they climbed out into a fitted kitchen. They knew it was a kitchen because it had a sink, and a bowl of fruit on the round, pine table. The walls were tiered with identical doors like the side of a scrumbled dunny truck, so you couldn't tell the stove from the fridge.

A great hunger came over them in this soothing place.

Fergus hunted for the fridge. Peach looked round for the vegetable rack. Fergus picked a peach up from the table and took a ravening bite. He gagged, a tooth-chattering choke, and spat out silicon and plastic.

'Wot de fook?'

The peach had a little label.

'IF YOUR GEIGER-PEACH LOSES ITS FRESHNESS,' Peach read, 'CHECK ALL FILTRATION SYSTEMS. IF IT TURNS BLACK, FOLLOW THE EMERGENCY PROCEDURE.'

Fergus found the fridge. It was full of tablets, packaged in cards, blue for food, red for drink. Fergus took out a twelve-pack of Guinness pills.

'CARE MUST BE TAKEN TO SUCK SLOWLY. ONLY ONE TABLET AT A TIME.'

Fergus popped all twelve into his palm, shovelled them into his mouth, went cross-eyed, and crashed blissfully into the sink.

'Sure, 'tis not too bad, dis contraceptive pint!'

Some need for absolute comfort, a comfort greater than either of them had known in their life above ground, greater than hunger, drove them through where the wall had been knocked out and arched, into the living room. It was lined with books on one wall, compact discs on another, and videos on the third. There were no windows to break these dykes of culture. Fergus scoured the videos. Peach went through the books. All his favourite authors were here: Krishnamurti, Rudolf Steiner, Salman Rushdie. And *Mein Kampf* and the ninety-three volume *Men Only* omnibus. For there was something dreadfully comprehensive in this wall of books.

'Be Jaysus, look at dis,' said Fergus taking down, from beside *Mazeppa, Massacre at Murphy's Hole*, 'I tink 'tis from de Mabinogion.'

They hunted for the video, suddenly desperate to see *Massacre at Murphy's Hole*, pulling back the sofa, shifting lampstands, peering down the back of the central heating, growing more and more angry till Peach looked up.

'Jesus, look at that.'

The plaster rose had been removed, the light-fitting was gone, for, like the Sistine Chapel, the whole ceiling was one vast video screen, framed in the original Victorian mouldings. They lay on their backs on the berber carpet and pulled the switch string. Unable to find the machine to slot in *Massacre at Murphy's Hole*, they'd just have to watch what the owner had on. The lights dimmed, and they heard music. It was the theme of the Rhinegold, where it reappears to overwhelm the Hall of the Gods in the *Götterdämmerung*. The screen flickered greyly. At first Peach thought it was footage of a World War Two newsreel. But wait a second, that was the Post Office Tower that stood, snapped like a Doric pillar, amongst the rubble of Oxford Street. Then faces, burned to white fists, poking swiftly at the screen. Then a long, slow-panning shot of devastated countryside, shredded trees, an upturned fence, a climbing frame like the skeleton of a tank. But Peach knew the contours, the geological silhouette of Hampstead Heath well enough to know that this was where he'd been walking only an hour ago. Switch to a scuttle of blast-whitened rats on a railway platform. They were watching the Future! And it went on and on, spiralling outwards through suburban streets, hibernating in heaps with cockeyed noticeboards in German, Turkish, Urdu, as the corpse of Siegfried was carried to Valhalla.

A strange warmth came over them. A deep satisfaction that combined the trembling relief of narrowly escaping an injury with a profound megalomania that lapped, swooned, swole, swept outwards and outwards like Wagner's theme for the End of the World. Peach forgot Morag, and his coming child. Fergus forgot his family of eight and his workforce of eight thousand. For they were the last two human beings left on earth.

They may have lain there for ever except the scavenging voyeuristic hand on the camera-handle moved their eyes to the most spectacular shot of all – a vast hole, bottomlessly black, buildings crumbling from its lip, where the first missile had hit.

'Jaysus, dere's a fine piece o' diggin',' whispered Fergus in his trance.

The word roused him. 'Diggin' dragged him from the carpet. He shook his head. He remembered his own hole. He shook Peach awake and drove him into the kitchen.

'Get dat fookin' digger goin',' he roared through the hole. 'Jaysus, I'm not payin' ye t' pick de clay from yer boots. Get dem shovels and get up here!'

And a moment later the great digger was screwing into the kitchen.

The shed was finished. The two side walls were eight feet high. The parapet of red engineering bricks was ornamental: consisting of a half-brick alternating with a full brick laid as a stretcher would be in a nine-inch wall. But because this was only a four and a half inch wall, it meant that the stretcher projected a quarter-brick on either side of the tiny parapet giving it a fine crenellated effect. Because the top three courses were of red engineering bricks, to contrast with the yellow stocks below, the little shed faced the heavens proudly and elegantly, a distant relative of Queens' College Cambridge. The transparent PVC roof was pitched from back to front, where the wall was lower, and overhung the eighteen-inch door by the quarter-brick length of the rebate. Slate would have looked better, matching both the brick and Peach's dreams of the shed, but then it would have been pitch-black inside, and his customer would not have been able to tell his lawnmower from his deck-chairs. It would have taken a quarter of an hour's groping to find his secateurs. The structure was too small to warrant a window, even the narrowest medieval slit, and to supply electricity would have been pushing the little shed into the realms of the pretentious. So clear, corrugated PVC it was. At least it let in the light from the right direction. It faced God.

There was only one problem with the shed now: the brickwork was up, the door was on, the roof was in place – but where the corrugated plastic of the roof met the brickwork there was an often sizeable gap caused by the unevenness of the old bricks. Whenever it rained, water would run down the inside of the shed, as if it were God's urinal, rusting the lawnmower, mildewing the deck-chairs and perhaps leading his customer to sue him. Peach had foreseen this problem. If the roof were slate, there would have been no trouble: he could have haunched the joint with cement. But he couldn't do this on PVC. Sooner or later, the haunching would crack, or just slide off. Tying felt or lead flashing into the joints of the brickwork, to overlap the roof, would have been time-consuming and still dodgy, as the wall was only one brick thick, and to lose a third of this four and a half inches to the non-bonding flashing would have weakened the joint. But for the gap between roof and wall – at points an inch and a half wide – the shed was finished, and he could be paid and off to his next job.

He covered the joint with sylglass, but it was already peeling off before he got to the bottom of the ladder. What he needed was a totally waterproof substance that adhered better than cement. Bitumen! It would stick both to the brick wall and the plastic, and seal the crack. But he had no idea how to use the stuff. The closest he'd ever come to bitumening was Book One of *Paradise Lost*. Outside Hell, you needed a cooker: a special bucket with a spout, on its own ring, and a couple of gas-bottles to burn under it. Which was expensive to hire and hard to get into a taxi.

In the corner of the garden was a pile of old timber left over from his building work, and waiting to be burnt and his customers, luckily, had gone away for a long weekend. The answer to his problem had been presented to him. He went down the hardware shop and bought a galvanised bucket. Then he went to Asphaltic, the biggest suppliers of bitumen and asphalt in North London. Their depot was on old railway land, a quarter of a mile off the main road, past garages and warehouses. Trucks towing asphalt-bubbling cauldrons steamed and smoked past him as he trudged down the barren track to the same yard. Builders' vans, and the big Asphaltic lorries themselves, unloading blocks of asphalt, enough to build a castle of tar.

'What's the smallest amount of bitumen you do?' asked Peach at the counter.

'A keg.'

'How much is in a keg?'

'A keg's a keg.'

'You don't do half kegs, or quarters?'

'No, mate. Waddaya want?'

'A keg please.'

He was sent outside with a receipt in his hand. Thirty-two quid! That was today's profit gone. But it was too late to turn back now.

He handed over the receipt and was led to a pile of large, dense, black barrels, wrapped round in brown paper. The barrels didn't contain anything. For the barrels were themselves what they contained. That is, they were bitumen cast in this shape when it was molten, and now solidified. These were kegs – the sort they had at barbecues beside the Styx.

'Where's your motor, mate?' asked the yardman kindly.

'Oh . . . er, I . . . um . . . left it up on the main road,' said Peach waving vaguely towards Kentish Town Road. '. . . It's all right, mate, too much trouble to bring it in now. I'll . . . I'll . . . take it up on my shoulder.'

The yardman looked at him incredulously.

'All right, mate.'

He stood Peach where the kegs were stacked three and four high. He chose one that was about Peach's shoulder height, and toppled it gently on to his shoulder. Peach's knees buckled and began to meander backwards across the yard. No one would imagine from just looking at them that they could be so heavy. He tossed the keg a fraction of an inch on his shoulder – to get it straight – and crashed into a post.

'You okay, mate?'

'Yes, fine,' gasped Peach. 'Just point me towards Kentish Town Road.'

Peach staggered out past the office, threading between the high axles of the customers' lorries. Trucks hooted as they roared past him with their three tons of asphalt already cooking. Peach was trembling with exhaustion. But he dare not put down his keg. For once down, he would never get it back on his shoulder. At last he reached the road and hailed a taxi. He laboured the keg into the back of the cab as gently as possible and collapsed into the back seat. He'd done a day's work already but was losing money faster than ever. He was also terrified that the keg would leave its dunny-painted smell in the back of the cab. Or damage the suspension. Or simply melt all over the floor before he got back to his job. But it didn't, and the driver didn't seem to mind having it on board, and even chatted to Peach about the art of bitumening. Peach gratefully tipped him a fifth of his non-existent profit. Money was flowing out of him like blood from a wound. But at least he had his bitumen on site. It was eight times more than he needed. But he didn't care. He was a bitumener at last. He was proud of his keg.

He piled the wood up in the corner of the garden and lit it. The only place to make his fire without killing the lawn was under an old oak tree. But its lowest bough was a good fifteen feet above the ground. That should be all right. The wood was dry and soon he had a good fire going. He let it blaze for a while to build up heat. Then when the flames began to die down, he sat his bucket on the white-hot embers. He tore the brown paper off the keg and tried to gouge some bitumen out of it with his trowel. But the keg was as hard as a black, glassy rock. He went for it with his clubhammer. For his bucket, now black on the outside, was red-hot within and the bottom was showing signs of falling out. With furious hammering he chipped off enough slivers and flakes of bitumen to half fill the bucket. That should be enough to do the roof. He chucked them in, and they immediately turned into a chuckling black liquid. Peach felt like chuckling too. His bitumening was going to be a success. This was probably the ancient way of doing it. Ancient and cheap!

Soon the bitumen was bubbling fiercely. But the strange thing was that it had reached a point where, no matter how fiercely the liquid spat and bubbled, the lumps in it would melt no further. And more worrying still, the bitumen that *was* molten seemed to be evaporating. Peach found a long steel reinforcing rod with a hook at one end and stirred and prodded the black liquid. But it was no use. The lumps still wouldn't go away. The bitumen that was molten would have sizzled away to nothing before he'd kneaded them out. He needed more heat. He threw an armful of wood on the fire. The flames swelled up around the bucket. But still the lumps wouldn't go away, no matter how much he ground them into the bottom of the bucket, which seemed to have grown softer than they were. He threw on more wood. The flames were now standing a foot above the rim of the bucket. The bitumen inside was popping and cracking like a whip. He stirred faster and faster – a black vortex in the centre of a fire.

Then all at once the embers settled, the bucket tilted, and a single flame jumped in. Just one – he saw it. For a moment this flame danced alone like a sylph on the black lake of Hell. The next instant there was a mighty whoompf, like a mortar going off. And the bucket hurled a rocket of dense black smoke, ten, fifteen, twenty feet up into the branches of the oak tree. But unlike an ordinary mortar, this rocket of smoke didn't go away. It didn't fly off from the bucket to some distant target in Belsize Park. The column of pitchy smoke stayed standing in the bucket pulsing and billowing like a black flamethrower and threatening a still greater explosion. It stayed as fixed as a baby devil who's got his head stuck in a bucket farting furious black smoke, all howling fire within. Neighbouring windows opened, then closed again. The woman next door sprinted for her washing, then thought better of it and dived for cover. It was Black Friday in Downside Crescent. Washing would be taken in dark and bituminous-smelling for half a mile around. The leaves of the oak tree recoiled, burning. Peach desperately poked his shepherd's crook through the smoke, and after several tries, caught hold of the white-hot bucket handle. He lifted the whole contraption from the fire. But instead of dying down, it only shot the smoke up a few feet higher. Peach let go of it and ran to find something to put it out. He had sand out in front, or there was water from the garden tap. The tap was closer, so he chose water.

He filled his builder's bucket from the tap and sloshed back down the garden, spilling half of it. The rest he threw into the bucket of burning bitumen. And a strange and terrible thing happened. The black smoke vanished in a trice but the fire did not go out. In its place stood a column of light, like a sparkling electrical storm reaching twenty feet up out of a bucket. It roared and sparked. A million little electric stars crackled open up and down its spine. It was like seeing Kundalini herself. It was beautiful, and out of control and reaching up into the tree. The first branch was already alight. Peach pulled his hair and danced on the spot. It might explode at any moment and blow him into next door's garden. And still the column of light towered above him, bellowing, as though Satan, smoky, churlish, eructating, had turned into shining Lucifer, electric bed-bugs running up and down his spine, and showing no sign of ever going out. And he Peach had done it.

Then he remembered – sand. Of course! Sand. He ran to the front and brought some through. As soon as he threw it into the bucket, the geyser subsided as if it had been put to sleep. He glanced round nervously in the sudden silence. Up to this point, he had enjoyed good relations with his customers' neighbours. Thank God his customers were away. But was the fire brigade already coming? He could hear no sirens. The tree went out.

In fact, the sand he'd thrown into the bucket made a nice

workable mixture with what bitumen was left. And it was still molten-hot. He hurried back up the garden with the bucket bouncing on the end of his rod, took his trowel in his teeth, and holding the bucket as close to him as he dared, climbed the ladder to his PVC roof. He took a dripping, bubbling trowelful and ran it along the joint between the wall and the roof. It adhered to the brickwork all right, but the plastic melted away like water.

M R STAG and his friend stood outside the door of Peach and Morag's squat. His friend carried a sledgehammer with which he playfully tapped at the crumbling parapet which surrounded the porch, careful not to get dust on his shiny shoes.

'Come on, come on,' yelled Mr Stag at the rotting door which Peach had painted sanyasi saffron, as though the decrepit old house had taken up the robe.

Mr Stag hammered at the door with his fist and several large flakes of saffron fell off.

'Come on, come on, you cowardly cunts! Open the door or I'll break it bloody down.'

'Squwattas,' observed his friend.

'I ask you – havin' t' break me own flamin' door down!'

'They ain't human, Malc. Drugs 'nd sex's all they think about.'

'Okay, Maurice,' said Mr Stag. 'Give it a crack with the sledge. Makes me bleedin' sick it does.'

Maurice stepped from his corner. He looked at the saffron door. It'd be all over in Round One. He gave it a clubbing right hook with his fifteen-pound sledgehammer and nearly drove his arms from their sockets. This door had no glass chin. It juddered, but stood firm. And like a true Buddhist, it didn't hit back. Only a few more sections of saffron dropped off.

'Bleedin' animals,' said Mr Stag's left-hand man, as he jabbed the top hinge with his sledge.

Martha, Peach and Morag were out. The house was empty. Peach's piano was still halfway up the stairs. It was three weeks since Tiger had got it there, and it had been getting harder and harder for Morag to climb around it, as her belly swole. Peach had sawn off the banisters from the piano up to the top of the house, as Arthur had told him to, but had left the lower ones to climb on. For three weeks he'd been desperately trying to get hold of Arthur. But Arthur was on holiday in Spain, due back any day. It must have been a good holiday, for the days had turned into weeks with no sign of him. But worst of all was the brick – the single brick that held the piano up. It was crumbling visibly under its monstrous weight. Peach had tried to drive wedges under the piano for extra support. But when he did this, the step splintered, the piano trembled, and a little more dust fell out of the brick. Peach and Morag climbed more and more carefully round the suspended piano, which now shuddered every time they passed and if someone slammed the front door, began to echo ominously.

'I mean what gets up my nose,' said Mr Stag as he tried an upper-cut to the bottom hinge with his shoe, 'is, they ain't got no respect for property.'

'Too much Tayo of Sex, Malc. Not enough honest work. Did you see some of them pictchas?'

The sledgehammer thudded into the door in lightning combinations of shots. The door staggered and sagged at the knees, its eyes went glassy and it swallowed its gum-shield down its letter-box, but wouldn't go down. The only thing that continued to fall was the paint, which hadn't been properly primed, and there was now a little pile of it, like a saffron towel, on the doorstep.

Inside the house the walls were shaking. Little stones were falling out of the brick and tumbling down the stairs with lumps of plaster from the ceiling. Peach's great black Lutheran upright was shuddering from its castors to its music rack and the echoes and janglings in its black sound-box were turning into a ghastly music.

'Give the lock a belt, Maurice,' said Mr Stag.

It was good advice from the corner. Peach had fitted the lock himself. Going for a last round knock-out, the sledgehammer passed straight through it, as the cartridge flew out, and the door crashed into the ropes – the stairs inside. Mr Stag and his friend stood in the doorway and looked up.

Three quarters of a ton of piano, cased in grim black mahogany, its loud pedal playing, its music rack flailing wildly, was hurtling down the stairs at them, launched, it seemed, from the first-floor landing down the cliff of steps.

'The cunts,' whispered Mr Stag in the moment's realisation before the piano passed through the door.

His friend screamed and leapt aside and backwards, over the wall into the hotel yard. Mr Stag turned, a second behind him, and seemed to run, with a sprinter's high-elbowed action, straight out into the air beyond the parapet, with the piano on his heels, thundering like Liszt's coffin, its strings, pedals, hammers and lid crashing to an inhuman crescendo.

Mr Stag continued out into mid-air, and landed in the street. The piano smashed into the parapet, knocking out a section of bricks and lodging perilously in what was left of the wall, half out over the pavement.

When Peach came home from work that night, he found the front door wide open, the house empty, and nothing inside it touched. And his piano swinging on its centre of gravity above the pavement. He dashed round to Arthur's and found him suntanned and fit. Arthur and his men came at once. The piano had knocked out the remaining banisters and they got it upstairs in no time. Peach looked at the front door. It was badly caved-in but he reckoned he could mend it with a bit of ply. All it needed for the moment was a new lock. But who, he asked himself, once more in the presence of the miraculous, had kindly opened the door as the piano swept past?

⋯→ ■►●◄■ ←⋯

nine

AUTUMN was coming, and Morag was getting heavy. In the corner, beside the piano, stood a pink cot on the headboard of which a newly canonised rabbit was blessing, with raised ears, the birth of three chickens. Inside the cot lay piles of baby clothes, all neatly divided – vests smaller than the palm of his hand, overalls nine inches long, miniature cardigans, and woollen boots that just fitted his thumb. These clothes were also neatly divided by age – nought, three months, six, nine, a year, the piles lengthening rapidly. At such a rate of growth it was no wonder that the clothes, which had all been handed down two or three times, were still as good as new.

Their squat had changed too. Mr Stag had never shown his face after that first visit, and Peach had repainted their room and the kitchen, and the stairs and the bathroom they shared with Martha. Though they could still be evicted any day, he'd swathed the dodgy wiring in insulating tape, shut up the hole in the roof, and fixed a seat on the toilet, taking joy in the tasks-in-themselves, and not their long-term benefits.

'How long till they crawl?' he asked Morag.

'Six months.'

'Well, that means if we've saved enough for me to have a long break when the baby's born, I can fix the banisters then.'

'Don't we have enough for you to knock off now, Peach. After all, you've finished the shed and there's not long to go.'

'How long?'

'A week. Maybe two. You need to rest *before* it's born, not after. "Rest before labour." We won't get a chance after, if it's anything like Ruth's Joel.'

Peach was rummaging for Morag's sewing-tape.

'Well, I've got one more job lined up. A very big one by the sound of it. Still, I might get it done in a week, if I get help.'

'Well, don't take it on, Peach, if you can't.'

'Don't worry. I'll get it done somehow. And come home the night it's due with a big wad in my pocket!'

'Well, make sure you're not crazy-paving when it's coming, and I can't get hold of you.'

'Christ, don't say that! I want to share everything with you, Morag. I read about some Kashmiri yogis who lash the husband to a tree while his wife's in labour, and he suffers all the birth pains, tied to the tree. He psychically transmits them to his own body. She feels nothing. Just delivers the baby. I wish I could do that, Morag.'

'Well, you'll just have to *be there*, Peach. You can hold on to me while I scratch your face and swear at you.'

'I suppose that's a more direct method of pain transference,' said Peach. 'Are you frightened, Morag?'

'No. Not really. You can't be frightened of what you don't know.'

Morag was squatting on the floor like Indian women do, stretching her legs downwards till her knees nearly touched the floor, then slowly lifting them again, to strengthen her pelvic muscles.

'But you know, Peach. There's one thing I *am* worried about. We still haven't sorted out *where* the baby's going to be born – here or in hospital. And it's getting very late.'

'I know. But how can we sort it out with Stag on the horizon – until the very last minute.'

'The doctor came around today and tried to talk me into going into hospital. Wouldn't say one way or the other whether he would attend here so I've booked in at the West London just in case. So I suppose it will be all right. I'd just like to know, that's all. I want it to be here. But not knowing is sort of holding me from feeling ready.'

'What can we do?' asked Peach.

The address of the big job was number 1, Imperial Way, NW11. With his *A–Z* in his shoulder-bag, Peach caught the 28 to Golders Green, then the 210 along Hampstead Way. He got off where the map indicated, and found himself entering the richest, most exclusive, and most imposing belt of housing in North London.

Before the hippies took over the word 'paranoia' to mean a faint muscular chill caused by dropping their dope behind the fridge, it was a clinical term which meant suffering from delusions of being watched, persecuted, about to be killed, or at the very least, arrested. It was 'paranoia' of this pure kind that Peach now began to suffer as he walked, from the highest numbers towards number 1, down Imperial Way.

Only a month before, while working in merely middle-class Swiss Cottage, he'd been coming back to his job from the café, when he'd noticed a puddle on the brick forecourt of a block of flats. And it had been three days since it had rained. His paver's interest had been aroused by this kink in reality, and he'd stepped over to have a look at it. The wind had been ruffling the puddle, sending eddies across it. The puddle looked like a fish stranded on a brick shore, shivering. You could see the darkened bricks beneath breathing like gills. What misguided paver had left such a deep puddle plonk in the middle of so large a paved area? Peach looked closer. No, it wasn't a blocked drain or subsidence. There was no rhyme or reason for it.

There was something poignant about this lost puddle, when there were no other puddles in the whole length of the forecourt. It was so absurdly deep, it was almost tragic. Then Peach's meditational interest had taken over, and for one, two, five, maybe ten, minutes he had stared into the puddle-in-itself, letting the merely external questions of falls and gullies drop from his mind. He'd stared until he *became* that particular puddle in the middle of that particular bleak forecourt, outside a stuffy block of flats, with the wind running eddies of fish-scale along his back. He'd stared long enough, in fact, for the police to arrive – two Special Branch officers leaping from a patrol car as it skidded to a halt. Someone behind the motionless Venetian blinds, or perhaps some two or three, had rung the station to report a man behaving suspiciously outside their block of flats. The officers asked him what he was doing. What could be more plausible than that he was casing the joint for a break-in? He explained to them that he was examining the puddle out of a paver's professional interest in such things. He thought of adding the puddle-in-itself, but he knew they wouldn't believe him. They didn't believe him anyway. They were in fact taking him to the station and charging him with Suspicious Behaviour. It was only when he'd told them that he was working a few doors away, and they'd driven him in the patrol car to his own site, knocked on the door, and his astonished customers had vouched for his good character, that they let him go. Now that *was* paranoia, in the clinical sense of the word, cold, deep, and totally justified.

And now, walking down Imperial Way, on a sunny morning in the week before the birth of his first child, looking for number 1, Peach felt the same paranoia beginning to overtake him – though there wasn't a soul in sight and he hadn't stopped to examine any puddles. For there were none: the footpath of this Private Road was well-paved, in expensive bricks, the falls perfect. He hadn't looked at any of the front gardens or drives too closely. The only sign of family life, or life itself, that Imperial Way afforded the pedestrian, was in the drives of the houses – a big, daddy Daimler or Rolls-Royce before the front porch, a mummy Range Rover for nipping down to the shops, parked by the pyracantha, and two or three nippy little Fiats, Polos or Metros, good for the traffic in town, climbing all over the gravel as children will. The mansions had such large grounds they could afford to go décolleté of walls, hedges, fences – those homely things the poor talk over – one estate-sized garden running promiscuously into another with only a line of conifers or a string of waterfalls to define the boundaries. It was left to the sheer presence of money and a burglar alarm as blatant as a chastity belt above the porch, to provide the sense of impregnability. A force-field of total security emanated from each house, on either side of the road. Where they met, in the middle of the road, these fields of surveillance repelled each other like the poles of two magnets, creating a void of terrible fear, which ran roughly down the centre line, into which the innocent sun shone, and down which Peach walked, following the Way of the White Clouds. Luckily Imperial Way was a quiet street, and he wasn't knocked down.

... 13 ... 11 ... 9 Imperial Way ... Each number took several minutes to walk past ... one mansion after another. It seemed as though, between 1918 and 1939, someone had built a brick replica of every stately home in England in the one street ... a council estate for millionaires. The further he walked down it, the more Peach realised that he must not take this job on. It was bound to be too big for him ... 7 Imperial Way ... 'My child's due in a week,' he thought desperately, arguing with a marble number-plate. 'This is not my territory. We've got enough to get by. There's no reason why I shouldn't just turn around and go back to the bus stop ... have a walk on the Heath. I must save all my energy for the birth. If the lady rings back, I'll tell Mrs Emmet to say I've come down with glandular fever. That lasts months. She'll find someone else. A big firm. Why me? I don't like it here. I want to *look* at things when I walk down a street. If I stop and smell that rose, I know I'll be on video in Scotland Yard. Might just as well walk up the drive and sit in that Rolls making engine noises. Vroom, vroom, vroom. I was merely attempting to joy-ride this rose, officer. Take me away. It's sure to be a big job. I must say No . . .'

. . . 5 Imperial Way . . .

But the sunny void at the centre of the road drew him on. Perhaps, deep down, his feet felt some human need reaching out to meet him from behind the burglar alarms and curtained windows, and walked towards it. Perhaps it was his own Fate, which he'd felt once on the piano stool, to which he could never say No . . .

. . . 3 Imperial Way . . .

After the open-plan gardens and sweeping drives of the other numbers, it was almost a relief — even though he wasn't going in — to see that number 1 Imperial Way had a fifteen-foot brick wall around it with six feet of barbed wire on top of that. And very professional barbed wire it was too — six dead-parallel strands, each exactly a foot apart and each one neatly wound on to its electric terminal, converging on infinity as they ran down the almost endless length of the wall. At twenty-foot intervals there were arc-lamps on high staunchions. Each staunchion had a collar of spikes. These same Tudor ruffs decorated each down-pipe along the front of the house, matching its 1933 Elizabethan façade.

'I must say No. I will say No,' said Peach to himself as he pushed an ivory button, and a bell chimed deep inside the house and the closed-circuit camera, built like a lasar gun, began to look him up and down. 'But it'd be rude to just not turn up.'

An elderly butler opened the door.

'I . . . I'm . . . Peach O'Hare . . . landscape gardener . . .'

'Ah yes. The Tradesman's Entrance is third on the right, sir — past the garages.'

Peach found the gate. It was made of flexile steel and had Tradesman's Entrance written on it. The gate rolled itself up automatically, when Peach approached it, and closed behind him with the smooth click of an electronic portcullis. Now he found himself in a narrow passage beside a garage and came out into the strangest garden he had ever seen.

He entered a terrace of Venetian marble – huge six foot by six foot slabs like the floor of St Mark's, which stretched for five hundred feet, running along the whole house-end of the garden, to a width of thirty feet. It was an altar of the High Renaissance. Alabaster lions, bigger than Nelson's, guarded the house at forty-foot intervals and along the outer edge of the terrace was a marble balustrade, into which were set funeral urns, taller than a man and also of marble, in which some late geraniums were still flowering cheerfully. In the centre of the terrace, opposite the living-room windows, was a flight of steps, fifty feet wide, overarched by a pergola made of sandstone flying buttresses, which turned, at the height of thirty feet, into a delicate fan-tracery supporting nothing but blue sky, meeting, sixty feet above the steps, in a prayer-pointed nave through which sturdy climbing roses, mostly wood and thorn, wound, descending to a kidney-shaped swimming pool donated by Picasso. Art deco deck-chairs shaped like folding ashtrays were dotted around the pool. The first golden leaves of autumn were already sunbathing in them. At the far end of the pool Bernini's St Paul stood on the edge holding an open book against his chest from which a jet of water spouted into the deep end.

On either side of the steps, and tumbling from the foot of the terrace down to the lawn twenty feet below, was a rockery of sunset-shot basalt, a carefully-thrown avalanche amongst which were dotted bonsai Rocky Mountain redwoods and giant sequoias, six hundred years old and eighteen inches high. On the back of one of the boulders, he glimpsed a trademark, printed like God's own signature on Sinai: GENUINE GRAND CANYON ROCKERY, POWDERED AND RECONSTITUTED BY WILF'S MARBLES MICHIGAN. The rockery carried on around both sides of the huge garden, forming what geologists call a 'natural amphitheatre', the centre and stage of which was the biggest, levellest, lushest lawn Peach had ever seen. There must have been two acres of it, cut close as a bowling green, with a pile like a Persian carpet. The lawn was bordered by an Elizabethan knot-garden of miniature hedges, which ran twining and interlacing its way around its circular rim in both directions, growing higher as it went, till, as it approached the bottom of the garden from both sides, it turned into a full-grown Tudor maze, twenty feet high and completely uncrackable, into which the path disappeared in a green shade, lit by stone Buddhas with fairy lights in their navels. This path, which ran between the hedge and the rockery, was made of cowrie shells set in cement in the Polynesian style. The path came out at the other end of the maze on to the tool-shed, which was a replica of the Taj Mahal, its rectangular lakes quietly brimming with Brussels sprouts and runner beans. A fine lattice of Turkish marble encased the compost, allowing it to breathe under its Blue Mosque lid. The greenhouse, at the very back of the garden, was a faithful model of the Palace of Versailles, its miles of symmetrical landscape reproduced in tomato plants, marrows and giant orchids.

As he stood in amazement surveying this garden, Peach could not see in the whole vast acreage one thing that needed doing. Nothing seemed to have been left out. Nothing was out of place. Unless it was three or four massive stones that were just lying randomly in the middle of the lawn, like toppled megaliths. And there was certainly nothing he could do about them. For they looked as if not he, nor a hundred men, nor even a crane could lift them, so massive, naked and grim were they. And even these stones were not wholly out of place in that sculptural garden, just lying there, amongst all the fine workmanship, like the original Unemployed Masses.

How long he stood staring at that wondrous garden he did not know, but at last Peach became aware that someone was staring at him, closely and quizzically, as though sounding his inner depth. A thin, white-haired old lady was standing by the living-room doors holding one of the alabaster lions by the ear. She clutched that alabaster ear both with great physical frailty and a will of iron. Her face was lined with wrinkles and squaw-eyed squints. The Crows of Wisdom had pecked about her face and sipped from her eyes and left their crow's-feet in her suntanned skin. Her bony, thin-muscled hands gripped the alabaster ear with the aid of several diamonds, rubies and sapphires, and a couple of giant moonstones as big as translucent knuckles. Peach had never seen such a wiry old lady. Life had tried to force her to stoop, but had only managed a slight bunching of her shoulder-blades. Her spine was still straight – straighter than her walking-stick. The clothes which must have once fitted now hung loosely upon her. Peach could almost feel the living skeleton beneath them, as taut as a coat-hanger. Her gold watch-band lay loosely on her wrist, as though it had turned to a bracelet, and Time, closed up in its watch, to a golden bead. Though she was tapping her stick impatiently. Her stockings were the old-fashioned cotton type, wan as semolina pudding, and wrinkled about her knees like the skin on boiled milk. Perhaps she'd just come from praying. Though, with her piercing gaze and thin, strong fingers, it was more likely she'd been gutting chickens.

'Good morning, Mr O'Hare,' she said. 'What took you so long?'

Amidst all this grandeur, Peach wouldn't dare tell her of the long wait at Golders Green for the 210, and yet . . .

'Well. What do you think of it, Mr O'Hare?' said the old lady, waving her walking stick at the garden.

'It's very . . . grand, Mrs . . .'

'Eden. Flora Eden.'

'It's very grand, Mrs Eden . . .'

'. . . but something's lacking, isn't it? That's what you were going to say.'

'Well . . . no . . .'

'And you're right, Mr O'Hare. I can see you know gardens. It's very grand, but something's lacking.'

She took Peach's wrist with a grip that was all bones, will and precious stones.

'And I know what it is.' She spoke with a refined savagery. 'This garden's the life-work of my late husband. He wanted it to be the Universal Garden. He could never take second best, my Horrie. He wanted Paradise. Well, we got it. Horrie always reckoned that the best of every nation, race and epoch was in its gardens, and he wasn't far wrong. So what he did was gather it all together in one place – sold what had become almost a multi-national to do it. Insurance, originally. He reckoned that if you put the best of every nation and time in the one spot, it would create a sort of New Eden, a place so grand, yet at the same time so peaceful, that people would have to take notice of it and change how they lived. It was a pity we had to have the barbed wire up, but our neighbours' children are into everything and those bonsais are worth a lot of money. In fact you're about the first person who's seen it. Anyway, Horrie wanted the Garden of Eden, as built by men. And he wanted it to be better than the original. But it hasn't come together. There's something missing. Horrie was a good man, but he lacked imagination. I think you can see where he went wrong. He was one of those people who think – you've got a garden, you've got to have a lawn. Though even he knew two acres was overdoing it. And that's what's wrong: the grass isn't saying anything. You can see that, can't you, Mr O'Hare?'

'Well, grass is . . . pretty universal,' said Peach.

'What culture, what race, what period of history does a lawn represent?' the old woman was almost shouting now.

'Perhaps if you let it grow long, to represent Nat—'

'Impossible! Not with all this monumental stuff around. Horrie brooded over that lawn for ten years. Tried sunbathing on it, croquet parties – it never felt right. Tragically, the penny only dropped the day he died. He'd just come in from mowing it. "Flora," he said, "we've got to have something low-maintenance." Then the lightning struck – crazy-paving, two acres of crazy-paving! Second-hand slabs, with a mix of pink and green, double-painted, laid by an expert. He charged me with it on his deathbed as a sacred mission.'

'But . . . but what will that . . . express?'

'The Present, Mr O'Hare! The Here and Now. England, Nineteen Eighty-Seven. That's what Horrie left out. Always did leave it out – the sweep of Modern Life!'

There was a thrill in the old woman's voice that stirred

Peach, even though the conception was so horrible. And even though he knew he couldn't possibly do it in a week, and that he must say No.

'Well, yes,' said Peach. 'I see what you mean, Mrs Eden . . . But I'm afraid . . .'

'And when you do it, there must be no damage to my husband's work. No cement stains on the marble or trampling on the borders. And I don't want your men using the back of the garage as— And any damage you do you make good at your own expense.'

'Yes, but you see . . . In fact, I'm very busy just now . . . and . . . and . . . my wife's expecting . . . in a week . . . I think . . .'

'Well, a week will do then, if you think it'll take that long. It's a bit slow for a big firm. To be blunt with you, I don't want to die before it's finished. But I suppose I can wait a week. When will you start, now, or tomorrow?'

'Well . . . you see . . . It's such a big job . . . It'll take a lot of organising. Materials . . . labour . . . machinery . . . and . . .'

'All right, tomorrow then,' grumbled the old lady.

She rummaged in her purse. It was the first time Peach had noticed this battered old receptacle – a sort of Gladstone bag with a razor-strap across the shoulder. She fished out a fat envelope and handed it to him.

'There's five thousand, advance. And don't be late in the morning!'

Peach walked back down Imperial Way feeling quite at home.

Peach neither went lung-gom walking on the Heath, nor home to climb on to his piano stool. He walked straight to the Garden Centre, which wasn't far. In the corner of the yard was a mountain of broken-up footpath. The council contractors brought in an endless stream of it. One of the yardmen spent all day stacking the broken slabs on palettes. A palette was a square yard in area. He laid out the slabs in a rough crazy-paving fashion as he stacked, so that each layer was a

215

square yard – nine layers to the ton. The palettes were then stacked by a forklift, four, five, six tons high.

Peach went to the counter and ordered three hundred tons for the morning.

'That's everything we've got out there, Peach. You've seen that pile, have you? Are you sure you've worked out your area right? – you don't mean three hundred yards?'

'No, Jackie, three hundred tons. Bright and early tomorrow morning.'

'Well, we're a bit booked up for tomorrow, love. And it'll take our trucks three or four days to shift that lot anyway. Can't you have it a load at a time? I know Imperial Way's just over the hill but—'

'Listen, Jackie,' said Peach, taking out Mrs Eden's fat envelope. 'Get a haulage contractor, two, three, if necessary – McGovern, Murphy, someone like that. Get ten tonners, twenty tonners, artics, anything. Just sling it in loose. They can tip on site. There's plenty of room. But get it there in the morning. And then I'll need sand. Let me see – three inches under two acres, that's . . . give us four hundred metres of soft. And I need that in the morning too. I want to start laying by lunch-time. Oh, and some cement – for the pointing – fifty bags! And here's something for a drink.'

And Peach jammed two hundred pounds in the Christmas Box.

Next was the question of labour. There was only him. Of course, he would hire bulldozers, JCBs, a steamroller for the groundworks. He could even hire a portaloo. But machines can't lay crazy-paving. Peach tried to work out how many men he'd need to do Mrs Eden's job in a week – five? ten? – more like thirty or forty. And that was assuming they knew how to lay paving. Still there were thousands of blokes out there who needed work. He'd teach them. Although it was unimaginable that he could finish this vast job in one week, he was carried away by a rising excitement. And so, like the rich man who lacked guests for his wedding, Peach took to the streets.

3-Tooth was having a strange dream.

He was lying under a bush — well, in that respect, his dream tallied with reality — and the beautiful vagabond girl was in his arms, her black leather pants and fishnet vest cast in abandonment on the grass beside them. Her pale, lithe body was flushing bright red as they approached the climax of love. He was stroking her wiry, black hair, which made her begin to moan somewhere down in her belly. Thrusting his tongue between her pearl-smooth teeth, he could feel the delicate-fleshed tracery of the inside of her mouth, where her moaning deepened as it came up out of her fine long neck. They were moving together in perfect unison. But just as they approached the pinnacle of pleasure, someone began shaking him, still in his dream, by the shoulder. It was Jimi. Unmistakable. Wearing the same outfit as on the cover of *Are You Experienced?* – all silk and sequins and peacock colours. And Jimi was sayin' somethin' to him, urgent like, in his ear. He was sayin', 'Get up, 3-Tooth, man. Wake up. I've got a gig on. Biggest gig of me career, man. 'N I need you, man. Tomorrow mornin' – A sharp! Recordin' a number on EMI. An' I want ya to dig it! So leave this chick, man. There's no time for sweet delectation now. Wake up, 3-Tooth, we got some crazy groovin' t' do!'

3-Tooth woke up. He was lying on top of his guitar with his legs wrapped around its sound-box, from which a deep A minor moan was coming. His arms were round its long fine neck, and he was french-kissing the tuning board, mistaking its six pearl knobs for teeth, which was three more than he had, thrusting his tongue between the spools of steel string. His buttocks were gyrating, strumming ecstatic music, and his plectrum had grown six inches. 3-Tooth pulled out his tongue, disengaged himself, and fell off his guitar with a dead plunk.

'Jesus, man,' he mumbled. 'Lucky the amp was off, or they would've bin diggin' it in the Hilton!'

217

3-Tooth looked up through his shades.

Peach O'Hare was shaking his shoulder urgently.

'Wake up, 3-Tooth. I've got a job on. The biggest job I've ever had. I need you. Tomorrow morning, eight sharp. Number One Imperial Way. I want you to do some digging. Wake up, 3-Tooth. We've got some crazy-paving to do!'

3-Tooth groaned.

'All right, Peach man.'

He took the slip of envelope with the address, rolled over in his guitar-bag and went back to sleep in search of his other half.

Allwrath took the corner into Highgate Road at a skilful six miles an hour. The Sacred Site was drawing near. He could sense God's excitement. Physically the six-foot kerbstone was grinding the rear mudguards into the bitumen in long, scraping hops. But psychically, It was driving the hearse onwards, a granite dynamo in the boot. Allwrath peered through side gates, down alleyways, into builders' yards and allotments, as he passed steadily by. A man on the corner of Dartmouth Park Road took his hat off to him in deep respect. He would know beyond any doubt when he'd found the Sacred Site. It would drag the hearse to a halt, a vast Earth-magnet under his axles. Sometimes he could even feel the Earth Goddess, Gaia Herself, shaking the rear suspension in Her sacred impatience to rise from the dead and dance with the Great God in the boot. Be it vacant lot, school playground or the Houses of Parliament, wherever he found the Sacred Site, Allwrath swore he would perform his ceremony, the Ultimate Ritual, and smash these Illusions to smithereens.

But always, like a bad dream in his rear vision mirror, the twelve black carloads of Rationalists were following him, brushing the nausea off their thinking suits. Gog knows, he'd tried to lose them, but this was hard at six miles an hour. Their Daimlers were driven by purring quantum theories and full tanks of differential calculus, whereas the old hearse was rattling like a tram down ley-lines, buried and forgotten under tons of concrete and asphalt. Why didn't they get on with it? Why didn't they just force him into the kerb and set upon God with their microscopes and graphs. He knew what it was: He was the Hypothesis they could never prove, which they were tracking mercilessly, to the Sacred Site Itself, intending to show that there is a void at the Earth's heart. But let them beware! Allwrath smiled grimly into his rear vision mirror at the wrath-reddened face of the Reverend Briggs.

But that grim smile was a mistake. You should never smile at a Fiend of Reason, even in a mirror. Allwrath missed the right into Swains Lane, and found himself rolling up Highgate West Hill, the steepest hill in North London. He climbed the gentle incline and hit the 1 in 20 gradient. His engine gagged. In his own stomach, Allwrath felt the full weight of God dragging them backwards. They subsided to five miles an hour. For all these months he had skilfully shepherded the hearse away from anything sharper than a 1 in 80, only to be rolling up this asphalt Everest. He pressed the accelerator into the floor and they sank to four miles an hour. The cortege was slowing too, keeping time with the hearse. They laboured past St Anne's at three miles an hour. His engine was screaming breathlessly through the clenched teeth of third gear. God slid backwards amidst a crinkling of plastic flowers. The hearse began to shake. Three miles an hour, and still the cortege kept a perfect twenty feet behind him. But what when his engine could pull them no higher? What when they reached nought miles an hour? His brakes were as feeble as his engine; they'd never hold such a mighty weight on such a slope. What when he rolled backwards into the first black limousine? Allwrath tried to swing the hearse into a desperate U-turn. But at two miles an hour, it didn't respond. The windscreen was shuddering the left-hand wiper loose. They reached one mile an hour, and they were still a hundred yards from the top. Then the shuddering and sliding stopped. The engine cut out. There was a moment's total stillness, as the hearse reached its highest point of upwards momentum, where it seemed it would hang for ever. Allwrath was just shutting his eyes when he saw Peach O'Hare light-footing it down the hill from the opposite direction, a euphoric smile, as usual, plastered over his face. Allwrath gave a desperate cry and jumped out.

'Peach. Peach . . .'

Just as the hearse began to roll backwards, Allwrath put his shoulder to the door-frame. This was enough to hold it steady. But he had not the strength to push it an inch upwards.

'Peach! Peach! Remember the bricks . . .'

Peach ran across the road.

'Allwrath! How nice to see you. Look. I've got this big job on tomorrow. I was wondering—'

'Push. Push,' grimaced the Druid as the weight of God began to drive him downwards.

Peach ran round to the boot. The coffin was straining at the door. He put his shoulder to the hearse and began to push. The hearse inched upwards. His shoulder ached. It seemed that the weight of the whole Earth was in it. Together they laboured the hearse round the corner past Holly Terrace, the black cars edging after them. Fifty yards to go.

'Look,' gasped Peach, 'Allwrath! Do you need a job?'

'I have a Mission, Peach,' panted the Druid. 'I don't need a job.'

'But I need labourers.'

'Keep pushing, Peach.'

'It's a huge job. I need help.'

'Sorry, Peach. The Sacred Site is near.'

Then Peach took his shoulder away from the hearse. It stopped, and became very heavy, twenty feet from the top. Then God took matters into His own hands, and decided to ram the Reverend Briggs. The hearse rolled backwards.

'All right. All right,' screamed the Druid. 'I'll work for you. Tomorrow. Tomorrow. Keep pushing, for Gog's sake.'

Peach put his shoulder to the boot, and together they stopped the hearse from rolling backwards. Then once again they began labouring it upwards. They reached the summit. Allwrath jumped in while Peach kept pushing, bump-started

220

the hearse, and slowly drew away on his Druid's Quest. But as he gathered speed, Peach ran behind him, writing in the hearse's dusty rear-window: 1 IMPERIAL WAY. 8 O'CLOCK SHARP.

The Reverend Briggs was driving. He had the hand-brake on, and they had stopped in a black queue a hundred yards from the top of the steepest hill in North London. Even the silky engine of the Daimler was growing hysterical. The Reverend Briggs peered at the summit of Highgate West Hill through the spokes of a medieval zodiac with which he had been steering his limousine. He lifted his head and it rolled backwards over his shoulder till he was looking at his parishioners. The Apostles of the New Covenant! Mr McGrundle was asleep in Mrs Nugent's lap, who was unpicking the wool of his jumper 'to knit Arthur a pair of socks, against that dreadful cold'. Mr Spikes was talking to a fly on the back window, about the summer's Test Series, which he'd missed. But the shortlived fly was a football freak.

The Reverend Briggs had skilfully reduced speed as Allwrath lost momentum. Another illumination was coming to him. His head rolled round on his shoulders like a drunken dinosaur.

'Dearly Beloved, we have been following Arthur's funeral for three years now, and I plainly perceive that the Lord approacheth the End of His Ministry. For behold, this hill, this mighty – ' he grappled with his *A–Z* ' – Highgate West Hill, is the new Calvary. We are driving up to the Place of Skulls, possibly somewhere on the corner by the Flask. Where our Saviour, obviously, if you observe His rear suspension, bearing the terrible weight of our sins, will perform the final Act of His New Covenant. Wake up. We are about to witness the Crucifixion!'

The mourners peered fearfully out of the windows. The Reverend Briggs grew exultant.

'And just as, on His Way to the Cross, our Messiah stumbled under the dreadful weight of His Cross, so now, see! – His sacred Hearse falters, shudders, cuts out, and collapseth to a halt. When lo! a passer-by, a blessed bystander, is summoned to help carry the weight of the Lord's Cross. He puts his shoulder to the Boot. He pushes. The blessed Hearse staggers forward. He groans. He pants. He pleads. The Messiah's Holy Vehicle reaches the crest, where the Good Lord jumps in, bump-starts, and pulls off towards Golgotha. Leaving the mere passer-by a blessed man. See how happily he skips off down the Hill. Look how he smiles uncontrollably to himself!'

The Reverend Briggs ground the limousine into first, reached the summit of Calvary, and set off after Allwrath. One of the mourners was pulling at his shoulder.

'Your Holiness. Something's wrong. There's someone signalling from the eighth car back.'

'Better see what it is,' muttered the Reverend Briggs.

He woke the chauffeur and pulled him behind the wheel. Then he climbed on to the back seat, and with Mr McGrundle and Mr Spikes supporting him by the knees, rolled back the sun roof. He poked his head out and was dazzled by the unaccustomed sunlight. He saw a Highgate he had never seen before.

'What beast the matter, Mrs Brown?' he called back.

'It's my husband, Mr Brown, your Worship,' called a hysterical voice from the eighth car. 'He's passed on.'

A wonderful, sunlit clarity smote the pastor. He looked sagely from Allwrath's fleeing hearse to the eighth black limousine, then back again.

'Well, Mrs Brown. He's chosen the right place to do it.'

By the time he'd finished making his arrangements for the following day it was getting late. He didn't have enough labourers, but with 3-Tooth and Allwrath he ought to be able to make a show. The bulldozer and steamroller he'd hired should get things moving. Something told him there were a million things he'd forgotten, but they could wait. He was unable to think, let alone worry, about what he'd forgotten. He was knackered but jubilant. He should go straight home now and rest. He burned to tell Morag about the stupendous job he had undertaken. Tomorrow would be the most daunting day's work he'd ever done. But finding himself halfway up Highgate West Hill on a late summer's evening, something made him turn down the lane that led to the Heath. He would walk across the Heath to Golders Green and go home from there. The lane brought him out by the top of Highgate Ponds. He crossed the causeway between the water like an Olympic walker. On his left, the fishing pond feathered its ripple-back like an exhausted swan. On his right, reeds and rusty railings swayed around the still pond where the wildfowl bred.

The elation that had rolled his legs down the hill only increased as they laboured up the other side. He had accepted a mighty challenge. Nothing was any longer impossible. The freedom which before he'd only found in the 'Pharaoh's Tomb' was spreading out into the physical world, was rolling across the Heath. He resisted the temptation to turn off the path into the wooded gully on the right. He always seemed to get lost in fantasies when he meditated on that part of the Heath, came crashing out of hawthorn mazes of daydream to find himself trapped past his shoes in little quagmires of mystified longing. Now he kept to the direct path, straight up the hill. A path of good, clean hoggins. As he mounted the hill, the first skyscrapers of the City came into view beyond its shoulder, on his left. But he ignored them, light-footing upwards like Christian towards the City of God.

At the top of the hill the path crossed the spinal ley-line. Peach paused a moment by the rubbish bin to thank the Higher Beings for his Great Task. Then he turned right and carried on up the hill in the direction of Golders Green. But it was still early, and having saluted Rudolf Steiner, Blake and Krishnamurti, he lingered by the gate to Ken Wood. In the old days Peach would have circled for hours under the tall trees, but he entered the woods less often now he was working. Partly because he was always late, but partly also because walking in the woods seemed to sap him now, lull him, even dishearten him with thoughts that he was wasting his time. As though, at best, he'd left the spinal path of headlong Evolution and was lost in this image of Eternity, this wood, which the Giant Man carried on his back like a sack of leafy peace, wondering if he'd missed the bus.

But now Peach lingered at the entrance to the wood. He should go home, but something held him by the gate. He was too excited to go home. And where better to plunge, if you are over-excited, than into Eternity? The mighty vision he'd always expected on the Heath was perhaps awaiting him now. The brain-juddering descent, the whole hog, in full technicolour. Excitement, exhaustion and the spiralling aimlessness inside the woods might work the final alchemy. Then he had an inspiration. He could stay in the woods all night! He would walk and chant in total solitude under the darkening trees, then, when he could walk no more, find a bench and sit in the dark with his eyes open, waiting upon God. What a way to spend the night before his big job! He could go straight to work from the woods. But perhaps he only wanted to do this because he was, in reality, terrified of tomorrow. Besides, his tools were at home. And then the dreadful thought struck him that his baby might arrive early. It might be born this very night. And what if he was sitting in midnight meditation on Hampstead Heath and missed the birth! His skin goosepimpled at the thought. He had to struggle with himself not to dash for Golders Green there and then. But that was crazy. The baby wasn't due for another week. And he had his job to finish first.

Peach entered the woods. He walked for half an hour but nothing happened. He was exhausted, emotionally and physically. He wouldn't be able to cope tomorrow if he didn't go home.

Beside the path, on his left, was a screen of holly trees and on the other side of them was a clearing under two giant oak trees. And in this unlikely place there was a bench which looked out over the rusty railings and bracken that bordered

224

the wood, across the whole Heath, and down upon the City of London, four miles away. Peach had termed the bench the Mystical Seat in the days when he came here often, and had had deep experiences on it. But its power seemed to have waned. He hadn't pushed through the prickled blades of the sentinel holly trees for over a year. But tonight he did, for he needed to sit down. As usual, vandals had thrown the bench down the slope into the bracken. Peach hauled it back up. It was an ancient, iron-framed bench with the coat of arms of the London County Council on its curled arm-rests. By the time he got it up and facing the City, he was panting. He sat down and looked outwards.

The dark trunks and boughs of the two oaks and the lighter foliage of the more distant trees formed a sort of large eye-hole in which an oval section of the City's skyscrapers was visible, bright and far away. Framed by the darkness of the tree-trunks and the rustling of the leaves a little farther off, this eye-hole had a deep stillness within it, here in the woods, and a bright and silent focus beyond. And through this clearness and interior stillness, this great eye-hole looked, not just at the City of London, but at the deep human Idea of it, from which it had come, somewhere in the mists beyond Dulwich. And as it focused the skyscrapers and cupolas and Kings Cross's mighty glass shed, the great eye-hole of the woods seemed to be registering a totally new City, though made of the very same sand, cement, brick, timber and human beings, out there in the boundless freedom of the distant sunlight.

Peach subsided into the stillness. Though his eyes were open, they registered little. It was the rustling eye that gripped the earth all around him, that was watching the scene unfold before him. Beyond the railings a clump of willow-herb rose from the bracken. Minarets of pigment with purple eaves, soft down on the lithe stalks, seeds bound to the flower with the frail, white hair of old men. From seed to decay they danced in a clump. The wood's eye considered them. What Peach saw was a conscious witnessing element in which they lived. This conscious element surrounded them like a liquor in which they were preserved; from which, indeed, they drew their life. Ken Wood's eye contemplated the clump of willow-herb and Peach felt the wondrous element pour into his mouth, subtler than air, filling his throat till it knew the taste of consciousness itself. It tasted of ecstasy. And suddenly his Throat Centre opened, and he was speaking to the clump of willow-herb.

He uttered a sound which he couldn't fully hear above his heart's beating, a sound as if all the sad mechanicalness of his body had gathered into one soft ratchet in the back of his larynx, leaving the rest of him spirit, and this ratchet was being turned by the sheer clarity of the wonderful witnessing element as it poured, without cogs or spokes, through his Throat Centre. It sounded like a frog shut in a music box. It was the Word made flesh. And as he uttered it outwards, Peach knew that this sound was the Name of willow-herb in this witnessing element. The breeze took the clump, and the willow-herb bent towards him in acknowledgement. The clarity wound up out of the bracken, through the lithe towers, round each pursed, purple gargoyle, and passed into the light.

And as it did so, Peach rose into his Forehead Centre. There he saw the endless building and rebuilding of the willow-herb. For *he saw it being thought*. And before his eyes, the stalks burdened with flowers turned to white clouds on sticks that instantly vanished into the light around them. And for the first time in his life, Peach *saw light*!

He watched amazed as even the railings vanished into the light, and reappeared an instant later, rebuilt, recast, totally new down to the last flake of oxide and fungal puff of blown paint. And the willow-herb had reappeared out of the Light, supple and refreshed. He watched the continuous building and rebuilding of everything on earth. Of the bracken and the white track. Of the trees in the distance and even the jogger thudding past unheeding. He saw the Light bend, compress, stretch, bunch itself, for it was the musculature of Mighty Beings, good at their work. He saw the continuous building and rebuilding of the oak trees. Of the bench on which he sat.

Of the dark ground on which his feet paddled. And of him himself.

And all the sorrow, all the pain he'd ever known condensed in the places at the backs of his eyes where tears form, where they were *wrung out* into a single clear drop of ecstasy in the centre of his forehead, where the bridge of his nose, like a cable anchored deep in his brain disappeared into a cavity which yearned to see. He looked outwards, not with his eyes, but through the drop of ecstasy, and the willow-herb, the bracken, the circling branches, and the Heath began to stream upwards towards the final Centre, the Crown Centre. Peach caught his breath. Whether it was fear of what was about to happen or a desire to stream upwards with the willow-herb and the Heath, he stood up. All around him the Light was pouring upwards. A resolution, a natural wish, an absolute determination, to turn this vision to human good, rose through him. And by its force, and no other, the Light left his forehead and began to rise – not into his brain, for his brain could not contain it – but into *the direction Upwards*. For the Final Centre, the Crown Centre, the Thousand-Petalled Lotus, he realised with the joy of sudden freedom, had nothing whatso-ever to do with his, Peach O'Hare's head, was not in his brain, was no skull-cap of vision for his private spiritual wardrobe, but was a vast Descent, whose only habitation in a human body is this *upwardness and uprightness*. The fierceness of the Descent burnt up the gentle element in which he'd spoken to the willow-herb. It annihilated the Light by which he'd seen the willow-herb being thought. And for an instant the building and rebuilding of everything on earth stood still. The building and rebuilding of the bracken stood still, and frond-tip fists curled in expectation. The building and rebuilding of the rusty railings by ambient spirit stood still as well-fixed iron. The building and rebuilding of the oak trees subsided. The building and rebuilding of Peach himself, body and soul, stood momen-tarily still. Peach shuddered for, only in him, this standing still meant dying, an oncoming blackness.

Suddenly London filled the Heath's vast eye, and Peach

stood in a radiant City. Its streets had no names and no direction, being sudden vistas into other men's and women's minds, which are endless and everywhere. But they were golden streets. For the vistas would only open with Forgiveness. And the savage thoughts cast off in the alleys and the abominations in the gutters had been understood by the windows, and forgiven by the doors. There were boulevards into the souls of plants and birds. There was a highway into the soul of London, that mirage of domes and skyscrapers forgiven by the honest outlines of Camden Town. Each street opened with a pang of cold blue air, for it meant a death. But down them he saw a million simple acts baked golden in the kilns of Forgiveness, and laid in courses, plumb, level, well-bonded, the innermost self on the outside, as quaint as Dutch eaves, and God sheltering in each dwelling. The streets opened and closed as Peach, arms outstretched, circled on his toes, looking into the souls of all things. He saw spires and mighty domes crusted with jewels, thickets of piers, viaducts and bridges, with friezes of spiritual light carved into them. But these, though magnificent, were less real than the common streets and houses, being as they were, made out of *shared dream*, rather than daily moments.

And still, and for ever, the City was a Descent into Upwards, so that even as he stood in its streets, arms outstretched, Peach felt that he was falling, his body's sense of gravity gone, held upright only by the act of falling, his feet on a golden pavement, till everything went black, and his body's fear grabbed him, and dragged him down into the bracken.

THAT night, sitting in bed with Morag, Peach could still feel the ecstatic stillness around him.

'I feel ready to be a father now.'

'What do you mean?'

'As though the world's turned inside out from what it was eight months ago. And everything that's inner is moving out into the world.'

'With the baby?'

'Yes. I feel more confident, I suppose. With all this work and everything. I suppose I used to be afraid of the real world.'

'The real world is all there is to be afraid of.'

'You're a visionary, Morag.'

'Yes?'

'And I hope vision makes up for everything. You know . . . a house, security . . . all that . . .'

'Oh, it does.'

All at once her belly gave an earth-quaking heave, so strong that Peach could actually *see* it through her nightdress. The limbs within her were large and fully-formed.

'You don't mind taking on such a big job then?' she asked him.

'No. It doesn't worry me at all. Except . . .'

'What?'

'Why don't you come with me tomorrow, or anyway come and see me during the day sometime. I don't want to be away from you too long this last week, Morag. And you'd like seeing the place. And 3-Tooth and Allwrath. They'll be helping me.'

'All right.'

ten

THE next morning fell clear and golden from heaven like the first dead leaf into a cut-glass vase. It was autumn. The early sun still promised summery warmth, but it was bundled up in mist. And you could feel that, when the mist unwrapped it, the sun would be a diamond, shining at a sharper angle to the earth than yesterday, honing facets of light whose underside was a blue, oncoming coldness. A new consciousness was gathering, approaching, waking, and looking, amazed with this sharp light, at golden walls and paving stones of which yesterday it had only been dreaming. Though the leaves were turning and starting to fall, something deeper was coming back to life from a vegetating dream. The leaves and flowers whose blossoming had been so mighty and inconceivable that, all summer long, it had swished and rustled by in an earth-dream, could now be seen down to the last leaf-nerve and vein of petal. Everything – bricks, tiles, stones, leaves, flowers – could sense that its spiritual prototype had drawn a fraction of an inch, a half a degree, nearer in this diamond light – and was glad, even if it meant death.

Peach felt light-hearted as he staggered down Imperial Way with his tools. Perhaps this was the spirit in which they built channel tunnels, space stations, nuclear reactors: make a few arrangements, spread a bit of money around, give your mates the wink, and – hey presto! – the cogs of the world begin to mesh around you.

He knocked at the door of number 1 at twenty to seven. The butler pressed a button and this time opened, not the narrow Tradesman's Entrance, but a gate which was wide enough and tall enough to admit half a dozen canopied elephants abreast. Mrs Eden was waiting by the sundial on the terrace. She was still in her nightdress and slippers, with a shawl of ancient lace around her shoulders. Her fingers on the sundial were nicotined yellow by the early sunlight. The dial-stick's shadow angled through her fingers like the morning's first black cigarette.

'Good morning, Mr O'Hare. You're late. Where did you leave your truck?'

'Down by the bus stop,' said Peach, leaning the ganger man's pick, shovel, sledgehammer, broom, spirit-level and Sainsbury's bag of hand tools against the marble balustrade. He was tired already.

'Well, get on with it then. No hanging about. I haven't got time to watch you drinking tea all day. I want to see the Work finished.'

Peach could almost see the capital W in the grandeur with which she pronounced Work, though he fancied, for an instant, that the word was underpinned by a grim twinkle. Peach was daunted. How could he possibly add to this monumental garden? How dared he even try? Yet the old woman seemed to believe that he was the man for the job.

'Drake will bring you and your men tea at eleven,' she snapped irritably. 'How many men do you have?'

'Ah . . . well . . . two . . . three . . . Including me . . . I'm not sure yet . . .'

'Well, they're late!'

She stalked into the house.

Peach looked at the monumental garden. A bird was singing in an apple tree behind the Palace of Versailles. Where should he begin? He took the pickaxe, descended the marble steps from the sanctuary of the patio, and started hacking at the two-acre lawn. But something told him this wasn't the way to

231

begin. He'd better wait till the machinery came. But Mrs Eden wanted him to *do* something. He hid behind the maze for twenty minutes, till it suddenly struck him – he hadn't worked out where he was to tip the sand and paving slabs when they arrived. He ran back up to the terrace. He pictured a vast shute made of scaffolding and planks, with tarpaulins to catch the dust, straddling the balustrade and tipping all his materials on to the lawn where he needed them. Leading to the mouth of this shute was a five-scaffold-board-thick pontoon of planks to protect the Venetian paving. Either that, or take it up where the trucks would be backing in. It was seven o'clock. The first truck was due in an hour. He'd forgotten all about these protective measures. Perhaps he could ring the hire shop and get them to send a truckload of scaffolding and boards. But he daren't ask Mrs Eden if he could use her phone for this, as it would betray his total unpreparedness for the job. He thought of running for the nearest phone-box. But it was miles away in a poorer suburb. And anyway, the machine operator from the hire shop might arrive after the first lorries had already done the damage. Peach ran back down the steps, round the cowrie-shell path, careful not to enter the maze, where he might be lost for the morning, to a replica of the Concert House at Bayreuth, which was the incinerator in which he found some old fence palings. Chanting 'Everything'll be all right,' like a mantra under his breath, he carried three armloads of these up the garden and began strewing them across the terrace, carefully interlocking them so that the weight of the vehicles' wheels would be spread over the greatest area. He laid several along the balustrade. They'd just have to unload the slabs by hand and toss them on to the lawn. The palings on the balustrade should catch any chippings that might scratch the marble. At three minutes to eight by the sundial, he remembered the lions. In their four-hundred-foot sentry duty along the back of the house, two of the creatures stood on either side of the gate, their alabaster ears cocked dangerously close to where the trays of the trucks would be passing.

Peach had his arms round the first one's mane and was trying unsuccessfully to drag it aside, when the trucks arrived. It was eight o'clock, autumn-sharp on the stone table of the sundial, and they'd all come at once, as he'd asked. The Garden Centre's little three-ton tipper was flagship in a convoy of five-, ten-, fifteen- and twenty-ton lorries, coiling artics balancing the palettes of crazy-paving on their open trays, high-sided demolition wagons, and even two pantechnicons, a stony rumbling coming from inside them as their drivers surged and jolted, moving house in Valhalla. The autumn air was suddenly sweet with the smell of diesel. And although the great queue of trucks had ground to a halt at Mrs Eden's gate, their engines were screaming urgently as though they were on the grid at a Demolition Derby. They backed up neighbouring drives and over lawns trying to get a better position. And he, standing alone at the gate, held the starter's flag.

The lorry with the steamroller was fourth in the queue and the machine operator was leaning from his cabin, shaking his fist at the sand-lorry's driver, who sat prissily ignoring him, revving his engine and belching blue smoke in his face.

'Where do you want it, guv?' said the Garden Centre's friendly driver.

Peach quailed. Perhaps he should just tip all the stuff in the street. But now the street was full of lorries, there was nowhere to put it. And if he did drop it there, it would take him, Allwrath and 3-Tooth a month to carry it in. Horns were blowing. Drivers with delivery notes were approaching him from all directions.

'Where do you want it, guv?' the Garden Centre's driver reminded him.

'Back across the terrace, mate . . . carefully . . . over those palings there . . . Do you mind unloading by hand? . . .'

'Not at all, mate.'

The driver gave the line of trucks a quizzical look, calculating how long it would take to unload that lot by hand.

'Well . . . you pass the stones down to me, and I'll sling them down on to the lawn.'

233

'All right, mate.'

The Garden Centre's little truck backed carefully through the gate, keeping well clear of the two lions. It rolled slowly back across the white cathedral floor with Peach running beside it, watching the six-foot hair-line crack form. Still, it was only a thin crack which should mask up easily with white cement. The driver patiently unloaded the crazy-paving by hand, passing the broken slabs down to Peach, who threw them over the balustrade. But it was further than he thought to the lawn, and the larger pieces bounced down the rockery like fractured gravestones, chipping some of Wilf's boulders and felling several giant sequoias. By the time they reached the cowrie-shell path, which Peach had forgotten to cover, they were smashed to pieces too small to do much damage. It took ten frantic minutes to unload the first three tons and by the time they'd finished, the air was angry with horns. Would Allwrath and 3-Tooth never come? They were his friends. It was ten past eight, and they were letting him down.

The little green tipper nipped out, and in backed a demolition lorry, so high it only just scraped under the arch of the gateway. It too was full of crazy-paving, about thirty tons. Its tall sides were dented from ancient stone-slinging battles. It reversed violently across the terrace, masticating palings. The driver climbed out and released the truck's gate.

'Do you mind unloading by hand?' asked Peach.

The driver looked at him as if these words came from some primitive language he'd long forgotten.

'Fuck that!' was his only reply.

He pulled a lever and the back of the truck began to labour upwards. Peach heard a robin singing in a moment of autumnal stillness. Then there was a roar followed by a grey, clattering avalanche that took out twenty feet of balustrade and two urns, turning their marble to high quality rockery stone. Wilf's reconstitutes returned to Grand Canyon dust. The cowrie shells below thought a grey wave of the ocean had hit them in their concrete bed, as the mighty tide crashed upon the path and rolled across the lawn. Peach groaned.

'Thank you,' he said to the empty truck as it roared out.

'Do you think that young man knows what he's doing?' Mrs Eden asked her butler as she sat at her dressing table.

'It sounds as if he's getting stuck into it, madam.'

'Well, she likes crazy-paving,' muttered Peach hysterically as he surveyed the ruins of the Venetian terrace. It was a quagmire mosaic of sculpted six-wheel drive. The next truck to back in contained twenty metres of sand. Peach waved it in, trying to restrict the damage to the tracks the first truck had left. But the driver ignored him, breaking his own path across the paving, and tipped the sand through the balustrade and down the rockery. It's amazing how much building sand stains; you could dye a black suit yellow in enough of it. When the sand truck pulled out, it left the balustrade and the patio behind it jaundiced as though a large dog had pissed on it. But Peach didn't have time to worry about this. The next truck in carried the steamroller. The low-slung wagon backed in sharp, taking off the lion's face, and for some reason of its own continued up the patio in the direction of the steps. Peach ran after it signalling wildly.

A thick-set man with a Neanderthal scowl climbed from the cab. He stared impassively at Horrie's garden, as if it were a monumental gear-box with trouble in the transmission. He stared at Peach. His tappets were rattling. Without seeking, or seeming to need, advice, he threw down the ramps at the back of his wagon, scaled the vast roller, climbed into the driver's seat, and started the engine. There was a belch of black smoke followed by a diesel scream.

'Where ya want 'er?'

Peach saw another problem he hadn't foreseen – how to get his heavy machinery down on to the lawn without doing any damage.

'Oh . . . ah . . . down there . . .' He pointed down the steps.

'But perhaps we'll leave it for now . . . It may be a bit difficult getting it down.'

'No trouble at all,' his machine operator informed him, staring at the Pyrian marble steps as if they were the crankshaft of some discontinued model.

The steamroller lurched forward and rolled down the ramp. The roller reached the patio and for a moment seemed to continue on downwards, as the white slabs subsided.

'Look . . . please . . .' said Peach, running along behind the steamroller. 'Park it here . . . For ten minutes . . . While I decide what to do . . .'

'She'll go down there no sweat,' said his machine operator helpfully.

The roller reached the lip of the top step and mashed it to a ramp of hard-core. Two, three, four, five . . . by the time the back wheels were on the downward slope, they were rolling down a smooth incline of well-compacted rubble. Peach's machine operator looked behind him as he rolled, surveying the smashed marble with a professional eye. It made a good base. Well packed already. It was pretty much ready for asphalting . . . Halfway down the steamroller started to slide, skidding from step to step over the shiny marble. The machine operator, who had driven everything from a combine harvester to a crane, kept the giant roller steady as it hit the bottom step, careened across the patio, and crashed into the pool with an earth-shuddering thump, where he came to rest, the roller still turning, like a mighty mill-wheel. The judder shook the garden. The keystone of the sandstone pergola, modelled on the delicate fan-tracery of King's College Chapel, fell out, and the sixty-foot nave collapsed upon the ruins of the steps with a roar of yellow stone and thorny wood.

Peach's machine operator climbed from the pool and surveyed his vehicle. Peach was staring at him, horrified.

'No trouble at all, mate. Winch job.'

The spray from his fall had lashed the house. Luckily, Mrs Eden was on the toilet.

236

'What was that?' she called through the door to Drake.
'Must be using dynamite to take up the lawn, madam.'
'Most unusual. Do you think he knows what he's doing?'

The trucks continued to come and go. Peach was past caring or counting the damage. A grey mountain of broken paving-stones now towered from the lawn to above the level of the terrace. Beside it was an ever-spreading avalanche of sand. And still the trucks kept coming. With his machine operator gone to get a winch, Peach was again left single-handed to contemplate the chaos, of which he was in charge. He waved his arms distractedly at the trucks, pretending to guide them in. But none of them seemed to see him. He felt like weeping himself. The old, cowardly impulse to ditch his tools and run, not stopping till he'd reached the safety of the Heath or the piano stool, came over him more powerfully than ever before. But simple terror held him to his post. He was in too deep. Besides, the police would track him down, on the Heath or on his piano stool. His landscaping days were over. He would be now spending his child's birth-day in prison. And only a long sentence would pay for this criminal damage. Tears started to his eyes. If only he had a friend to talk to – to make a start perhaps, digging up the lawn, laying a few stones, even a yard or two, just as a gesture. But they'd let him down. In the end, the spiritual man is always alone – though not, unfortunately, disembodied – and the material universe was showing its true metal. Then there was Mrs Eden. He dreaded her true metal even more than the material universe's. It was she he'd offended against most deeply. It was her dead husband's life's work he'd destroyed. At any moment now she'd stagger from the house and attack him with her huge black handbag. If even one of them would turn up!

All at once, from the direction of the bus-stop, Peach heard the opening bars of 'Hey Joe' – two aggressive E major chords followed by a wrenching gear-change into C, from which a callused fingertip bottle-necked up the top string into the screaming mouth of the sun. Though it was already loud, it was still coming from a great distance away. And though he couldn't hear the words, Peach knew them by heart –

'Heeeeeeeeeey Joe! . . . I heard ya shot

Ya old lady down . . . da doom da doom da da doooom . . .

Heeeeeeeeeey Joe . . .'

Peach ran to the gate.

3-Tooth was walking sideways up Imperial Way, his amp under his arm, turned right up to get a bit of echo out of this tunnel of suburban sunlight, his back still following a template of the Edgware Road pedestrian subway, his guitar under his other arm, playing and singing as he walked, drowning out the engines of the lorries and setting off a burglar alarm three doors down.

'Sorry I'm late, man. Heeeeeeeeeey Joe . . .'

'What?'

With 3-Tooth standing beside him, Peach could feel his eardrums tearing at the roots.

'Sorry I'm late, man,' shouted 3-Tooth, without stopping playing. 'Bus driver never heard the bell, man . . . took me a mile past me stop – he was so deeply into it, man . . . an old head-banger – banging 'is nut against the windscreen, man . . . forgot t' let me off . . .'

'Switch it down a bit, 3-Tooth. Please.'

'What?'

'Switch it down . . . The lady . . . No, lower, lower . . . The lady'll think . . . no, lower . . . she'll call the . . . Anyway, let me show you what's to be done.'

Peach led 3-Tooth to the top of the demolished steps, and pointed to the lawn.

'Yeh, all right,' said 3-Tooth, shaking him off. 'Won't be a second, man – just workin' somethin' out here . . .'

And he switched up the volume again and sang

'Heeeeeeeeeey Joe . . . where ya gonna

Run to now? . . . da doom da doom da da doooooooom . . .

Just let me work this riff on out, Peach. – Nice gaff, man . . .

238

Da doom da dooom da da doooooooom – Nice big garden . . .
Heeeeeeeeeeey Joe! . . .'

'What's that?' snapped Mrs Eden, cracking her egg in the
kitchen. 'What ever's going on out there?'

'Sounds like he's got his compressor going, madam. Should
I go and have a look?'

'Perhaps you'd better, Drake.'

Still playing, 3-Tooth strutted to the centre of the terrace,
above the ruins of the stairs, his hips swivelling in time to the
music as 'Hey Joe' reached its orgasmic conclusion. He surveyed the vast rockery amphitheatre, round which the echo of
his five-watt amplifier was still booming. He raised his hand
to still a torrent of applause that had turned to sand and
broken paving-stones, as 'Hey Joe' flew off west beyond
Hendon. 3-Tooth shouted into the sun.

'Now I know what it's like, Jimi!'

He looked from side to side at the desolation.

'Tha stage is big 'n empty, man. The band's too smashed t'
play. Yar on yer own. Always have bin – always will be.
Someone's bin friggin' with the lights, too – turned 'em right
up. They're tryin' t' dazzle ya, man . . .'

He lifted his shades and was hit by the sunlight.

'But I'm with ya, man. Always have bin. Always will be.
And I'd like t' dedicate this next number t' you, man. It's one
ya oughta know . . .'

3-Tooth strummed his guitar once.

A thunderous A minor shook the tools in the Taj Mahal and
rattled the panes of the Palace of Versailles.

'THERE MUST BE SOME WAY . . .'

Suddenly Peach, who had been struggling with 3-Tooth like
a distracted road manager, saw someone standing in the wings
of the living-room curtains. It was Drake, the aged butler. He
was staring at the seat of 3-Tooth's black leather trousers,

through which his unwashed jowls, trailing shreds of under-
pants, seemed to be munching their way with a circular
motion. He should run and fetch his mistress. But all he could
do was grip the curtains and watch.

'THERE MUST BE SOME WAY . . . . OUTTA
HEEEEEEEEEERE . . .'

Peach sobbed. 3-Tooth was a maniac. He must stop him.
With all his strength he wrenched the tiny black amp from
under his friend's arm. It spat blue tongues at him.

'Help me, 3-Tooth,' he shouted. 'For God's sake, help me!'

And with a flex-tearing heave, he threw the amp up, and
almost over, the barbed wire on top of the twenty-foot wall.
Unfortunately, trailing feedback, it missed the top strand, and
wound itself by the naked wire round one of the electrified
staunchions that sustained the barbed wire. All nine hundred
feet of fence gave a jump. Then it began to hum with the
menacing roar of a mighty electronic instrument, just switched
on. Even 3-Tooth stopped playing. He looked up. He could
see the electricity bowing along the taut strands of barbed
wire. On a sudden inspiration, he plucked bottom E on his
guitar. His amp fizzed on the staunchion. And the bottom
strand of barbed wire began to wobble in an electric field of
immense force – from which came a note, the deepest musical
note ever created by a living being. It made the Tibetan
mountain horn sound like a gnat's fart. And it was an E! With
an ecstatic, three-toothed smile, 3-Tooth plucked A. His amp
writhed on the staunchion. And the second strand of barbed
wire came to life. And it was an A! It was unbelievable. It was
supernatural. Then D. Then G. Then B, playing up the fence.
Then finally, the top strand of barbed wire – top E! Nine
hundred feet of electrified guitar string with little, spitting
barbs. Every dog for five miles flattened its ears and ran. Radio
One vanished momentarily from the air. Mrs Eden's freezer
began to defrost itself.

'Hey man, there's somethin' weird 'bout this wire, man,'
shouted 3-Tooth.

'It's in tune,' said Peach, aghast.

'It's Jimi,' shouted 3-Tooth. 'He's comin' down t' jam with me at last!'

'Please, 3-Tooth, no . . .'

3-Tooth looked up into the fence and saw the Crucified Lead Guitarist walking amongst the wire.

'Okay, Jimi. I'm with ya, man. A ONE . . . A TWO . . . A THREE . . .'

Again he struck A minor. His lead turned blue and was woven in electric tongues. His amp lashed on its staunchion. And a mighty wave-motion passed down the six-foot, six-strand, barbed wire fence, down one side of the garden, across the back, up the other side, around and over the house, popping fuses and making Mrs Eden stagger, and back to the staunchion – they were surrounded by A minor. Then a G, a quick B minor, and down to a bottomless F.

'THERE MUST BE SOME WAY . . . . OUTTA HEEEEEEEEEEERE . . .'

'My God! What's that?' said Mrs Eden.

She was talking on the phone to Lady de Sage.

'Can you hear me? A bad line? It's that Mr O'Hare you recommended. He seems to have some strange machinery. I ought to go out and have a look how he's getting on, but—'

Peach ran to the gate. He'd tell the rest of the trucks to go, and not come back. He'd pay them off. Then he'd threaten 3-Tooth with his pickaxe, and make him stop. He'd drag the machine operator away from his winch even if it meant a fight. He'd give them both a shovel. He'd *order* them to the lawn. He'd *make* them dig. They were supposed to be helping him, weren't they? He'd just carry on. He'd keep working till he was sacked or arrested. Probably both. But he wouldn't give up.

Instead of another lorry, a battered hearse came lurching through the gate, followed by twelve limousines, their black paintwork stained with the dust of hard travelling. The hearse rolled to a halt and Allwrath jumped out, his crowbar in his hand.

'I've come to help you, Peach. I've come to pay a Druid's debt.'

'Look, Allwrath—'

'I bring the energy that built the Sacred Circle in ancient times. I bring the Earth-energy, and God Himself. I will work.'

'Well—'

'Unfortunately I have been unable to shake off these demon-iac philosophers.'

Doors were opening. Cramped limbs were being stretched. Three men in black were urinating up the pyracantha.

'Perhaps . . .' said Peach.

'I have noticed,' whispered Allwrath, 'over the last few weeks, that I seem to have some strange sort of power over them. Perhaps . . .'

'. . . They could work too!' said Peach.

Some were already looking for the plot. Others were singing hymns. One was talking to the headless lion. Allwrath pounded the patio with his crowbar, shattering another stone. Then he cried with the granite voice of the High Priest of the Ultimate Circle.

'I want you to do exactly what I tell you!'

'Saviour!' cried the Reverend Briggs hastening forwards on his knees waving a bottle of port he had secreted for the occasion.

'Each one of you take a pick and a shovel. Ladies too. And follow me.'

Then he whispered to Peach.

'Give us a hand with this coffin, Peach. I don't like the look of those sledgehammers.'

They slid the coffin from the back of the hearse. It hit the terrace with a splintering crash.

'Oh Arthur,' wept Mrs Nugent. 'Are you all right in there?'

'Peace, woman,' hissed the Reverend Briggs savagely. 'Hath not the Lord lifted the weight of the world from his shoulders?'

Peach and Allwrath slithered the coffin down the ruined stairs, and dragged it past the pool from which the rear wheels of the steamroller were still turning like an abandoned mill, on to the lawn, followed by the faithful in their black suits and dresses.

'Now, what's the job, Peach?' asked Allwrath.

'Well, the lawn needs to come up . . . And then there's all this crazy-paving to be laid.'

Allwrath held his crowbar above his head.

'Very well, my black Voltaires. Very well, Mrs Hume, Mrs Locke! Start digging. I want this lawn up by lunch-time!'

'Is the lawn going to Heaven too, with Arthur, your Worship?' asked Mrs Nugent.

'Just dig,' cried the Reverend Briggs, seizing a pickaxe and remembering his allotment.

Pent-up grief and long confinement in the black limousines awoke the energy of even the most elderly mourners. Mr McGrundle stopped trying to hear the sea in a section of the cowrie-shell path that had remained intact, rose from the ground and began picking like a navvy. Mrs Nugent stopped knitting kneedlelessly, dropped the tattered tangle of Mr Spike's jumper, and began to dig like a young woman. Tufts of turf flew. Heavy, rooted clods were cast aside. Today was the second Good Friday and they were harrowing the green, green grass of Hell with their Saviour, while on the terrace high above them a diabolical being in black leather trousers and shades was creating infernal music.

'ALLLLLLLL ALONG THE WATCHTOWEEEEEER . . .'

'Who's that, your Worship?'

'Must be one of them Jehovah's Witnesses,' panted the Reverend Briggs.

While the Reverend Briggs and the mourners dug, Peach and Allwrath surveyed the lawn prior to paving.

'You know, with you here, Allwrath, and all these people you've brought, I might even get this all done today.' Peach had tears of joy in his eyes.

But Allwrath wasn't listening. A strange light shone in his eyes. For his eyes were looking through lawn, through maze, through path, through pool, through steps, into ancient times. And they saw a mighty ring of megaliths, some of them bigger than a house, lying on the ground. And ancient Druids, of mighty power, drawing a vast ring, a sacred ring, around them. And carving the Sun and the Moon, and ancient runes, into the stone. And speaking to the granite itself. And the mighty megaliths slowly reared themselves upright, by the sheer power instinct within stone itself, with no help from human hands. Allwrath's eyes were watching the rebuilding of the Ultimate Circle. And Gaia began to speak from Mrs Eden's lawn, into the soles of his feet.

'Peach! Peach O'Hare, my friend. This garden . . . This place you have brought me to . . . has a vast power . . . is—'

And indeed, whether it was the force-field of 3-Tooth's nine-hundred-foot electric guitar, or whether it was the toppled steamroller awaking memories of extinct mastodons, or whether it was the presence of the Druid himself and his six-foot kerbstone, the mighty stones that lay on the lawn were *twitching*, as if they were trying to lift themselves from the ground.

'The Sacred Site! . . .' whispered Allwrath.

'No! One Imperial Way?'

'The Sacred Site of the Ultimate Circle!'

Allwrath's eyes shone mystically.

'No,' said Peach. 'Not now, Allwrath. Please . . .'

But the Druid directed his crowbar at Peach's pile of crazy-paving.

'Behold! – '

The thirty-foot mountain of crazy-paving was shifting and rattling of its own accord. Each broken slab was shuffling impatiently against its neighbour. And from the hill of sand came glints and twinkles as every last grain grew excited.

'They smashed the Holy Stones, and used the chippings for aggregate in their paving slabs. But see! The chippings have come alive in their coats of grey, rationalist cement! And the particles of Newton, look! – are grains of sand in Israel's eyes! Peach, against my own will, you have brought me to the Ultimate Circle, I stand on the Sacred Site. And I even seem to have followers. Now God will awake in his kerbstone. And Gaia is about to arise from the Earth. I can feel Her coming up through my feet, Peach. I have only to build the altar . . .'

'Altar?'

'Yes. Altar, Peach. We Druids always use an Altar for . . .'

'What?' asked Peach weakly.

'Human sacrifice, Peach. It's a most important ingredient in the ritual. God will need blood after His long sleep . . .'

'Look, Allwrath. Please don't bother. I've changed my mind. I can do the job myself. Please take your . . . Druids, too. This is my site, and . . . Who . . . Who were you thinking of sacrificing?'

Allwrath glared around him.

'Whoever it was who usurped this Holy Ground and dared call it Private. And put up this howling wire of Reductionism around it—'

'That's my customer, Allwrath. I'm not having my customer sacrificed in her own garden!'

The customer herself was standing at her French windows beside the frozen figure of her butler, surveying her garden beyond 3-Tooth's swivelling bum. The squaw-eyed squints above her high cheekbones had deepened into a furrowed stare. The fine old wrinkles about her mouth were drawing themselves up into a net laden with – rage? unholy joy? murder? It was impossible to tell looking in from the outside, for the autumn sun had turned the plate-glass window to a golden mirror.

'We will dig till lunch,' cried Allwrath swinging his crowbar. 'And after lunch we will build the Altar. The Holy Stones are to hand!'

And he pointed his iron staff at the mountain of crazy-paving.

'But Allwrath! That's crazy-paving, *my* crazy-paving – three pounds fifty a yard . . .'

'It *was* crazy, Peach. But its mind has been healed. Dig on!'

And the black crows of Reason pecked at the turf with their picks and flapped their iron shovels, slinging the clods into the rockery. By lunch-time the whole lawn had been dug up.

They leant on their tools and rested.

A woman as beautiful as the golden day and nine months pregnant came through the gate and picked her way down the ruined steps. Her bag was full of sandwiches and two flasks of apple juice. She waved to Peach. 3-Tooth respectfully played a little quieter.

'NO REASON TO GET EXCITEEEEEEEEEED . . .'

The fully-developed child in her womb danced in the enveloping A minor.

Peach's machine operator, who was still having trouble with the winch, stood up and wiped the grease off his hands on to his trousers, respectful in the presence of the birth-machine.

'Morag,' cried Peach with undisguised joy.

'I've come to see how you're getting on,' she said, setting down her basket of sandwiches. 'Goodness! What a big job!'

'Yes. Well . . . We've made a show!'

'Would you like some sandwiches?' she asked the watching workforce.

They flung down their tools and gathered around her. The Reverend Briggs distributed the sandwiches amongst his sweating flock. They had caught a bit of sun on this morning of the Crucifixion. The red faces with which they worked on their wholewheat sandwiches would soon be golden.

Allwrath ate his sandwich apart. He sat on the ground beside the long-neglected megaliths talking to them of the coming sacrifice. They digested his words in boulderous rumbles.

The machine operator stood in a ploughed field, one amongst many human machines, their cogs of rounded flesh, their spinal drive-shafts working inwards, ploughing fields of naked humanity where a great tenderness swayed and ripened. He chose a houmos and salad sandwich.

In respect for Morag and her feast, 3-Tooth unplugged his guitar, but kept plucking, so as not to lose the supernatural riff. Jimi himself had walked along the great barbed wire guitar, down the lead, across the strings and into 3-Tooth's body via his hands, which played undreamt-of chords. He and Jimi had become one. It didn't matter if the sound was off for a while. It was being heard beyond the Universe. They were digging it in the Black Hole.

Peach and Morag sat eating on the coffin.

There was a moment's simple, golden stillness.

'So tell me what you're doing here,' asked Morag at last.

'Well . . .' said Peach.

'All right! Back to work, my black-winged Wittgensteins!'

Allwrath was stalking savagely down the garden.

'Up, you vultures of Voltaire. Let's build! Let's get this Altar up!'

Rejuvenated by Morag's sandwiches, the faithful rose willingly and followed their Lord to the Harvest.

Peach's machine operator picked up a shovel, amazed by its simplicity, and began to move sand.

3-Tooth plugged himself in again. The barbed wire howled. 'THERE ARE MANY HERE AMONG US, WHO THINK THAT LIFE IS BUT A JOOOOOOOOOOOKE . . .'

'Now listen . . .' said Peach, also rising.

Sitting on the coffin, Morag felt a faint contraction shiver her womb. She shuddered and started clearing up the sandwich wrappers.

'Start spreading that sand around,' shouted Allwrath. 'We'll put It here.'

Peach looked on.

At first the crazy-paving went okay. Allwrath paced out a mighty square beside the recumbent stones. It took up half the old lawn. The mourners spread a three-inch thickness of sand over it. Then they began setting out the broken stones, rather higgeldy-piggeldy for high-class crazy-paving. But Peach and the machine operator darted amongst them, straightening the slabs as they went along. Soon the square was laid, and moderately level. Peach could have wept with gratitude. At this rate they'd have the whole lot done, pointing and all, by this evening.

But instead of starting on the next square of earth, Allwrath made them spread the next three inches of sand on top of the first square, and started laying the stones on top of that.

'Allwrath! . . . Please! . . . On the ground . . .'

But Allwrath ignored him. He formed the mourners into a human chain passing slabs along from the mountain to the ascending pyramid. For that's what it was: a rising pyramid of crazy-paving. One square on top of the other, each square slightly smaller than the one beneath it. Soon it was twelve feet high, and the more agile mourners were perched on the steps of the pyramid passing the broken footpath ever upwards to Allwrath and the Reverend Briggs working on the summit.

Morag dusted the crumbs off the coffin, and suddenly realised where she'd been sitting. The pangs were starting to bite. She could suddenly feel the baby's head, like a rock over which some tender part of her was being stretched. She staggered a little looking for something to hang on to. Peach ran up.

'Peach, it's coming.'

Peach stared distractedly at the gate.

'What, Morag?'

'The baby!'

'Oh my God! Oh sweet Jesus! Oh no! Not now, Morag. Please, not now!'

'There's nothing I can do about it, Peach,' she snapped.

'Of course not. No. But can't you just hang on a minute. I can't leave now . . .'

'Fuck you,' she shouted.

'Do your squatting exercises. Here. Hold on to this . . . coffin . . .'

'I hate you, Peach.'

Breathing heavily, she squatted by the coffin, gripping its brass handle. She pulled her dress up around her thighs and pushed her legs downwards, trying to relax her pelvic muscles, then drew them up, shuddering like a new butterfly.

'I won't be a sec,' said Peach.

'God damn you. Hurry. Hurry.'

Peach ran off.

'3-Tooth. 3-Tooth. Stop! Stop playing. Come quick.'

But 3-Tooth was now Jimi, and Jimi didn't answer him.

'Allwrath. Allwrath. For God's sake. Stop now. Help me . . .'

But Allwrath's Altar was nearing completion. The pyramid now stood thirty feet high. He would stop for nothing now. There was only one layer left to go – the size of a single paving-stone. Allwrath laid it in place, and climbed on to it. He lifted his crowbar high into the air and shouted down to Peach, to the neighbouring gardens, to Hendon beyond.

'Here, where I stand, is where God, still sleeping in His box, will soon be standing!'

'You'll never get it up there,' shouted Peach in distraction.

'*I* won't get Him up, Peach,' Allwrath yelled back. 'He will climb by Himself. For the time has come for Him to awake. I'll get you all to hold hands in a circle . . .'

'Allwrath. Stop. Please. Come down. Morag's in—'

'I summon God,' the Druid announced to the neighbours' tennis-court.

Then, step by massive step, he began to descend the pyramid. Sweeping Peach aside, he strode up the garden towards the coffin, to which Morag clung in her labour.

The Reverend Briggs fell to his knees, signalling his congregation to follow him.

'Behold, the Messiah's final act! We are about to witness His Death and Resurrection. Just as, in Jerusalem, He had no tomb to lie in and borrowed Joseph of Arimathea's, so now he strides towards Arthur's box!'

Allwrath stood above the coffin of Arthur Nugent, which he struck fiercely with his crowbar.

The Druid was so possessed by Earth-power that he didn't

see Morag in her labour, holding on to the coffin beside him.

'Oh Jesus! Oh Peach. Come quick . . . Oh . . .' Rocking to and fro with her eyes shut, she was oblivious of the Druid beside her.

'O God,' he cried. 'O Stone of Life! Awakener of Gaia, Goddess of the Earth. Rise now! Your Faithful High Priest Allwrath calls upon you to ascend your rebuilt Altar and to stand once more . . . at the centre of the Sacred Circle!'

The lid of the coffin began to bobble up and down. There was a heavy shifting inside it.

The Reverend Briggs grappled with Mrs Nugent, restraining her from rushing to the side of the opening box.

For there was a mighty rumbling inside the coffin. Then the lid was flung back, and the kerbstone from the bus stop outside Woolworth's, Glastonbury High Street, reared up and stood on one end.

'Arthur!' screamed the organist's wife.

'Golly,' thought the Reverend Briggs. 'We knew he had stone ears. But not the whole of him!'

The standing kerbstone lurched sideways, smashing through the side of the coffin.

Fearing it was something splintering inside her own body, Morag screwed her eyes tighter shut, and, still gripping the brass handle of the coffin, which had come away in her hand, screamed from her own darkness.

'Peach! Peach! I can't bear it. Where are you?'

'THE WIND BEGAN TO HOOOOOOOOOOOWL . . .' howled Jimi Hendrix through 3-Tooth's gaping mouth, high in the barbed strings of his supernatural guitar.

When you want to move a paving-stone that's too heavy to lift off the ground, you stand it up, and roll it from one side to the other, 'walking' it on its corners. So now, rolling from side to side, the six-foot kerbstone *walked*, by its own power alone, up the garden towards the pyramid.

'When He climbs the Altar, the whole Earth will awake,' cried Allwrath exultantly.

250

'Oh Arthur, do you still love me?' sobbed Mrs Nugent. 'Are you *all* stone?'

'Hush, woman,' said the Reverend Briggs. 'His body must already have risen. What we are seeing is his spirit, the spiritual form of his soul.'

The great stone reached the foot of the pyramid and, carefully tilting one corner of itself on to the first level, began to climb. It was a slow but breathtaking ascent. Breathtaking but inexorable. At last the kerbstone stood at the top of the pyramid, on the peak of Its Altar, at the centre of the Ultimate Circle. It swivelled itself slowly around, to face them. It had no face itself, and no mouth. But it spoke words that creaked and shook and rumbled and thundered out of the very grain of the granite itself:

'O GAIA. O GODDESS. O EARTH, MY WIFE . . . ARISE!'

For some time now a distant humming and roaring had been coming from under the earth. The roaring grew louder, approaching relentlessly. No one had heard it before under the howl of 3-Tooth's guitar. But now the earth between the pyramid and the swimming pool began to shake. Large cracks ran all over the ground. The clods of earth shook themselves to dust. A huge shuddering and moaning was coming from below.

'Gaia,' cried Allwrath ecstatically. 'Gaia, Gaia . . .'

The little pebbles were scurrying all over the ground, so great was the vibration. The moaning grew louder. The earth parted. And a mighty, corkscrewing, diamond-tipped drill-bit burst into the light, plummeting five, ten, fifteen feet into the air, dragging behind it a monstrous digging machine with Fergus O'Fury himself at the wheel.

'Gaia?' your man in the white dressing-gown was asking him.

A man in a dishevelled cassock was burying his face in the earth, shrieking, 'It's the Devil! See his red hair!'

Your electrician up dere wit de big red voltometer had finished testin' de electric fence, for it had just fallen silent.

251

And dere, amidst de gawpers, stood his old friend, Peach O'Hare, lookin' as lost as he did dat first day he set out to find some work.

With no good earth to get its teeth into, the giant drill-bit remained erect, gently screwing a hole in the sky.

Fergus O'Fury brushed the earth from his hair, dusted the shoulders of his jacket, and stepped down from his machine.

'Good night t' ye all,' said Fergus to the gaping faces. 'Can ye tell me if dis be Hendon Central . . . or dereabouts?'

Allwrath glared at him. The Reverend Briggs crossed himself. 3-Tooth plucked a dead string. Peach held helplessly on to Morag, who was moaning in her own darkness. No one answered him.

'Can ye tell me where I am den?' Fergus asked again, with a gallant smile.

'Number One, Imperial Way, North West Eleven,' answered a shaking, iron-willed voice from the top of what had once been a flight of steps. Clutching the remains of the balustrade, Mrs Eden descended, climbing over a shattered buttress, kicking a gargoyle-head aside, her heavy black handbag on her shoulder, her old tights grimacing whitely. For one moment, Peach groaned louder than Morag.

'Mrs Eden . . . Mrs Eden, I'd just like to say . . .'

'What are you doing, Mr O'Hare? What are you doing in my dead husband's garden? What are you doing to the Most Perfect Garden On Earth?'

'. . .'

'. . . You are bringing it to life, Mr O'Hare. You have taken a dead monument and made it breathe. Never mind a few bonsais. It is inspired, Mr O'Hare. You should concentrate more on the designing side of things. What you have achieved in one brief day is the difference between . . . reading *House and Garden*, and naked inspiration. Have you ever meditated, Mr O'Hare? Are you a religious man? I'll give you some before-and-after photographs to show your future clients. A

252

new-age pyramid in the middle of a heap of ruined modernity and reproduction trash! – Those hedges will grow back, if I leave them alone – The original Garden of Eden may well have looked like this, Mr O'Hare . . .'

She stood in front of Peach gripping his hand. He could feel the vibrant skeleton in her handshake.

'Mr O'Hare, I would like to thank you personally for . . .'

Morag, who had been as respectfully quiet as she was able during the old lady's speech, let out a piercing groan. Peach began to cry.

'Oh God, Morag. I'll never get you to hospital now . . . Or home either! It's too late. I'm sorry, my precious. What . . .'

'What's that?' asked Mrs Eden.

She peered at Morag. She saw her condition. She began dragging the rings off her old fingers and flinging them on the ground.

'Drake,' she shouted. 'Drake! Bring me some hot water. Towels. A pair of scissors. And a blanket. At once. This young woman's fully dilated.'

Fergus O'Fury pressed through the crowd, wiping his big, clay-thickened hands on his trousers.

'I know dat man,' he said, nodding at Peach. 'He's me friend. De man who got me goin'. I'll stand by 'im, madam. And 'is missus. Sure, I know a little about dese tings, havin' had eight birts under me own roof. I know de crack. I'll deliver de little one, dere.'

Mrs Eden took one look at his huge, work-grained hands, and placed the hot water in them.

'You hold that,' she said. 'I was a midwife before I married Horrie. That was before Pethedine, epidurals, inductions, and often hospitals. We lost a few, but we knew what we were doing. Sixty years it is, since my last delivery. But I believe I've still got it in my hands.'

Everyone could see that. In fact she had a little wet head with black hair gummed to it in her hands now. Morag screamed.

'What shall I do?' asked Peach, who felt as if he'd been helpless all his life.

'Just keep holding her like you're doing.'

Morag was gnawing his arm as though she wanted to eat it.

There was a tug, a tiny, gurgled whimper, a howl of relief from Morag, and a little red body rolled out of her like a blood pudding covered with stars and the wet, torn skin of darkness itself into the old lady's hands.

Morag pulled her dress up over her breasts, which were tight with milk. Mrs Eden set the little body on Morag's belly, where it rose and fell as she drew breath, and surveyed her tits with amazed blue eyes. Then it sneezed out some mucus and Morag took it in her hands and placed its mouth over her swollen nipple. It gave one more whimper, spat out more womb darkness, and began to suck ferociously, as Mrs Eden cut its dead life-cord.

Peach tentatively placed his hand on the baby's back. It was terrifyingly small. He cupped the little bum in his palm, which was suddenly filled with a sticky black substance.

'Baby's first stool,' observed Mrs Eden.

He absent-mindedly wiped it off on his trousers. Then smelt his hand. This black defecation of Morag's blood-food smelled sweet!

The baby sucked, and spat, and coughed, and sucked again in sweet autumnal silence. Mrs Eden deftly bathed Morag's womb. Morag smiled at Peach, aglow, then looked back to the baby. Peach felt an overpowering impulse gathering within him. A desire to give his gift. His hand ached with joy above the little body. He would give it the best thing in his life. He rose and made his way through the quiet crowd, which parted before him. He walked down the garden alone. He heard his baby cry tentatively in the deepening autumnal silence. He climbed the pyramid, slowly mounting the steps of broken paving stones to the top of the Altar. He reached the top and flung his head back and stretched his arms up in gratitude to the Divine Source then spread them down to the shape of the Cross, the fulcrum of which was his heart. Then he sat down on the very tip of the pyramid. He was outside the 'Pharaoh's Tomb' now, sitting on its apex, his back straight, resting against God. He drew a deep breath and became still. He was completely happy. He was doing the work he knew best.